Nimrod

Ryan Roberts

Published by Earth Island Books
Pickforde Lodge
Pickforde Lane
Ticehurst
East Sussex
TN5 7BN

www.earthislandbooks.com

First published by Earth Island Publishing 2022

ISBN 9781739795597

Printed and bound by IngramSpark

chapter 1

*

nice guys finish last

Today is the last day of my junior year of high school. This morning Frankie Friel got on the loudspeaker and announced to the entire student body of Somerville High School that my mom is The Woman in White, the eccentric lady who walks around town clad all in white. He was the only one who knew—until now. Frankie lives across the street from me; we've been friends since we were little kids. More like frenemies, actually, because he's always pulling stunts like this one with the goal of embarrassing me. When he tosses insults my way, it makes the other kids laugh but it's not because he's funny. Far from it. They laugh so he doesn't set his sights on them, which only feeds the beast, because the more laughs he gets, the more he makes fun of me. The stuff he says, for the most part, doesn't bother me...except when he talks about my parents.

Most of my classmates are out of their seats conversing with one another as Miss Tucker, our biology teacher, has given us the final ten minutes of the school year to sign each other's yearbooks and talk about our summer plans. Getting my yearbook signed is the perfect cover, the one I've been waiting for since this morning. I cradle my yearbook in my left arm and walk over to where Frankie is standing. When he sees me, he flashes a smirk, letting me know just how proud he is of himself for letting out my secret and I rear back, years of pent-up aggression loaded in my fist, aim for his chin, and knock the smug look right off his face.

Walking the halls en route to the principal's office is an out-of-body experience. It's like I'm floating above, watching myself as if I'm in a movie. As I begin to worry about my imminent fate, most likely suspension for the beginning of next year, I realize I hear clapping. I look to see that all the kids and teachers from every classroom have stepped out into the hallway and are applauding me as if I've just saved the world. Even the custodians are clapping for me. I had just done to Frankie Friel, thorn in the side of everyone he's ever come in contact with, what we've all fantasized about doing. My luck does not change inside the principal's office. He softly explains that he's keeping me here as a mere formality (his words), to give the appearance that he's disciplining me when in reality he's thanking me for doing what so many of his colleagues have been wishing someone would do since Frankie first stepped foot in this school. He even throws a few yells in my direction for the sake of authenticity, in case anyone is listening outside his office. After my mock punishment is over, he thanks me for my service and says, "Rod, you're free to go."

"Rod, you're free to go," Miss Tucker says, snapping me out of my daydream.

As I look around the empty classroom, I realize that the rest of my classmates have left to get a head start on their summer breaks and I am hit with a sense of dread, more damaging than any punch in the face could be. While most teenagers run with anticipation toward their two-plus months away from the monotony of school and the feeling of being trapped inside the same four walls for seven hours a day, that's the way I feel about going home.

"Hey, Nimrod, need a ride?" Frankie asks, pulling up next to me in his black BMW. Daydream aside, I'm a nice guy, not the kind to go around punching people. I haven't forgiven Frankie for the dick move he pulled this morning, but I know that he's been extra callous since his mom walked out on him and his dad and he's been lashing out. That doesn't make it right, but in Frankie's own self-absorbed way, this ride is his form of an apology, so I get into the passenger seat and accept—both the ride home and the apology.

* * * * * * * *

Frankie pulls into the parking lot of the volunteer fire station and tells me I can walk the rest of the way. It's not far, only about a six minute walk to my house, but I look at him, confused.

"Kiley lives that way," he says, pointing to the right. "If I drive you home, then I have to double back and it'll add another five minutes onto my drive. And I *really* wanna get there. Did you see what she was wearing today?"

Nice guys finish last, right?

Although a six minute walk has just been tacked onto my journey, I'm still ahead of schedule. Most days I take the bus home, which won't find its way to my neighborhood for another twelve minutes or so. It's way faster if you have a car (I don't) or get a ride home with someone. Frankie isn't usually so hospitable but I guess he was feeling guilty for outing my mom as The Woman in White, which is why he gave me a ride (three-quarters of the way) home. The library is right down the street from here so I decide to use my free time to walk over and see if the books I ordered have arrived. My mom doesn't like it when I'm late—it rattles her nerves, which don't need any extra help in that department—so I'll make it a point to be in and out.

On my way down Olive Street, nearly to the library, a sign for a new business catches my eye and stops me in my tracks: Follow the Sun Yoga. My hero, Sting, is a big practitioner of yoga. Yes, *that* Sting. Sting the rockstar. Also Sting the environmentalist, Sting the actor, and Sting the yogi. That's what they call people who do yoga. I used to just refer to him as a yoga person until Rachel Readlinger overheard me saying it in the cafeteria and made a big scene out of me not knowing they were called yogis. With Sting being a major proponent of yoga, and my life's goal being to meet him, this yoga studio's arrival in my town, where nothing new ever happens, leads me to believe this could be more than a simple coincidence. Library books be damned— I need to investigate.

Using my hands to block the glare of the sun reflecting off the window of Follow the Sun Yoga, I attempt to see what goes on inside a yoga studio. Of course yoga goes on inside, but I wonder if they practice the same styles of yoga that Sting does: Ashtanga and Jivamukti. The problem is, I have only read that these are the styles he practices, so I am not sure how I would be able to tell one way or the other.

"What are you, some kind of pervert?!"

I can't be sure because it all happened so fast, but there's a strong possibility that I let out a high-pitched yelp, which I have a tendency to do when startled. I turn to face my accuser and see that it's a girl around my age. I'm sure I've never seen her before—she's not someone you forget. It's not uncommon for me to become tongue-tied in the presence of a girl, but this one in particular, with her long bangs, heavy black eyeliner, and unencumbered confidence, makes me more nervous than usual.

"Who...me?"

Of course she means me. I am the only person around, certainly the only person peering into the window of Follow the Sun Yoga, so she's clearly talking to me. But I needed to say something, *anything,* to buy some time to attempt to get my mouth and brain to work in unison.

"You're the only one I see here peeping into the window, unless you've got a friend hiding around the corner somewhere."

"No, definitely not. I don't have any friends."

Real smooth, Rod.

"Well I'm sorry to hear that, but if I can offer a little advice, the way to make friends isn't by sneaking around looking into windows."

"Oh...yeah...no."

Ugh.

"I wasn't sneaking a peek," I offer. "Well, technically I was, but really I was just trying to see if Sting is in there."

"Is Sting your dog or something?"

"No, Sting the rockstar. Not that I thought he was *in* there. It's just that he's super into yoga and I'm a big fan of his, so I was just—"

At that moment, my phone rings, prompting another of my trademark high-pitched yelps. It's no surprise who's calling me as there's only one person who ever calls me. Before I'm even able to get out a hello, my mom is already ranting in full-on panic mode. There's no use in trying to calm her down, not when she's like this, so I just repeat "I'm on my way home" a few times before hanging up.

"Mom problems?"

"Oh yeah, you heard that, huh? Sorry about that. My mom just—"

"No need to apologize," she says. "If anyone knows about mom problems, it's me."

"Well, I've gotta go."

"See ya around, Sting."

"Not if I see you first," I say, hating myself for not being able to hold back on a Peeping-Tom-inspired joke. I am *so* not smooth.

chapter 2

*

favorite son

When I walk in the house my mom is standing right there waiting for me; so close, in fact, that I nearly knock her over with the front door. She tells me how happy she is that I'm home. What she actually means is that she's relieved. She hasn't been happy in twenty years, since my brother died. She blames Green Day for his death but that's a story for another time. His name was Colin. I never met him, being that I'm only sixteen.

"I thought the school year was never going to end. Sometimes I think I'd be better off pulling you out of that school and keeping you home with me full time. I feel so much better when you're in range," she says, handing me my walkie-talkie.

Anytime I'm not in school, my mom insists that we each keep a walkie-talkie on us, the same pair I used to play with when I was a kid. This way she can get in touch with me anytime she needs me (which is often) and it also prevents me from venturing outside of the walkie-talkies' frequency, hence staying 'in range.' My mom is old school so she doesn't own a cell phone; she doesn't believe in them. Not only is she old school, she's also old. That's not me being rude; she really is old compared to the parents of other kids my age. So is my dad. I already mentioned my dead brother, Colin. Well, when they had him, they were the normal age for having kids. But that was a long time ago. He died nineteen years ago, when he was just twenty. The pain of losing a son and spending the rest of their lives without one was too much to handle so three years after Colin's death, when my dad was fifty and my mom was forty-seven, along came Baby Rod. That's me, only I'm not a baby anymore and Rod isn't the name they gave me. At the risk of sounding like a basket case, Green Day, along with the death of my brother, is also to blame for my nickname.

When my mom asks me why I'm so late (and by 'so late,' she means three minutes later than usual), I attempt to change the subject. I'm not supposed to take rides from Frankie. They don't mind me going over to his house to play video games but getting in the car with him is a different story and would probably give my mom an aneurysm.

"Did you know there's a new yoga studio in town? Right across from the library."

Of course she doesn't know. My mom walks all over town but for some reason she refuses to walk down Olive Street. She'd rather walk twenty minutes out of her way than take that street. It's no use asking her why not, because she'll never say. She's got a lot of...quirks.

"It sounds like it could be fun. Maybe something you'd be interested in trying? I could even try it with you if you want."

As I'm saying this, the look on my mom's face tells me it's more than she can handle. She doesn't do well with change. My mom is a creature of habit and I know better than anybody that there's no way in hell she's going down to that yoga studio, but the thought of seeing that girl again got the better of me and I decided to take a shot.

"I wish you wouldn't be late, you had me worried sick. Now can you get me a glass of juice? Mommy's really thirsty."

"Sure, Mom."

The pills my mom takes dry out her throat, so she asks me to make her juice quite often. I'm happy to do it. Did you know that most juice you buy in the grocery store has hardly any juice in it at all? Store-bought juice usually contains only 10% juice and the rest is added sugar and other random ingredients. When I learned this, I told my parents, thinking they'd be as appalled as I was, but they're old school and they like their Tropicana, so knowing that it's barely juice at all that they're drinking didn't stop them from buying it. This led me to start making my own juice. Since I didn't have an electric juicer at the time, I would squeeze oranges and lemons with a hand juicer I found in my parents' cabinet, which I don't even think they realized they had. It's this little white doohickey made of glass that has JUICE embossed across the front. That's how I figured out what it was in the first place, as I had never seen one before. Its base looks like a tiny rowboat with a handle on one side. Coming out of the floor of the rowboat is this thing that looks like half a football with jagged lines running vertically along its length. That's where you press the orange or lemon, and then the juice trickles down and sits on the bottom, waiting to be poured into a pitcher. You have to press a lot of fruit to fill a pitcher so adding water helps and also makes it less sour. After I started making my own juice, I would pour it into their empty Tropicana containers (which became empty after I poured the original contents down the sink). I would do this without them knowing, of course, and at first my dad drank it and said, "I think Tropicana changed their recipe. Why can't they leave well enough alone?" which is an expression I find silly. Why settle for "well enough?" Why wouldn't you want something "super awesome?" After a day or two, my dad began enjoying my secretly homemade juice even more than the regular Tropicana he was used to. My mom didn't really notice at all, because she usually only drinks juice after she takes her pills and by then she doesn't notice much, not for the next few hours anyway. Eventually I told them I was replacing the Tropicana with juice I'd made by hand and I think they were a little weirded out, because what thirteen-year-old kid makes his own juice and sneaks it into empty Tropicana containers to trick his parents? Since then, I've been on juice duty.

There's no juice left in the fridge so I have to make more, which takes a little while. Not nearly as long as it used to because now I have an electric juicer. My parents got me one for Christmas last year so now I can make all kinds of juices. It still takes a while to cut up all the fruit and then clean the juicer afterwards, which you have to do after each use or it gets all kinds of funky. By the time I get back downstairs, my mom is asleep on the couch, clutching an old family album filled with pictures of our family taken before I was alive. Looking at those photos is like looking at a completely different family and not solely because they are pictures of my parents with a boy that isn't me. The strangest part is how different my parents look. Not just younger. My dad was in shape back then and could do things like play baseball with his son, the one who isn't me. My mom had a great big smile on her face in most of the photos, which is hardly ever the case these days.

My dead brother, Colin, was the golden boy. Star baseball player, great student, doer of no wrong. I, on the other hand, am good at...making juice. With my mom asleep on the couch, likely for the rest of the afternoon, I set her glass of juice on the coffee table, bring mine upstairs with me, and google: how to tell when a girl is flirting with you.

chapter 3

*

sting-chronicity

You probably think it's strange that a kid my age is into Sting. Well if it is, it's only weird that a kid my age *these days* is into Sting, because back in the late 1970s and all throughout the 1980s, practically every kid my age was into his band, The Police. Stewart Copeland, the drummer for The Police, made a documentary called *Everyone Stares,* which I watched on YouTube. In it there was a scene in which, after one of their concerts, Sting couldn't get out the back door of the building because there were so many teenagers crowding the place chanting, "STING, STING, STING!!" Police (both actual police officers and the other members of his band, The Police) were trying to help him escape. He looked totally freaked out but you could tell he reveled in the adoration of his fans at the same time.

The first time Sting appeared on my radar was while watching my all-time favorite movie, *Bee Movie.* It's an animated movie written by Jerry Seinfeld, who my parents really like for his TV show, which they used to love watching with Colin back in the '90s. Every time Seinfeld's name comes up, my dad makes the same lame joke: "I love Jerry, even though he spells his name wrong." My dad spells his name, Gerry, with a g. Personally, I think Jerry with a j looks better, but a g makes more sense if it's short for Gerald, like it is for my dad. Then I learned it could be short for Jerome, too. This is what dad jokes do: they force me down rabbit holes that have no destination. So let's move on. *Bee Movie* had a major impact on my life for a myriad of reasons: **1.)** it was my introduction to my hero, Sting; **2.)** it's the reason I stopped eating meat; and **3.)** there's the name connection. We'll get to the other two later but for now let's stick with Sting.

There I was, a little kid watching a movie with his mom. Toward the end of *Bee Movie* there's a courtroom scene in which the main character, Barry (who is a bee), is suing the human race for stealing honey from the bees and Sting is called to the witness stand. I had no idea who he was but I thought it was cool that his name was Sting, so I asked my mom about him. After Colin died—for which she blames Green Day—my mom stopped listening to music. I was young and didn't realize that music was something she avoided; it was just normal to me that we never had it playing in the house. That's all I knew so I didn't think twice about it (or even once, for that matter). But this day was different. My mom suddenly became more animated than I'd ever seen her, telling me about Sting and The Police. She was wide-eyed, talking with her hands, and her voice contained an unfamiliar excitement. She opened the entertainment center underneath the TV and pulled out a CD by The Police. My mom brought me up into Colin's room and played The Police on his old stereo, the only one in the house. She had me by the hands as we listened and danced together. It was truly one of the happiest moments of my life. And it was over as quickly as it began. The moment the CD ended, it was as if my mom snapped back into reality, *her* reality of not allowing herself to feel joy, as if that would somehow be an affront to the memory of Colin. I was a little kid so I didn't understand this at the time; it's something I worked out later as I replayed the scene over and over again in my head, not knowing what went wrong, wondering if it was something I had done, wondering if it would ever happen again. The following day all of the CDs were missing from the entertainment center.

The fifth and final album by The Police (and the one we danced to that day) is called *Synchronicity,* a concept developed by Carl Jung, a renowned psychiatrist (or maybe psychologist—I can never remember the difference) back in the late 1800s/early 1900s. The concept holds that events are "meaningful coincidences" if they occur with no causal relationship yet seem to be meaningfully related. In other words, Jung believed there was a large pattern to life, that it wasn't just chaos. Heady stuff, huh? I've tried reading Jung. I borrowed a copy of his book *Man and His Symbols* from the library at least five times but I've never been able to read it all the way through. Sting seems to be a big fan of his work. On top of being one of the biggest rock stars in the world, he's also quite bright.

We never spoke of that moment again, but whenever I watched *Bee Movie* (which was a ton), my mom would disappear as Sting's small part in the movie approached and I understood that Sting had some kind of power that I did not fully grasp. That day was the beginning of my fascination with him and in years to come he would continue to appear in my life at pivotal moments involving my mom, leading me to believe that he holds the key to unlocking the happiness that is buried deep within her. I feel that Sting and I are connected— these moments of synchronicity are too genuine to ignore, and I know in my heart that if there is a way that I can meet him, I'll be able to unlock the mystery and help my mom turn back into the happy person she was when Colin was still alive.

chapter 4

*

at the library

I live in a small New Jersey town you've never heard of called Neshanic Station, where every day is exactly the same. Without a driver's license, the only thing to do in Neshanic is daydream about getting a car and leaving this town behind. Perplexing to me is the number of people who get their licenses yet end up staying here for good. I imagine many shared my fantasy of getting out until one day they conceded, accepting their small-town fate of being born, living, and dying all in the same place. My birthday is in September; this year it's just a few days before the start of my senior year. I'll be turning seventeen, which in New Jersey is when you're able to get your driver's license. Able, that is, so long as your mom doesn't have an earth-shattering fear of you getting behind the wheel. Guess who won't be getting his license in September?

My mom is having a better day today. Yesterday she hardly moved from the couch at all, not even to eat dinner, so my dad ended up eating both his meal and hers when he got home. Today she's out on one of her walks, so now is the perfect time for me to get over to the library to pick up the book that Mary, the librarian, has for me. You may consider sneaking off to the library while my mom is out deceitful, but I don't have a job (she won't allow it) so I can't afford to buy books from Amazon, and I have to get them somehow. Plus, I enjoy spending time with Mary.

I used to spend practically every Saturday at the library. My dad felt guilty that I spent so much time looking after my mom and cooking the majority of the meals so he wanted me to take one day a week to get out and do something for myself. He called it my "free day." The problem is, in my boring town, there isn't much to do. I started going down to the library and ended up really hitting it off with Mary. Not in a creepy way. She must be 70 years old, which is just a guess—I'd never ask. We would talk about books, movies, etc., and then I'd end up helping her rearrange the entire fiction section, which was a ton of work but we had a blast doing it. After a while my mom, who didn't like me being gone every Saturday afternoon, changed my free day to Sundays, the only day the library is closed. I brought this up to her but she just kept saying, "I'm sorry but it's out of my hands." My dad said he'd talk to her but either he didn't get around to it or the talk didn't go well. Either way, now I have to be creative about getting myself to the library.

Every time I leave, I set a timer for an hour and a half and I always make sure to keep my walkie-talkie on me, just in case. My mom's walks can, and often do, take longer than this but they are never shorter, and I err on the side of caution to ensure that I return home before she does.

There's a shortcut to get to the library that shaves a good five minutes off the walk from my house. Two homes on Maple Ave. share a driveway and if you cut through it going in between their detached garages, it leads you through an alleyway that lets you out at the library's back door. I discovered it one time while my dad and I were out looking for my mom when one of her walks was lasting longer than normal. Now I use it when I'm in a pinch.

Usually when I arrive, Mary asks if she should put on 'our songs,' which is code for a Sting CD we both love. Listening to music goes against what you probably think of as library etiquette, having to be quiet and all. I once asked Mary if she could borrow *My Songs*, Sting's new (at the time) album, from the county library. The Neshanic Station Library is tiny and there are a lot of things it doesn't carry, but

Mary is always happy to call over to the county library in Somerville to check its inventory. If it's in stock there, the librarian will send it to us in Neshanic, since they use the same computer system (which Mary hardly knows how to use, hence the phone call). Since the only CD player in my house is in Colin's room and my mom has nothing but disdain for music, I told Mary that there was a good chance I wouldn't be able to listen to it at home, but that I'd heard Sting say on *The Tonight Show starring Jimmy Fallon* that the liner notes contained explanations of the meaning behind the lyrics, which piqued my interest. I didn't mention to her that I'd planned on scouring said liner notes for clues as to what power this English rockstar seemed to hold and how I could harness some of it to help my mom become happy again. When *My Songs* arrived, Mary brought in a portable CD player from home so we could listen together. Since then it's sort of become our thing. She puts it on as we chat and if there are any old fuddy-duddies (her words) at the library, we just wait until they leave. It's usually not a problem because there's hardly ever anyone in there.

Sting is, as usual, the focal point of our meeting today but this time his words rather than his music have brought us together. Mary stands in the doorway upon my arrival, her arms outstretched, holding a beautiful hardcover copy of *Lyrics* by Sting, which I had asked if she could get. Just like she did with *My Songs*, she had it transferred over from the county library. The title likely explains it but in case there's any question, this book contains all of Sting's lyrics from his first album with The Police, *Outlandos D'Amour*, to his most recent (at the time of the book's publication) solo album, *Sacred Love*, along with his commentary. A collection of music-less poems to most, but a book of clues to me; the hope I feel blanketed in when Mary places *Lyrics* in my hands is immeasurable.

Mary hands me another book, telling me she simply could not resist. It's Sting's memoir, *Broken Music*. Flipping through both with Mary looking on excitedly, it hits me that these books weren't borrowed from the county library. There aren't any of the usual markings that library books contain: no stamps identifying them as property of such-and-such library, no barcode to scan for checking it out on the computer. Mary must read the look on my face because before I'm able to protest she states, "They're a gift, from one reader to another."

My mouth opens but before any words come, she adds, "And don't even start with this pay-me-back nonsense. You coming here to spend time with a lonely old lady is priceless and I won't hear another word about money," which makes me smile because since stepping through the door I have yet to utter a single word.

It's one of the kindest gifts I've ever received, from one lonely person to another.

"Thank you so much!"

"You're very welcome. Did you happen to see that the new yoga studio across the street is officially open? You haven't been by in a bit; I can't remember if it was open the last time you were here."

Don't ask me why but I decide to play dumb when Mary brings it up.

"A new yoga studio, you say? Interesting."

chapter 5

*

boulevard of broken dreams

Set diagonally across the street from the library is a general store which, in all my years of living in town, I've never stepped foot inside. Housed in a modest white building, a sign hangs above its immense bay window that reads simply: The Store. It must be the original sign as it looks ancient and the majority of the paint is chipped off, making the words barely legible. There looks to be an apartment up top because I doubt the neighborhood general store has two stories' worth of goods for sale. I've asked my parents about it a few times over the years, mostly about why we've never gone in there—not even once. My dad always says it's "because they're the competition." He works at the Wawa over on Route 202. The Store has another building attached to it that changes hands more than I can keep up with. Off the top of my head I can remember a nail salon, a bait and tackle shop, an antique store, and an insurance company, I believe. I don't pay much attention because businesses come and go so frequently in that spot and none of them have ever been useful to me. With all of the turnover to its adjoined neighbor, it's a wonder The Store has lasted all this time. People in Neshanic Station must really love their cigarettes and lottery tickets, which is all The Store is good for according to my dad. "You want a good sub, you come to Wawa," he says.

The latest business to set up shop next to The Store is Follow the Sun Yoga and I forgo the shortcut home, instead taking the long way up Olive Street with hopes of catching a glimpse of the girl from yesterday. I'm beginning to actually feel like the peeping Tom she accused me of being, though not enough to change my decision to walk past. Suddenly I gain a new perspective on the phrase "be careful what you wish for" as I see her crouched against the wall of the yoga studio, talking on the phone, looking as if she's crying and it's at that moment that she spots me too.

"I've got to go," she says into the phone, quickly sliding it into her pocket. "Hey, still looking for Sting?" she asks, quickly wiping her eyes in an attempt to mask her tears.

"Oh no, I figured he's back home in London by now. Sorry, I didn't mean to interrupt anything."

"Okay, I was kidding about the whole peeping Tom thing..."

So she was kidding!

"...sort of."

Spoke too soon.

"Now I realize that you're actually a stalker," she says with a sly (and gorgeous) smile that confirms (I think) that she is being sarcastic.

"I can assure you that I am no stalker. Well not of you, anyway. You're safe. Sting...lock your doors, buddy."

"The only thing I know about you is that you have a seemingly unhealthy infatuation with Sting. Give me the antithesis of that. You love Sting more than anything. What in this world do you most despise?"

"Green Day," I say, surprising myself with the swiftness of my response.

"Wow, I wasn't expecting that. And what, if I may, did Green Day ever do to you?"

"They destroyed my family." As the words come out of my mouth, I wonder what power this sarcastic mystery girl possesses that can get me to tell her something so personal without hesitation. I reflexively check the timer on my phone to make sure I'll still be able to beat my mom home.

"Expecting a call?"

"No, definitely not. I was just checking the time. I need to get home before my mom does. She's a bit...overbearing."

"My mom is the opposite of overbearing. Heck, she's not even bearing. The only time I hear from her is when she feels like making me cry, as you just witnessed."

"Look at the bright side—at least your mom doesn't treat you as if you're five and make you carry around a walkie-talkie, filing a missing person report if you travel out of range."

"So *that's* what the walkie-talkie is for," she says, acknowledging the embarrassing kids' toy clipped onto the waistband of my shorts. "I thought you might be an EMT or something."

"Nope, I've got a weak stomach, I couldn't handle all the blood."

"I'll keep that in mind. So, what's your name anyway, or should I just call you Stalker Boy?"

"I'm Rod, nice to meet you," I say.

"Cat," she says. "It's a pleasure."

Cat. What a wonderful name. I've never met a Cat before. Obviously I've met many felines, but no humans named Cat. Thank god I didn't just say that aloud. At least I hope I didn't. I begin to get nervous and second-guess all of my thoughts.

She's wearing a black jean jacket, white shoes, and a black knit winter cap. Cat is the kind of person that makes it look natural to be wearing such an outfit in the summertime. That look takes a certain kind of cool to pull off. And confidence, too. Two things of which I don't possess an iota.

"So, Rod, tell me more about Green Day destroying your family. You've got me intrigued."

Last night, after googling 'how to tell when a girl is flirting with you,' I traveled down a rabbit hole, as I am prone to doing, and learned that when attempting to flirt with a girl (something I have absolutely zero experience with), it's best to ask questions about her rather than talk about yourself the entire time.

"So, do you go to Somerville High School too or did you just move here this summer?"

"Just moved here. Well, I'm only staying for the summer. My Aunt Amy just opened this yoga studio and I'm staying with her in the apartment above to help her get it up and running. She's the best person ever. She's my Sting, if you will. I don't know anyone around here, except now I know you."

"Where do you live during the school year?" I ask, hoping to sound natural but fearing that it's coming off like the world's most boring interrogation.

"I live in Holmdel with my mom and her boyfriend. It's about forty-five minutes from here."

"Man, I wish I could stay somewhere else for an entire summer. I mean, I love my parents and all but I never go anywhere. An adventure like that sounds amazing. My mom's heart would definitely stop within twenty-four hours of my departure, though."

"Our moms sound like complete opposites, Rodney."

My knees buckle under me a bit when she calls me Rodney. No one has ever called me that before and for some reason it's the best thing I've ever heard.

"It's a dream to get to spend the summer out here with my Aunt Amy because she's my best friend and my mom and I are like oil and water. But I'd be lying if I said it didn't hurt that she didn't even bat an eye when I brought up coming here for the entire summer. My nurturing mother didn't even pretend she was going to miss me. She actually came up to my room smiling after my Aunt Amy made her pitch for me to come. Please don't judge me for using such a tired cliche but the grass is always greener. Perhaps your mom's overprotective nature is the only way she knows how to show you love."

Not only is Cat beautiful and confident, she is also quite profound. As I try to think of a response that won't make me seem like an idiot, her eyes wander up the street, causing mine to as well. My heart then drops into my stomach as I see my mom, adorned in her white walking attire, making her way up Pleasant Run Road past the volunteer fire station maybe three hundred yards from where we're standing.

"There she is again," Cat says. "I've seen her walking around town a few times now. I'm dying to know what her story is."

In a panic, I look at my phone and my feet are moving before the words "I've got to go" leave my mouth. I head for the library to take the shortcut home. Pleasant Run Road, the street ~~The Woman in White~~ my mom is making her way up, will soon intersect with Maple Avenue, where I will be momentarily. I need to hustle and cut through a few backyards to avoid running into her, quite literally. The adrenaline takes over, pushing down the worry that it's possible my mom saw me standing outside the forbidden general store, talking to a girl. Day one of summer break has already surpassed all of last year's excitement.

chapter 6

*

secret journey

Since I was little, I've been embarrassed of my first name, which is likely the reason it's been so easy for me to accept nicknames even if they haven't been the most favorable. Sure, every kid would like a sweet nickname like Ace or Falcon but that wasn't in the cards for me. In the second grade, our class put on a performance of Noah's Ark and I was cast in the esteemed role of Skunk #2. I didn't have any lines and my acting career was over as quickly as it began. Though my time on the stage was brief, it still garnered me the nickname Stinky, thanks to Frankie Friel. As far as nicknames go, Stinky stunk. It stunk *and* it stuck. Little did I know that all I would have to do to shed this stink was ruin a field trip and turn the entirety of my class against me.

Back in the sixth grade, our class took a trip to the Empire State Building. This was a huge deal and all the kids looked forward to it from the first day of school, because for the majority of the students, it would be the first time they'd be going into New York City without their parents. From Neshanic Station, New York City is just over an hour away, so lots of kids had been on day trips into the city with their parents for various reasons: to catch a Broadway play, to visit the tree in Rockefeller Center at Christmas, or even for an afternoon of Sunday shopping. The possibilities are endless in the City that Never Sleeps. Well, not for me. I'd never been to New York, as my mom proclaimed it to be a place filled with strangers and thieves.

She told me there was a darkness to New York City and she never wanted me stepping foot in that wasteland of a city (her words).

I'd never gone on a class trip before, either; I'd always been inconspicuously absent on field trip days (even those not venturing into NYC), as my attendance would have been far too stressful on my mom. Not being able to visit the Empire State Building didn't matter much to me. Growing up hearing nothing but negative stories about New York City, I had little desire to go.

On November 11th of that very same year, Sting was set to release his twelfth studio album, entitled *57th and 9th*. He began promoting it toward the end of the summer and I visited his website every day in anticipation of its release. When I first realized that his new album was to be released on the same day that my class would be visiting the Empire State Building, I thought I'd hit the jackpot. My mom would undoubtedly keep me home from school that day, so I surmised that I could stay home and listen to Sting's new album online (in private through earbuds, of course, adhering to my mom's unwritten rule against music in the house). I then learned that the album title was a reference to the New York City intersection Sting crossed every day to get to Avatar Studios in Hell's Kitchen, where the album was recorded. Things really changed after I hopped on Google Maps and found out that the cross section of 57th Street and 9th Avenue was just 2.1 miles from the Empire State Building. At that moment, I began planning my secret journey.

There was no way in hell my mom would ever allow me to travel into New York City, even under the supervision of teachers and chaperones, but this was more than coincidence; it was synchronicity at work. I knew I needed to get myself on that trip so I went to work on my dad in his most vulnerable state: while watching baseball. I watched his beloved Phillies with him, as I often did, but instead of keeping my nose in a book until he cheered a home run for or jeered one against the Phils, I played on his love of history and (thanks to Wikipedia) threw him facts about what was once the world's largest building as if they were fastballs. Things like, "Wow, what a hit! That batter is the size of a building. Speaking of which, did you know that the Empire State Building is so large it was assigned its own zip code, 10118?" Or, "Man, that was totally a strike, what's that ump looking at? It's almost like he's calling the game from atop the Empire State Building, which, by the way, was originally planned to be fifty stories but was later increased to sixty and then eighty stories. Neat, huh?"

The Phillies were dreadful that year, finishing second to last in their division, ahead of only the Atlanta Braves. Because so many of their games were meaningless by September, my dad's interest began to wane, so he took the bait, marveling at my newfound enthusiasm for the Empire State Building and soon becoming interested as well. Mary found me a great book about it that I borrowed from the library and while the Phillies were getting blown out, which was often, my dad and I dug into the history of New York's most famous Art Deco skyscraper. Eventually, I gathered the courage to bring up the field trip. Although he knew it would cause my mom much heartache, he also felt guilty that I spent most of my free time caring for her, acting like the parent instead of the kid, so he signed my permission slip and we made a promise to keep it between the two of us.

I suffered terrible pangs of guilt for deceiving my dad *and* keeping the field trip a secret from my mom. I justified it knowing that if this was truly synchronicity, as I believed it to be, and I ended up realizing my dream of meeting Sting, I could find out once and for all what his role would be in unlocking my mom's repressed happiness. On top of that, as much as history bores the life out of me, I had enjoyed spending time with my dad and I could tell that he was proud of my passion about this subject. Even if that pride was based on a lie, it still felt good for at least one of my parents to be proud of me for something, anything, other than just being Colin's (failed) replacement.

The night before the trip, I was confident that I had everything planned out. Everything, that is, except for what I would do once I arrived at the intersection of 57th Street and 9th Avenue. That was the one part I couldn't figure out, but I trusted that it was my job to get there and that the rest would be taken of by Sting. I listened to the song *Secret Journey* by The Police ad nauseam that night and trusted in Sting's lyrics:

You will see light in the darkness
You will make some sense of this
And when you've made your secret journey
You will find this love you miss

Our entire sixth grade class rode a chartered bus into New York City, two of them in fact. Once inside the Empire State Building, I made sure to make myself the very last student in line, which wasn't difficult because when you're the Invisible Man, blending in is part of the job (it's *fitting* in that's the challenge). Finally, when it was my turn to step through the metal detector, I turned to Mrs. Sullivan, my English teacher who was a chaperone on the trip and told her that I had to use the bathroom. In an attempt to hurry me through and catch up with the rest of the class, she told me there were plenty of bathrooms inside and that I would just have to hold it. That's when I played the D card: diarrhea. In a huff, she told me that it was "probably from eating all those vegetables on the bus." She was referring to the two carrots I had eaten as a snack. The same snack had caused Frankie to call me Bugs and continuously shout, "What's up, Doc!" from his seat in the back, which led Mrs. Sullivan to turn to me and ask "why I had to egg him on." Despite carrots not being a known culprit of diarrhea, I was not about to point it out to her. She motioned toward the restrooms in the lobby and told me to catch up with them on the other side as quickly as possible, as she had to corral the rest of the students and could not plan her schedule around my stomach's indiscretions (her words).

The moment Mrs. Sullivan and her lack of nutritional

knowledge crossed to the other side of the metal detector, I slipped out the front door, pulled out the Razor scooter that I had smuggled inside my backpack, and commenced my secret journey to make my mom whole again. I was short on time, knowing they would figure out I was gone by the time the first headcount was taken, so every second mattered.

New York City is equal parts confusing and intimidating, but although I had never before set foot in this concrete jungle, I was a man on a mission and I was prepared. I had the route from Google Maps memorized as if it were the alphabet. Head northwest on West 33rd Street toward Broadway for half a mile. Turn right onto 8th Avenue; continue for 1.2 miles. Turn left onto West 57th Street. Each city block contained more citizens coming and going than the entire population of Neshanic Station and I was bobbing and weaving through every single one of them as if I were Muhammed Ali. I knew I would be facing harsh repercussions for defecting from the field trip but this was no game—this was a matter of life and death. If I was right and the release of Sting's new record on the same day that my class would be a mere two miles away was indeed the key to unlocking my mom's happiness, I would soon be freed of the metaphorical shackles I wore and would be allowed to be a teenager; one that could make my mom smile, like she did when Colin was alive.

It didn't take me more than fifteen minutes to reach my destination and once there I learned that it was simply an intersection of two busy New York City streets. Yes, I know that's exactly how it was described but I was sure there was something more to it and I was determined to uncover the mystery. I went into nearby cafes whose names I don't remember, where they served overpriced coffee and scones; none of their patrons was a British-born rockstar. I combed Balsley Park and found lots of benches, a kiosk that served pizza and ice cream, and a play area for kids, but no Sting. I looked for a blind holy man, like the one in the lyrics to *Secret Journey*, but all I found was a crazy-eyed homeless man who aggressively insisted that Jesus was coming back and that I had better REPENT!

A storm was on its way. It was only eleven in the morning and the sky was turning black. I was running out of time, out of hope, and out of a clear vision on what to do. And then I remembered the lyrics to *Secret Journey*, the last chorus containing one line different than the others:

> *You will see light in the darkness*
> *You will make some sense of this*
> **You will see joy in this sadness**
> *You will find this love you miss*

In a last-ditch effort, I scootered over to 441 West 53rd Street, the site of Avatar Studios, where Sting had recorded *57th & 9th*. I knew he would be there and that this was the light in the darkness that I was searching for. Any punishment coming my way for breaking off from the group and ruining the class trip would be justified in a matter of moments when I met Sting and could find joy in my mom's sadness while finding the love that I miss; love that she only had enough of for one son. I was a mere two blocks away from my destination when Green Day, the black cloud perpetually looming over my head, intervened.

"There he is! I see him!" It was the weasel voice of Frankie shouting as he ran up the street pointing at me. Mrs. Sullivan shuffled down the street behind him trying in vain to keep up, her signature muumuu dress flapping behind her in the wind. "There's the nimrod right there!

The nimrod in question was me, dressed in a black t-shirt with the word "nimrod" written in lowercase black letters inside a large yellow circle—a giant bullseye giving me away. At the time I had no idea it was a Green Day shirt. I mean, what kind of band doesn't put their own name on their t-shirt?! It was a hand-me-down, like everything I wore. It's strange because my mom treats Colin's room as if it's a museum, one she guards like a hawk, not allowing anything to come or go without her approval and yet my parents have always dressed me in his old clothes. I had no say in the matter. My guess is that it was a money issue as it's always been tight.

There and then I became Nimrod (eventually shortened to Rod), the jerkwad who absconded from the rest of the students and ruined the class trip for everyone, stealing their chance to climb all one hundred and two of The Empire State Building's stories.

* * * * * * * * *

Early on during Little League, I decided to hang up my baseball cleats and my dad was disappointed. He loved baseball more than almost anything and Colin had been a star player his entire life. As bummed as my dad was, he also realized that I sucked, which alleviated some of his despondency. When he picked me up from school the day I ruined the field trip, forced to leave work early, the let-down in his eyes spoke more than words ever could. Eventually he would come around to understand that my heart was in the right place as I explained to him why I did what I did, but man, did that take a while.

As for my mom, this stunt of mine led to her ordering me to dig up the walkie-talkies in the attic and her obsession for me to stay in range was born. Technically, I didn't get grounded for my actions, but like one of those silly unwritten rules in baseball, it was understood that I was pretty much permanently grounded from that day forward. I'll never know if Sting was at Avatar Studios that day. Green Day made sure of that—another prime example that, for whatever reason, they are hell-bent on ruining my life.

chapter 7

*

dead end job

There's a scene in *Bee Movie* in which the main character, Barry, is talking to the woman in charge of doling out jobs the day after they graduate from high school—the day they officially become worker bees. She's explaining that they'll be assigned a job and they'll work that job every single day for the rest of their lives.

"So you'll just work us to death?!" Barry asks in a panic.

"We'll sure try!" she responds, as she and all of the bees laugh. All of the bees except for Barry, that is, who is horrified.

My dad is a worker bee. He works two jobs. His full-time job is as manager of the Wawa in the next town over. He also works part-time at Lowe's. A lot falls on my dad's shoulders since my mom doesn't work or drive. One thing you won't hear him do is complain. Sure, he'll talk about being tired when he comes home ("My dogs are barking," is a particularly favorite phrase of my dad's once his shoes come off), but it comes off as conversational rather than grumbling. Since I don't have a job or a driver's license, I'm not much help, so I try to do what I can around the house to pitch in. This mainly comes down to doing the majority of the cooking, which I've come to enjoy. This morning I'm making my dad's favorite, sweet potato oatmeal. It's a recipe I learned from *Forks Over Knives: The Cookbook*. Stumbling upon the documentary *Forks Over Knives* back in freshman year was a game changer. I was already vegetarian by that point, even flirting with veganism, but I was in it solely for ethical purposes, not thinking of the health factor whatsoever. Before seeing the film, I existed on a steady diet of tater tots, spaghetti, and gray soy burgers. Afterward, I adopted a whole-foods, plant-based diet.

Sweet potato oatmeal has become a staple of mine so I know the recipe by heart, which is good because it's 5 a.m. and my brain is on autopilot. My dad's shift at Wawa starts at 6 a.m. If I didn't get up early to make him a healthy breakfast he would just grab something at work (his words), which I know means Hostess Cupcakes or donuts or something equally unhealthy. As much as waking up at the butt crack of dawn during summer break feels inherently wrong, it comforts me to know he'll have at least one healthy meal today.

I probably already mentioned that my dad is a big guy. That's an understatement. My dad is huge. While I don't know exactly what he weighs, I imagine he's around 400 pounds. It's hard to gauge and I'd never ask, but since I weigh 135 lbs. and he seems to be at least three times my size, I come up with four hundred. He wasn't always this big. He was in good shape in the old family photos my mom carries with her practically everywhere she goes. My dad is a tall guy, around 6'2", and he was lean in the pictures where he's playing with Colin. After Colin died, my mom turned to pills to numb her pain and my dad turned to food, though he takes his fair share of pills, too. Rather than to control emotions, the pills he takes are for cholesterol, blood pressure, and heartburn. He's never told me this but I read about it on the Internet; apparently it's pretty common for people to "eat their feelings," and that's clearly what my dad does. I love my dad and I worry about him. I'm well aware that as people get older, their bodies change and they usually end up putting on weight (well, everyone but Sting, who seems to be in better shape with each passing year), but my dad doesn't even look like the same person as the guy in those pictures. His hair is completely white now, he's so big he has trouble even standing up out of his chair, and his walk is getting dangerously close to becoming a full-on waddle. Simple tasks are a struggle for him and I just wish that my parents' decision to have me as a replacement child had made them happy so that they hadn't resorted to slowly killing themselves with pills and junk food.

"Is that sweet potato oatmeal I smell?" my dad asks, coming into the kitchen with a brimming smile on his face. Even being painfully overweight and perpetually overworked, my dad has a positive attitude. I do my best to remain optimistic too, a trait I learned from Sting in his commentary on his song *Brand New Day*: "My long-standing strategy in life has been one of optimism, even in the face of some daunting realities."

"Yessir, your favorite."

"Tell me, bud, what's a kid your age on summer break doing up at 5 a.m.?"

"Well, this recipe feeds four so if I slept in and made it when you're already at work, too much of it would go to waste," I say. "Plus, it's more fun to cook for other people than to cook for myself."

"You were out like a light by the time I got home last night," he says, walking past and rustling my hair, like he's been doing since I was a kid. "I'm hoping that means you did something fun yesterday."

"Sorry about that. I tried waiting up so we could watch something together but I guess I passed out. I did get down to the library for a bit but Mom was having kind of a rough day so after that I mostly hung around here to keep an eye on her."

"She's been having a lot of those lately. One day I hope you get to be a kid and stop having to take care of me and your mom all the time."

"I don't mind. It's got its perks," I say as I shovel a forkful of oatmeal down my throat.

"Well I'm your dad and I'm giving you an order. Go do something fun today. Some fresh air will do you some good. Why don't you go over to Frankie's?"

Going to Frankie's won't be fun and I won't get any fresh air because all Frankie ever wants to do is smoke pot and play video games, but I agree to send him a text and tell my dad that maybe I'll stop by Frankie's after cleaning Miss Jones's litter boxes.

"Ahh...it's litter box day, huh?" he remarks grimly.

I nod, matching his sentiment.

"Well, that's not exactly the wild-and-crazy I had in mind so hopefully, for your sake, Frankie is around and up for hanging out. I'm not working at Lowe's tonight so I'll be home for dinner. How about I bring home a couple of pizzas and we'll watch a movie?"

"A couple of pizzas? Is someone coming over?"

"Nope, it's just us. But it's been a long week and I need to refuel with pizza. Lots of pizza!" he says with a smile across his face as large as a pizza. There isn't much in this world that makes my dad happier than pizza does. "Anything you want me to grab for you?"

"No thanks," I say. "I'll make something for myself later."

"A teenager who doesn't eat pizza. You're a diamond in the rough, bud."

* * * * * * * * *

Joanne Jones lives on Chestnut Street, the next street over from mine, right near my bus stop. Since she can't hear very well, she tells me there's no sense knocking on the door or ringing the bell because she won't hear it anyway. Instead, she has me come to the side door near where she sits and watches her programs (her words). Did I mention she's got an antiquated alarm system that never works properly? Entering her house rarely goes smoothly.

"Hi, Miss Jones. I'm here to scoop the litter boxes," I say as I plant myself in front of the alarm and methodically enter in the numbers.

Crap. She's asleep and, of course, the code isn't taking. I've got sixty seconds before this thing trips and alerts the police, something that's happened to me a handful of times. I know what you're thinking—why would she have her alarm set when she's in the house? Trust me, I've asked her this very same question on multiple occasions. The only semblance of an answer I've been able to get out of her is "you can't be too careful these days," and then she'll go on to say something mildly racist followed by a diatribe about how much better things were in her day.

"Miss Jones. Miss Jones! MISS JONES!" I'm now shouting as the alarm is about to go off and nothing is waking her from her slumber. It begins to dawn on me that she may be dead. I turn to get a closer look, unsure if I'm going to have to check her pulse (a task that I am in no way qualified to do) and end up stepping on one of the cats' tails. It lets out an awful screech. Then something hits me on the back of the head.

"OUCH!"

"Get out of here, you hoodlum! You think you can rob an old lady in broad daylight? I'm a retired real estate broker. I know people!"

"Miss Jones, it's me, Rod. I'm here to scoop your litter boxes," I plead, hoping she'll hear me and refrain from launching any other inanimate objects at my head.

"Jesus H. Christ, Rod. You scared me half to death. I thought you were a burglar. What are you doing sneaking around like that? Don't you know my intestines could pop out at any moment? Christ Almighty!"

"I wasn't sneaking around. I tried waking you but then I... never mind. Listen, your alarm is going off. I couldn't get it to disarm."

"What?"

"Your alarm! It's going off! Can't you hear that?"

"Well why didn't you shut it off when you came in?" she asks, matter-of-factly.

"You're right, why didn't I think of that?" I say, not quite loudly enough for her to hear.

"You're dripping wet and are making a mess of my floor," she gripes, disarming the alarm with no trouble at all. "What did you do, come straight from the swimming hole?"

"I believe that's milk from the bowl of cereal you threw at my head."

"Dang it, I wasn't done with that. Well, go ahead and scoop the boxes. You can clean this mess up when you're done. And you can get me a new bowl of Corn Flakes, too. I'll be right over to make sure you're scooping it right."

"It's okay, Miss Jones, you don't have to watch me scoop. I know what I'm doing."

Joanne Jones is old. Super old. She's a cat lady but doesn't have as many as you'd think—just four. Mittens is the only one I see (and occasionally step on), but I know the others are alive because the litter boxes get too full for it to be just one cat doing all the damage. Joanne can't scoop the boxes herself because **1.)** she's ancient, like I said, and **2.)** she has some kind of hernia and says her intestines will pop out if she bends over too far. Every time I see her, whether it's day or nighttime, she's wearing a nightgown. Around the nightgown a wide cloth band is fastened, which I assume is meant to hold her intestines in place. I don't know if that would even work and I try not to think about it but it's difficult not to because she's always going on about it. She tells me all kinds of gross stuff that I don't want to know, and because she can barely hear a thing, she talks super loud. I sit on a tiny stool and scoop through the litter boxes with a slotted soup spoon. It takes forever. The spoon is small and is not made for scooping cat litter. I actually bought a proper cat litter scooper with my own money and brought it over once but the next time I came back it was nowhere to be found. Sometimes I consider the idea of looking in her silverware drawer, but I'm too afraid of what I may find.

Every three days, when I come to scoop the boxes, Miss Jones tells me all about the special litter she uses and how it's the best kind and that not a lot of people know how to use it correctly. When she tells me that people "don't know how to use the litter correctly," it conjures an image in my head of people trying to pee in the litter box with her standing nearby shouting at them about how to do it the right way. What she really means to say is they don't know how to "scoop it correctly" but it's pretty cut-and-dry: you see a lump of cat poop or some cat pee and you scoop it up. Miss Jones is always going on and on about a woman she had working for her who had seen the clumps of pee and had mashed it up instead of scooping it. "She mashed it up! Do you believe that? Who's ever heard of such a thing?" I have. I heard about it the last time I was here, and the time before that, and the time before that. Since she repeats the exact same things every time I'm here, I make a little game out of it and try to predict what she's going to say before it leaves her mouth. These little games we play are what keep the lonely sane.

Miss Jones has had a lot of different people come over to scoop her litter boxes but she says no one is as good at it as I am. She means this as a compliment so I smile politely when she says it, but it's pretty depressing when your only known talents in life consist of juicing and litter box scooping. Those should look great on a college application. My guess is that the people that came before me got sick of hearing about her gross ailments and about the girl who mashed up the pee instead of scooping it, so they stop coming. I'm not trying to be mean when I call her ailments gross. I always try to be a nice guy but they really are vulgar. Last time I was here she told me that she goes to a podiatrist, which is a foot doctor, so he can cut her toenails for her because she can't bend over to do it herself on account of her intestines being ready to eject at any moment. Hearing an old lady shout that is off-putting in itself, but then she informed me that she's unhappy with her doctor because he used to soak her toenails so they would get soft before he cut them, but lately he hasn't been soaking them first; instead, he's just been going for it. Now I trust that you're in agreement with my "gross" assessment.

chapter 8

*

walking alone

As I leave Joanne Jones's house, clutching the five-dollar bill I earned for my services, I've all but forgotten about the alarm tripping incident so I'm startled for a second upon seeing a police officer approaching as I exit the side door.

"Hey, Rod, is that you? How's it going?"

"Oh, hey, Officer Stewart. Good, I guess. What are you doing here?"

God, I ask the dumbest questions. I know exactly what he's doing here. I'm too incompetent to properly turn off an alarm in the sixty seconds allotted for such an action and that alarm alerts the police so they have to come out to check and make sure everything is all right. *Duh.*

"Just here to check on the alert we got about Miss Jones's alarm going off. That old thing being stubborn again? The alarm I mean, of course. Not Miss Jones," he says with a smile and a wink approaching a Sting level of smooth. "Hey Rod, can I ask you something off the record?"

I've never been asked anything off the record before, at least not that I'm aware of. I do everything I can to channel my inner Sting and not blurt out, "YES, PLEASE."

"That would be fine by me," is all I'm able to idiotically muster.

"That kid who lives next to the park. You know him, right?

What's his name again?"

"Oh, Frankie. Frankie Friel. We used to be best friends when we were kids. Now we've kind of grown apart but we still hang out sometimes. I'm actually heading over to his house now. Well, maybe. I don't know. It's not set in stone."

Why did I just tell him all of that?! So not Sting-like.

"Is Frankie in trouble for something?" I continue, fearing that I may have just incriminated him for something. *Crap, am I a snitch*?

Immediately, my brain jumps to five years from now. I've just graduated college and am visiting Frankie in jail. He's in gen pop (which is what they call it on those *Lock Up*-type shows) and life inside has changed him. He's got dead eyes, face tattoos, and his bulging prison muscles deter anyone from acting on the impulse to call him Carrot Top, as his hair has somehow turned an even more obnoxious shade of orange since being locked up. He has no idea that the anonymous tip that landed him behind bars came from my lips. The guilt eats at me, enough to drive me to bring him homemade meals every time I come back to town for a visit, always disguising the fact that they're plant-based because that hippie shit will get a guy killed in here (his words).

"Rod, you still with me?" Officer Stewart asks, jolting me back into reality.

"Oh, uh, sorry. The cat litter fumes must have gotten to me."

"And here I thought I had a thankless job. So listen, I don't want to put you in a weird spot and I don't have proof that it's him, but we've got to do checks of the park every once in a while and I keep finding empty vape cartridges in the gazebo that David Morgan and the historical society are restoring, leading me to believe someone is smoking pot and leaving it behind in the park. I'm old school so I think vaping is the dumbest creation since auto-tune but I'm not looking to bust anyone's balls. I'm quite sure it's him. If you wanted to give him a head's up and just tell him to use the garbage can, the one that's all of ten feet from where he's dumping his stuff, I won't have to do a whole bunch of unnecessary paperwork. But littering is such a selfish move so I'll do it if my hand gets forced."

"Oh yeah, sure. Of course. No problem. You can count on me. No problem. Of course. I can be sly. I'll say something at him when I see him. To him when I see him. Definitely. I hate litterbugs too. And vaping." *Hi, I'm the world's least sly person, nice to meet me.*

"Thanks, Rod. Please say hello to your folks to me. Actually, there goes your mom now," he says as I turn to see my mom walking down my street heading out for a walk. Neither of us wave because she doesn't look over.

Officer Stewart tells me he better get inside to check on Miss Jones, asking if her intestines are still inside of her body.

"For now," I reply, which actually makes him laugh.

"You've got my number, right? Don't hesitate to call if you ever need anything."

"I will. Thanks, Officer Stewart."

* * * * * * * * *

Now seems to be as good a time as any to tell you about my mom's walks. After Colin died, she wanted to visit his gravestone at the cemetery every day but, like I already told you, she had written off driving and he was buried kind of far away in Edison, where both my mom's parents were also buried. She also stopped working at this time, which is when my dad had to take on a second job so he wasn't able to drive her there. Within walking distance though was the site of a memorial to Colin, the spot where they found his body. It's this massive tree where his friends and classmates would leave pictures of him or things that reminded them of Colin. So, my mom began to walk there every day.

The memorial tree isn't super far away from our house. It's only a little over a mile but it's not a straight shot so it takes about forty-five minutes on foot to travel there. Through the main part of town is a fairly easy walk. My mom would walk up Marshall Street, past Don's Service Center, which is an old-school auto body shop. The owner, Don, looks like he's straight out of the 1950s with his blue Don's Service Center t-shirt tucked into his tapered blue jeans, black cowboy boots, and his hair perfectly gelled and parted to the side. The shop is red and looks like an old barn. Ours is a residential neighborhood so the shop is surrounded by houses. If you weren't looking for it, you wouldn't know it was there other than the fact that the cars he's working on line both sides of the street for about one hundred feet. There are always so many that sometimes I wonder if he ever finishes working on a car at all, which leads me to imagine that Don is an entrepreneur disguised as a small-town bumpkin who actually owns stock in Uber, making money hand over fist as his customers are forced to take ride-shares while their cars sit at his shop for weeks on end. At the end of Marshall Street, my mom would make a right onto Maple Avenue and from there walk straight for a quarter of a mile or so. Just for reference, this is the limit of the walkie-talkies' range from my house. Eventually Maple becomes Elm Street, right about at the post office. A little past that is the old train station, which is now someone's house, then the flea market grounds where they used to hold a big old-fashioned flea market every Sunday. They stopped doing it a few years ago, which is too bad because I used to love going there as a kid with my dad. It was mostly people selling stuff they didn't want anymore but one person's junk is treasure to a kid. I used to load up on Matchbox cars, Curious George books, all kinds of stuff. Now the grounds sit empty but instead of putting up useless condos like towns around here are so eager to do, the Neshanic Station Historical Society proved that the land carried historical significance; some important general and his men had camped out there on their way down the Raritan River during the Revolutionary War, so it's preserved and now has a sign where you can read about the facts I just butchered, if you're so inclined.

Past the old flea market grounds, my mom would cross over the White Bridge via the pedestrian walkway to the right of its one-way passage for cars. Its paint has seen better days, most of it long since chipped away, but the venerable bridge proudly serves its purpose as one of the two entrances/exits to our little town, the other being through Pleasant Run Road, which comes in under the train tracks on the other end of town right near the volunteer fire station. On the other end of the (not so) White Bridge is River Road, a long and winding roadway that runs parallel to the Raritan River. I don't know that I'd call it dangerous, but I definitely wouldn't deem it a safe road for a walk. Walking up River Road takes a while, a good twenty minutes at least, and at the end of it, when she'd get to the fork in the road, my mom would make a left at the church; host to Sunday services, weekday preschool, and Bingo night every third Thursday of the month. The tree where Colin's spirit rests (my mom's words) is just beyond the church on the left.

My mom made this trek every single day for years, forty-five minutes each way, even in the rain. I don't know if she made the walk in the snow. It'd be a challenge to make it up River Road walking in the snow but I bet she tried. My mom had to stop walking to Colin's memorial when she was pregnant with me and couldn't resume until I was no longer a toddler, because there's no way she could push a stroller all the way there, which I'm sure made her sick at heart. Maybe my arrival filled the void that Colin left but it didn't take long for her to realize that I, the replacement child, was inferior to Colin, because when I was four years old, her desire to visit his tree every day returned and she started having me accompany her. It was a super far walk for a kid and my legs would get incredibly tired. My mom would carry me for a little bit but I was big; I was four, so I wasn't a little kid anymore—not small enough to carry, anyway. She'd attempt to make a game of it, getting me to chase her up the road to try to catch her. I made it there with her a few times but one time a police officer— Officer Stewart, who was just a rookie back then—drove past and turned his car around to come talk to us. He seemed pretty freaked out seeing a lady and her child walking on River Road because there's virtually no shoulder and it's rare to see someone walking on that road.

He asked if we were all right and what we were doing walking. I think he could see how tired I was because he kept trying to cheer me up. He asked if my mom and I wanted him to drive us home in his police car, telling me I could turn on the sirens if I wanted to, and because I was four, I thought that was the most awesome idea in the world. My mom didn't want to go and started to panic, so Officer Stewart and I had to try to calm her down, which is no easy task for anyone not named Xanax. Eventually we ended up getting her into the police car but I had to sit in the back with her and hold her hand to keep her calm, which meant I didn't get to turn on the sirens. Officer Stewart came inside and talked to my dad for a while when we got home. After that, I didn't go to the memorial site with my mom anymore.

My mom kept going, though. Sometimes she'd ask our neighbor, Mrs. Utatchi, to come over and sit with me. Mrs. Utatchi spoke English but not too well. Either that or she just didn't like talking to me. She'd come over and watch TV until my mom got back. She really hated my cat, Jessie. Every time Jessie came into the room, Mrs. Utatchi would yell at her, stuff that I didn't understand because it was in Vietnamese. Whatever she said, Jessie understood enough to know she wasn't wanted because she'd take off as soon as the yelling started.

Remember when I told you that Frankie announced over the loudspeaker at school that my mom is the Woman in White? For some reason she always wears white when she visits my brother's memorial. She looks as if she's dressed for church rather than for a walk. Maybe it makes her feel pure, like an angel or something. Who knows? She always has on a white top and a long white dress that extends to her ankles. If it's cold she'll wear a coat which is orange, not white. It was one of those Carhartt work coats that you see a lot of construction workers wear. It used to be Colin's. She also wears black or brown boots so it's not like she is *fully* covered in white, but enough white for her to receive the nickname the Woman in White. I don't know who started calling her that. It could have been anyone, as a lot of people see her walking. At first, she was only walking to the memorial and back but after a while she began walking all around town on these extensive walks. While out on her walks it's like she's meditating or something, because she gets this far-off look on her face and doesn't focus on anything in particular; she's always looking straight ahead. Sometimes people yell out the window at her, I guess to try to see if they can get her to look over or get any kind of reaction, but she never looks.

Sometimes my school bus passed her while she was out walking. None of the kids knew that she was my mom because she doesn't attend many events, it's usually just me and my dad. So they'd say things like, "Look, there's the Woman in White," or, "Hey look, it's a real-life crazy person!" I never stood up for her and told them she was my mom. I know it probably sounds like I'm ashamed of my mom but it's just...well, it's complicated. There really isn't a good time to say "Hey—that's no crazy lady, that's my mom!" I guess I could have and I wanted to, I really did, but I always froze and lost my nerve just before I was about to speak up. I feel extremely guilty about that. Frankie is the only one that knew she was my mom. A few times I was convinced he was going to tell everyone, because he had that sinister look in his eyes that he gets sometimes, but he never did and I was always grateful to him for keeping my secret. 'Was' being the operative word.

Fortunately, it's not too often that we see her on the way home from school. My mom usually walks in the mornings, so if we do see her in the afternoon it means she slept in or took an extra pill and was zoned out on the couch for too long. That means she starts walking later than usual and sometimes won't get home until really late. A few times, my dad had to get in the car and go look for her. I remember one time it was around midnight when he finally got back home with her. I was pretending to sleep but I was awake and was utterly freaked out.

Ever since I first met him on that walk when I was four, Officer Stewart has always gone out of his way to be nice to me. I'm sure he feels bad for me, knowing that my mom is a little eccentric. He'll always stop and chat with me but if I'm standing at the bus stop or walking with Frankie, he just winks at me as he drives by, probably so he doesn't embarrass me. Other than Sting, he's probably the coolest guy I know and since I technically don't know Sting (not yet anyway), I guess he is actually the coolest.

chapter 9

*

brat

The majority of my time playing video games at Frankie's consists of me staring blankly into the screen as he plays, volleying insults between the characters on the screen and me. It's okay by me. *Mario Kart* is cool and I like baseball games but I'm not big on playing video games otherwise. Most times I'll daydream about hanging out with Sting or what it would've been like if I were born in a different town, perhaps with a kid or two around with whom I could relate. Today, though, is different. I'm still daydreaming but the only thing on my mind is Cat.

"Spoof! Spoof! SPOOF!"

As Frankie yells the word spoof at me, whatever the hell that is, while trying to avoid letting the pot smoke escape from his lungs, his eyes bug out of his head like a fish with popeye disease and I use every fiber of my being not to laugh in his fishy face. Once he exhales a tractor-trailer-worthy emission of pot smoke, he lunges at me, causing me to protect myself with clenched fists.

"Jesus, man, were you going to hit me?" he whines, reaching past me and grabbing the toilet paper roll next to me on the couch. Yes, couch. My room contains a bed, a tiny desk, a bookshelf, and a path just large enough to walk from one side of the bed to the other. Frankie's is nearly the size of the entire top level of my house and contains as much furniture as my TV room.

"No, definitely not. I was just...you startled me. I couldn't understand what you were yelling and then you looked like you were coming right at me."

"I was yelling spoof. God, you're such a Nimrod."

For the uninitiated, like yours truly, a spoof is a cardboard toilet paper roll filled with dryer sheets. There is also a dryer sheet covering one end, held on with a rubber band. After inhaling a massive amount of pot smoke, the smoker then exhales into the spoof so that if his parents were to walk in, they would be duped into thinking the smoker was just drying his clothes in his room (a room which doesn't contain a dryer, but why would you even bring that up you idiot?...or so I'm told).

"If my dad walks in and I get busted, it's totally your fault," Frankie says, revving up for another hit from his complicated pot-smoking apparatus. "Maybe if you weren't such a square and actually tried pot you would know these things."

"Ahh, if ever a reason to start," I offer.

"You talk weird, dude. No wonder I'm your only friend."

Frankie and I have been friends for a long time but if given a polygraph test (or if someone just straight up asked either one of us), I imagine we would both admit to being nothing more than friends of convenience. We've lived across the street from one another our entire lives and are roughly the same age. It doesn't get more convenient than that.

When we were kids, we were genuine friends. Sure, we'd have our fair share of disagreements, but what friends don't? Being so close in proximity and age, and both being only children (my mom gets bent out of shape when I refer to myself as an only child but as long as I've been alive, I've been the *only child* in my household, so what would you call me?), it was nice to always have someone around to play baseball or go trick-or-treating with, or (for Frankie) to have someone (me) to whom he could show off all of his new sneakers, clothes, video game systems...you name it. Frankie's dad owns a car dealership on Route 202. His dad is the kind of guy who is always bragging and showing off his new "toys," as he calls them, whether it's a new car, the in-ground pool they had put in a couple of years ago, a batting cage he had installed in their yard, etc. And wouldn't you know it—Frankie is a chip off the old block. When I was younger I thought Frankie's dad was cool because he always had the newest stuff and I would get a little jealous that Frankie was always wearing new clothes to school while I was stuck wearing all of Colin's hand-me-downs.

The bragging Frankie's dad does has always driven my dad nuts. My dad refers to him as the Blowhard. My parents were fine with me hanging out with Frankie and occasionally going places with him and his dad (well, my mom would spend the entire evening being a nervous wreck, waiting for me to return home). My dad tried to be a good sport and went along to a Phillies game when they were playing the Yankees (Frankie's and his dad's favorite team), but Frankie's dad spent the entire game cursing and taunting my dad in the name of good fun (Mr. Friel's words). The socializing between dads ended that day.

"Hey, can I ask you something? Since you smoke pot right in your bedroom, you don't have any reason to smoke in the park, do you?"

I could've told Frankie his mother was on fire and the only way for her to be saved was for him to simply wink to acknowledge the fact that another living soul was in his room making sounds. She would've burned to a crisp. I repeat the question twice before finally receiving a well-thought-out, "Huh?"

"Well it's no big deal or anything. It's just that I ran into Officer Stewart and he was telling me he found some vape stuff in the park and asked if I knew anything about it."

Frankie just arrived in his fire truck.

"Dude, what are you talking about?! Are you and that cop, like, friends or something?"

"No, we're not friends." *Wait, are we friends?* That would be okay by me. In fact, it would be awesome.

"Hey, Nimrod! I'm talking to you. Or should I call you

NarcRod? What did you tell that cop? You better not have narc'd me out!"

"I totally didn't narc you out." Nor am I the kind of person who will ever feel comfortable using phrases such as "narc you out."

"That idiot cop doesn't know what he's talking about," Frankie continues. "My dad can buy and sell the entire police department if he wants to. That pig better stop running his mouth or my dad will slap a lawsuit on him. If I get caught smoking pot I'll get kicked off the baseball team and will lose my scholarship." The scholarship he's *hoping* to get, that is.

"Listen, Officer Stewart is cool. He just said that whoever is doing it should just put the stuff in the trash can. If that happens, he's not going to say anything to anyone. And I won't say anything to anyone either. That's a promise."

"Of course you won't tell anyone because the only people you hang out with are me and your grandparents—I mean your parents. I don't even know why I hang out with you. You're a total nimrod."

Have I mentioned that when Frankie gets upset and/or doesn't get his way he turns into a petulant, spoiled brat? He says crappy things constantly, but the claws come out when he feels backed into a corner.

"My dad ordered some pizza and I know there will be some extra," I say, trying to calm him down. "Do you want to come over and have some? We can watch a movie and eat some pizza like we did when we were kids."

"Yeah right, there won't be any extra pizza. By the time we get there your dad will probably have eaten the boxes too. If you weren't a little narc for them, the police would arrest him for being such a fat ass. Hey, maybe that's how he can lose some weight. Go to jail and eat gruel three times a day. Knowing him, he'd probably love it and eat all the other prisoners' gruel too," he taunts, taking a step toward me.

"Stop talking about my dad right now."

"What did you say, you little narc? I should kick your ass right now."

"Why don't you give it a shot, Frankie? I'd love to see you try," I say, staring him directly in the eyes.

"Get out of here, NarcRod. I'm done with you. Have fun taking walks with your freak mom and eating pizza with your fatso father."

chapter 10

*

sting-chronicity II

Living across the street from Frankie all my life has provided me with a handful of helpful life lessons. I may not have a clue who I am or who I want to be, but I can tell you without hesitation who I don't want to be: Frankie. Not in any way, shape, or form. In a way, this is a gift, because I believe that knowing who you don't want to be is as valuable as knowing who you do want to be. So I'm 50% on my way to figuring things out. Frankie subscribes to the notion that any attention is good attention and, as much as it pains me, I have to hand it to him—he knows how to make everything about him. Up until an hour and a half ago, all I could think about was Cat and the way her jet-black hair looks almost blue when the sunlight hits it a certain way. Now all I want to do is wash my brain of all the crappy things that Frankie said about my dad. I don't care if he calls me Nimrod or a narc or whatever-the-hell, but talking about my parents is going too far. One of these days I'm going to grow a set and write Frankie off for good.

BEEP BEEP BEEP BEEP BEEP BEEP BEEP BEEP BEEP

And now I have Frankie to thank for causing me to obsess over his insolence and forget all about the vegan pizza I had cooking in the oven. No better reminder than the smoke detectors screaming at me. This is the second time today an alarm has gotten the better of me. Today is not my day.

"Baby, do you hear that?" asks my mom over the walkie-talkie as I hustle from my room to the kitchen.

BEEP   BEEP BEEP BEEP BEEP BEEP BEEP BEEP BEEP

"Yeah, Mom, of course I hear that. I'll bet Mrs. Utatchi can even hear that our smoke detectors are going off."

"Mrs. Utatchi what? Honey, what's going on? Are you okay up there?"

BEEP   BEEP BEEP BEEP BEEP BEEP BEEP BEEP BEEP

"I'm fine, Mom. My pizza is burning. Let me grab it out of the oven."

"Okay, baby. Well, it woke your father up from his nap."

"I wasn't sleeping, I was resting my eyes!" my dad adds from the background.

Why can't people just admit that they dozed off? Why the shame in being tired and nodding off for a few minutes?

BEEP   BEEP BEEP BEEP BEEP BEEP BEEP BEEP BEEP

"He says he wasn't napping. He was resting his eyes."

"Yeah, I heard him, Mom." Now I'm talking to her on this stupid walkie-talkie kids' toy while I stand on top of a chair trying to fan the smoke detector with a dish towel in hopes of getting the godforsaken thing to stop its incessant beeping.

"He said he heard you," my mom reports to my dad.

And now she's in a conversation with my dad *and* me with her finger unnecessarily holding down the talk button. Lovely.

"Tell him to come down and watch something. We can watch a Christopher Guest movie," my dad offers.

"Not Christopher Guest again. We just watched *Mascots* the other night. Let's watch…"

BEEP   BEEP BEEP BEEP BEEP BEEP BEEP BEEP BEEP

"GUYS!" I snap. I need to yell down from the top of the stairs to get them to both hear me since my mom won't let go of the button. "You guys pick what you want to watch, I'll take care of this up here, and I'll be down as soon as I can to watch whatever you decide."

"He seems upset," my mom whispers to my dad.

"Mom, you're still pressing the button. I can hear what you're saying."

I didn't think anything could be more annoying than the sound of a smoke detector that will not stop beeping. My parents dispelled that notion in record time.

* * * * * * * * *

My mom is in her spot on the right side of the couch, so I sit down in mine on the left. The center spot is open; that's where Jessie used to sit when she was still alive. Now I use the middle spot to rest my tray of chips and salsa. I offer some to my mom which she declines but my dad says he's in, that chips and salsa sound like the perfect snack to wash down a couple of pizzas. Just in case, I always make sure to bring three plates with me so I pour some tortilla chips onto a plate for my dad with some salsa on the side and I look up to the TV and see that they've decided upon *Friends* for tonight. Clearly this was my mom's choice. My dad doesn't dislike *Friends* enough to veto it, but he'll most likely watch until he finishes his snack and then he'll either doze off again or he'll bury his nose in whatever book he's currently reading, usually something about baseball or an old war.

Friends is a good show. It's a bit dated since it's from the 1990s so I end up not catching some of the references but even still, it's pretty darn funny. It's a real trip seeing Matt LeBlanc so young since I know him from the show *Man with a Plan,* which I've watched on Netflix at least five times all the way through. He's got gray hair in *Man with a Plan* but in *Friends* he looks so young and skinny with a full head of dark brown hair. The show is about six friends (hence the name) who are all around the same age, late twenties I believe, each trying to find his or her way while living in New York City. Most episodes are set in one of their apartments or in the coffee shop where one of the characters works. I've got to admit that it does seem pretty awesome to hang out in a coffee shop with your best friends drinking coffee and shooting the breeze all the time. I don't drink coffee but maybe when I get to be their age I will. Hopefully I'll have a group of friends to hang out with by then too.

Despite the vegan pizza I burned to a crisp and Frankie's tactless words, the night is beginning to turn around, as this is actually one of my favorite episodes of *Friends*. Phoebe, the flighty blonde character who is my mom's favorite, finds out that Ross's son goes to school with Sting's son (yep, Sting!) and does her best to convince Ross to get her tickets to Sting's concert. I don't blame her; tickets to Sting's concerts are insanely expensive. Coming home from a Phillies game with my dad earlier this month, we saw a billboard on the Pennsylvania Turnpike advertising an upcoming concert in Atlantic City. I must've talked my dad's ear off about it because he told me to look up the price of tickets and that if they were reasonable, he would consider broaching the idea of him and me going together to my mom. Since I'm the last kid on Earth without a smartphone, I had to wait until I got home to look up ticket prices; my flip phone is an antiquated piece of crap. The entire ride home, my heart nearly beat out of my chest as I daydreamed about being at a Sting concert and finagling my way backstage to meet him. That dream was dead on arrival when I discovered that tickets for the nosebleed section were $150 and my dad said he wouldn't pay that much money to go all the way to Atlantic City to sit so far back we'd have to watch Sting on a screen. Perhaps Phoebe from *Friends* had had a similar experience, hence the attempt at getting free tickets. Ross informs her that the boys don't get along, so she takes matters into her own hands and goes to talk to Sting's wife, Trudie Styler, pretending to want to talk about the boys in order to get tickets. This ends in a restraining order against Phoebe.

The first and only time I ever witnessed my mom dancing, which I already told you about, is directly attributed to Sting. The only time I've heard her sing—also thanks to Sting. Another Sting-chronicity, if you will, that involved a different episode of *Friends*.

On a night just like tonight, minus the blaring smoke detector, my parents and I were watching *Friends*. Matt LeBlanc's character, Joey, is a struggling actor always in search of his big break. In this particular episode, he is over the moon about a modeling job he landed in which his face was going to be used in a series of ads promoting a free health clinic that would be displayed all over New York City. At this point, he did not yet know which ailment he would be the face of but he hopes it'll be for Lyme's Disease. It's not as funny when I describe it but trust me, it was hilarious. Inside a subway station, Joey sees a beautiful woman that he once worked with and hits on her, as Joey is known to do. He's just about secured a date when all of a sudden the woman gets a horrified look on her face, makes an excuse, and dashes out of there. Before Joey can comprehend what went wrong, he turns around to see his face on an ad for VD which, my dad informed me, is what they used to call STDs back then. The next scene is a montage of Joey's face plastered all over the city announcing to everyone that he has venereal disease, with a song playing in the background with the lyrics "don't stand so close to me."

Back then I knew who Sting was, from *Bee Movie*, and my fascination with him had begun because of the effect he had on my mom. But at that point, I knew him more as a cultural figure as I had only heard his music that one time my mom and I danced to it in Colin's room. I was still quite young and while I wouldn't say my mom's disdain for music had been passed down to me, I would say that I had some negative emotions attached to music from seeing how much it upset my mom. On that night, however, not only did I hear my mom singing along, faint as it was, I also noticed her eyes were closed and her head was bobbing along to the beat. I'm used to seeing her in Xanax-induced trances but this one, brought on by music, was totally new to me. I turned to see if my dad noticed these happenings as well, because they were a big deal, but as usual he was asleep in his chair. I knew that if I acknowledged what was happening my mom would snap back into her reality and god knows how she would've reacted. It didn't play for long but it was a catchy tune and the lyrics stuck in my head, so I typed the words "don't stand so close to me" into Google and the first thing that popped up was a video from The Police for their song of the same name. That night my fascination with Sting went from curiosity to restraining-order-worthy. I was convinced then and there that he possessed a power that I lacked. I was brought into this world to be a replacement for my parents' first son, the star athlete, who created a colossal void in their lives when he died. Colin left behind some large baseball cleats to fill and my story was to be the sequel to Colin's short film. Take one look at the photos of my parents from when Colin was alive and compare them to how they look these days, with me as their son, and it's quite clear that I have failed to live up to those lofty expectations. But if I could figure out how this English rockstar fit into the puzzle, perhaps I could make my parents—especially my mom—happy after all.

chapter 11

*

bring on the night

It's 3 a.m. and I'm beginning to come to terms with the fact that sleep is not going to happen. A good hour was spent attempting to understand *Man and His Symbols* for the hundredth time. If I can better understand Carl Jung's ideas, perhaps I can make sense of why Sting is the one who has on multiple occasions had an effect on my mom. After finally succumbing to the reality that I am simply not bright enough to comprehend Jung, I daydream for a bit about what it would be like to actually meet Sting. I wonder if his fan club ever offers contests in which the winner is awarded a trip to *Il Palagio*, the vineyard home he owns in Tuscany, for a week of yoga, tea, and conversation with Sting, his wife, Trudie, and their interesting friends: musicians, actors, environmentalists, etc. Something like that would definitely help my mom begin to heal. I make a note to myself to add a Sting fan club membership to my list of things to purchase if I'm ever able to save any money.

Finally, I was able to fall asleep, which I know because I was just startled awake. There's no better indicator that you were sleeping than being woken up. I'm a bit of a light sleeper. It comes with the territory of having an overbearing mom. Geez, that sounds mean. What's a kinder word than overbearing? Needy? That sounds even worse. Let's stick with overbearing but please know that I mean it in a gentle way. She can't help it. She lost her first-born and has never fully recovered. I'm not sure anyone who goes through something like that ever does. My dad doesn't seem as depressed as my mom on the surface, but this is the guy who scarfed down two entire pizzas followed by some chips and salsa immediately upon waking from his food coma.

I thought I heard a noise, which is a true bummer because I was having an awesome dream in which I was the host of a plant-based cooking show on YouTube and...wait...there it is again. There's definitely some kind of a moaning sound coming from my parents' room. Oh no...it's happening. They're doing it. *It*. I've heard some of my classmates swap stories at the lunch table about hearing their parents having sex, but I've never had anything to add to the conversation. Frankie used to tell me that he would hear his parents going at it and then sneak over to their door so he could hear it more clearly. I always found that to be a little strange but hey, to each their own. Frankie may have wanted to get a closer listen but I opt to stick my head under my pillow and pretend this isn't happening. Honestly, I figured my parents gave up that activity a long time ago.

Even with my head under my pillow, I can still hear the moans coming from their bedroom. Now I'm beginning to think that they are not moans but are actually groans. Yes, there is a difference. Moans denote pleasure, groans pain. Crap, now I need to go check. This can go one of two ways and neither outcome is going to be good. I get to their bedroom door and knock, quite sheepishly.

"Umm...guys? I think I heard an animal or something outside. Did you guys hear it too?"

"Hey, bud," my dad groans. *Yep, definitely a groan.* "Sorry to wake you. I've just got a stomachache. Too much pizza."

"Oh no. Can I get you a glass of water or something?"

"Yeah, that might help. Thanks, pal."

We live in a bi-level house, so when you enter through the front door you're on a landing and have a choice to go either upstairs or down. Seven stairs up and seven stairs down. Our kitchen is located upstairs, on the same level as our bedrooms. Also upstairs is a living room, which is a silly name for this room because no living is done there. It contains two couches that no one ever sits on and a coffee table that holds books that no one ever reads. The only time any of us go in there is to cut through to get to the dining room.

As I get to the kitchen to retrieve the glass of water for my dad, a figure in the living room catches my eye and I let out a girlish scream. The figure doesn't move and when I peek out from the kitchen wall I jumped behind for cover, I see that it's my mom. I go in and ask her what she's doing in the living room so late but she doesn't respond or even acknowledge my presence. She's got a sleeper hold on her old photo album so I know she was out here looking at pictures of Colin. Her eyes are open, which tells me she's zonked out on her pills.

More groans from my dad's bedroom. They're getting louder.

"Hang on, Dad. I'm on my way! Mom...don't move," I say, half joking.

When I arrive at my dad's bedroom, I knock and then enter. He's not in bed. The bathroom door is open and the light is on.

"Dad, I'm coming in. Are you decent?"

And then comes the sound of vomiting. In the span of a few hours I've heard two of the most wretched sounds known to man materialize out of the upstairs of my usually very quiet house: an enraged smoke detector and the sound of a man spewing his guts out.

* * * * * * * * *

My dad is unable to hold down a glass of water. He's been throwing up for a good twenty minutes and tells me the pain woke him up around midnight and grew increasingly worse until his groans woke me up three hours later. It could be the crappy lighting in his bathroom but I swear his skin is starting to turn yellow. As I plead with him to go to the emergency room, his mouth tells me no but his eyes tell me yes. My dad comes from a generation of prideful men, men who refuse to go to doctors when they're sick, who won't stop to ask for directions when they're lost, and who would rather give a wrong answer than to utter the words "I don't know." Sting has a lyric in which he sings, "I'm too full to swallow my pride." Well, tonight my dad is too full to *not* swallow his pride, so I tell him that I'm calling an ambulance.

"No, bud, really...that's not necessary."

"How is it not necessary? You're in too much pain to stand, you can't stop puking, and you're turning yellow."

"That's my sun tan."

"When was the last time you were in the sun?" I ask.

"I walked from my car into our house earlier. I think I got some color then."

Physically he's in bad shape but at least he's still got his sense of humor, terrible as it may be.

"I really don't need an ambulance. It'll only upset your mothe—" before he can finish his sentence, the vomiting starts again and now it looks bloody.

"I'm calling an ambulance right now."

"Please, bud, we can't afford it. Those things cost a fortune. I think you're right, I do need to go to a hospital. But I can drive. I have to."

My dad is in no shape to drive and the desperation in his voice breaks my heart. He's right; we can't afford it. We're barely making ends meet as it is and my dad carries that weight on his shoulders. It's time for me to step up and help my dad, who does everything for me and my mom. I've got a plan.

* * * * * * * * *

Officer Stewart arrives in record time. He gave me his cell phone number a few years back, on one of those nights when my mom's walks went deep into the night and my dad and I ran into him while out searching for her. I never planned on using it as I never wanted to be a burden, but desperate times call for desperate measures. I'm really glad I did because my dad is a big guy so having the extra help of Officer Stewart is a lifesaver in getting him down the stairs and out the door. While they're getting situated in the police cruiser, I run back in to get my mom but first I stop off in my room to grab my phone, its charger, and my Sting books from Mary, figuring we could be sitting in the waiting room for a while. Now all that's left is the tall task of getting my mannequin-like mother out of the house. Her pills are sitting next to her on the end table by the couch so I throw those into my pocket. Lord knows she'll definitely need them when she realizes where we are once we get to the hospital. They say it can be dangerous to wake someone who's sleepwalking and I don't know if that applies to my mom's current sedated state, but I don't have time to google it so I do my best to get her up and out the door as gently as possible.

"Hey, Mom," I whisper. "Dad and I are going to take a ride and we'd like you to come with us."

I have to repeat this a couple more times, with my hands resting gently upon her shoulders, but finally her eyes focus on me and she responds.

"Colin? Oh my baby, Colin! I've missed you so much. I've prayed every day that I'd see you again!" she weeps.

"Mom, it's not Colin. It's me, Rod," I say, fighting back tears of my own.

"Oh dear, I must have been dreaming," she says, coming to. "I thought you were my Colin."

If you were to meet my mom for the first time, you would think that her first son was named My Colin. She always refers to him that way. Never My Rod; in fact she really doesn't call me Rod at all, most likely because it's not the name she gave me. I try not to be petty or jealous of my dead brother, but hearing her refer to him as My Colin all the time does cause a tinge of resentment.

Fortunately, my mom's confusion gives me the chance to keep talking to her, reminding her of the here and now——what day it is, that

I'm Rod, that we watched a bunch of episodes of *Friends* tonight, and before she knows what's happening, she's in the backseat of Officer Stewart's police cruiser.

"Wow," my dad says from the backseat. "You made that happen fast. One day you'll have to teach me your ways, kung fu master," he says in a mildly racist accent that he in no way means with any harm. He's old and that kind of stereotypical accent was funny back in his day. It doesn't make it right, but it also doesn't make him a racist.

"Thank you so much," I say, looking at Officer Stewart. "I can't tell you how much this means to me."

"Happy to help. And hey, now you finally get your chance to turn them on," he says with a wink, signaling toward the sirens.

chapter 12

*

king of pain

We sit in the waiting room for what feels like forever. It doesn't seem like a busy night, at least not in the waiting room. Sitting diagonally to the right of us is a father and his two sons who look to be of Mexican descent. The father is wearing a Yankees hat. He's got a thick, black mustache and a hardened but pleasant face. He sits with his legs outstretched and crossed at the feet with his hands clasped together on his lap, calmly staring off into the distance. His older son sits to his left. He looks to be just a couple of years younger than I am and he hasn't looked up from his phone since my mom, dad, and I sat down. The younger son, seemingly the reason for their hospital visit, must be about five or six years old and sits holding an ice pack over his right eye, his left eye fixed on the screen of his own phone. The older boy seems to speak the best English of the bunch because he's the one fielding the questions from the woman at the front desk and from the nurse who just came from the back to speak to them. To our left is a man who looks as if he may be homeless. He has an unkempt beard, his clothes are tattered, and he appears to be quite drunk, as he's babbling incoherently, occasionally bursting into maniacal laughter. The last thing I want to do is make eye contact with him but with all of the gibberish and laughter it's a challenge to not look in his direction.

Officer Stewart emerges from the back area of the hospital, the part we're waiting to get into, and informs us that a nurse assured him we'd be seen soon. He apologizes, saying he has to get back to his patrol but that he'll pop in tomorrow before fist-bumping me and my dad and nodding to my lethargic mother. Police officers catch a lot of flak these days but Officer Stewart is a good person. He's always been incredibly nice to me and my family and is the kind of person who seems genuinely interested when he asks how I'm doing. I don't know how someone (Frankie) can say that all cops are terrible, because Officer Stewart is anything but.

Finally, a nurse appears and calls out my dad's name, Gerald Williams. I know he's in a lot of pain because he skips his go-to dad joke: Gerry...that's me...but it's spelled with a G. Instead, he just groans when his name is called. I help get him out of the narrow waiting room chair, in which he just barely fits, and into a wheelchair. I grab my mom's hand and we head back into the emergency room following the nurse who's pushing my dad's wheelchair. The nurse asks what brings him in tonight and proceeds to scribble down some notes on her chart as my dad fills her in. She then takes his vitals and tells us that a doctor will be in to see him shortly. My dad asks if I brought along anything to read and I feel like a selfish jerk for only grabbing books I would want to read. Knowing he wouldn't be interested in a book of Sting's collected lyrics, I hand him the memoir, *Broken Music*.

The next thing I know, I'm startled awake by a commotion. I must have dozed off and now my dad is irate, arguing with the nurse and what looks to be a doctor.

"I'm sorry, Doc, I truly don't mean to be rude but I need someone else to see me. I'm not a superstitious person but this is too much," my dad pleads.

"Mr. Williams, I understand your concerns. Trust me, I've been hearing them my entire career. You're very tired, it's late...actually, it's early in the morning, and your abdomen is causing you a lot of discomfort. Let me help you. It's just a name, not an omen."

"Dad, what's going on?" I say, wiping the drool from my face and making my way over to his hospital bed.

"Hi there, I'm the resident doctor on duty. You must be Gerry's son. You were sleeping when I came in so I didn't have a chance to introduce myself."

"Oh, I wasn't sleeping. I was just resting my eyes." *I don't even know who I am anymore.*

"Go ahead, tell him your name, Doc," my dad chimes in, uncharacteristically rude.

"I'm Doctor Payne, spelled P-A-Y-N-E. It's a pleasure to meet you."

"Hey, I'm Rod. Nice to meet you too. Is my dad gonna be okay?"

"Your dad should be fine. We have a pretty good idea of what's likely to be causing the discomfort in his abdomen but we do need to run some tests so that we can know for sure. And we can't get your dad the treatment he needs until we are able to run those tests. We've got him hooked up to an IV to rehydrate him, as he lost a lot of fluids with all of the vomiting. We've also got a low dose of morphine going to alleviate the discomfort."

That's the third time that Doctor Payne has avoided using the word "pain," instead making sure to refer to it as "discomfort." He's a seasoned veteran with regard to people being freaked out by his name. Of all of the professions for a guy named Payne to pick...he picks doctor. I've got to hand it to him; he's got thick skin.

"What do you think is wrong, Doctor Pay...um...Doc?"
Real smooth, Rod.

"Well, Rod, I'd rather not speculate. I'd like to run those tests and get back to you with a definitive answer ASAP. But your dad here has to give us the thumbs-up."

He then turns to fully face me while turning his back to my dad and whispers, "If there's anything you can do to ease your dad's mind and assure him that it's just a name, that he's in good hands, I'd really appreciate that. I'll check back in about fifteen minutes if that sounds like a plan to you, Rod."

"Sounds like a pain, Doctor Plan."

But first I'm going to jump out the window.

"It's Dr. Payne, but I know what you meant. And thanks, Rod."

I've already told you that the closest thing I have to a hero is Sting. Whether you like him or not, it's impossible to deny that Sting is one smooth cat. He's British, for one, and all British people sound cooler than Americans. That's a fact. He's also a handsome guy and women have always loved him. They love him now and they loved him when he was in his twenties as the lead singer of the biggest rock 'n roll band in the world. They even loved him before that, if the song *Don't Stand So Close To Me* is truly autobiographical. The lyrics are said to be about his days as a school teacher when some of his female students got the wrong idea about the teacher/student relationship. Beyond his looks, he writes smooth songs. I don't know much at all about music but the first time I heard his song *Walking on the Moon*, it made me feel like I was floating above the music and riding atop the notes he was playing on his bass. Lame as it may sound, it made me feel like I was walking on the moon. At the risk of repeating myself, there's just no better word to describe him than smooth. My point is that my hero may be the smoothest man alive and I am anything but. Perhaps that's one of the things that draws me to be a fan of Sting's: he's everything I'm not. He practices yoga and plays concerts to 20,000 adoring fans, and I call the doctor by the wrong name, uttering the one word that the entirety of the room has been trying to avoid.

My dad and I chat for a bit as my mom sits in the corner looking at family photos—none of which include me—and he agrees to let Dr. Payne run the tests that he needs. More than likely, the morphine running through his system is to thank for changing his mind, as I'm not known for being persuasive. A few minutes later, when Dr. Payne returns, he's very pleased to hear the news. He thanks me and then he and the nurse get started on figuring out what's going on with my dad's stomach.

Dr. Payne eventually finishes his tests and heads off. With my dad out like a light and my mom fortified inside her castle of memories, I decide to explore the hospital a bit. After aimlessly wandering the halls for a while, I remember that my dad gave me a few bucks earlier in case I wanted to grab something to eat, which was a good move as I'm famished. I follow the signs to the cafeteria and when I walk in, it reminds me of the one in my high school. Even though I haven't been inside many cafeterias to state this as fact, it's likely that most have a similar setup. How much variety can there really be when all you need is an area where the food is served, a counter where you pay for the food, and some tables and chairs at which to consume your meal?

The options that don't contain meat or dairy are sparse, which happens often so it doesn't come as a shock. Surprising, though, is the lack of healthy options. The same could be said for my high school's cafeteria but that makes more sense; when trying to feed herds of teenagers, it's a quantity over quality situation. The cafeteria here looks like it could have been catered by McDonald's. In a hospital you'd think they'd be promoting health and wellness, though I suppose that healthy people aren't good for business. Perhaps that's the angle. McDonald's provides the food that's going to be consumed by the friends and family of the hospital's patients, and once they eat enough of it, they themselves become patients. Everyone wins except, that is, for the people eating the food. Now I'm beginning to sound like one of those conspiracy theorists on YouTube. I'm not saying that those guys aren't good for an entertaining rabbit hole to venture down for a night. But watching those guys for kicks is a whole different animal than becoming one, so let's strike that McDonald's theory from the record.

My first stop is the hot trays at the buffet-style counter in the center of the room. There are piles of bacon in one tray, mounds of sausage links in another, and the last is filled with eggs that lean more gray in color than yellow. Hard pass. I make my way over to peruse the fruit selection and see a basket of the worst kind of apples, Red Delicious, and a few bundles of unripe bananas. It's hard to go wrong with a banana and the pickings are slim so that's the first addition to my tray. The bakery section consists of bagels, cinnamon buns, and croissants. Next to those sits a punch bowl filled with single-serving butter packets with a smaller bowl of assorted jellies to its right. Looks like a bagel with grape jelly and a banana kind of morning. The cooler is full of soda and energy drinks with some forgotten water bottles lingering at the bottom, but I can use some caffeine so it's hot tea for me. My meal somehow comes out to $9.75 so I hand the cafeteria employee the ten dollar bill my dad gave me, pocket my measly twenty-five cents change, and head off to find a seat.

The seating area is nearly empty. There's a table with three cafeteria employees eating breakfast together out of Dunkin' Donuts bags. Even they don't seem to be impressed by the selection that their workplace offers, which says a lot because I imagine they're offered an employee discount. The only other patron in the place is Dr. Payne, who is sitting by himself, looking at his phone while sipping a cup of coffee. He doesn't notice me which I'm glad about because I wouldn't know what to say anyway, so I take a seat on the opposite side of the room and get to work on my banana before it has a chance to go and ripen.

Halfway through my bagel, which, if I were a betting man, I would say is of the day-old variety, Dr. Payne stops at my table to say hello.

"Rod, right?"

"Yes. Hey, Dr. Payne."

Phew, got it right this time.

"I thought that was you. How's the bagel?" he asks.

"Oh, it's okay, I guess."

"Okay I guess is a nice way of saying it's stale."

"Yeah...not the freshest I've ever had."

"The food isn't exactly four-star here but the bacon isn't half bad. I give it a C+, so if you're still hungry, it's not as bad as that bagel you're working on."

"Thanks for the suggestion. Not a big meat guy though," I reply.

"Good for you, Rod. So listen, we ran some tests on your dad and should have some answers in a few hours. But since you're here, let me ask you, how's your dad's diet?"

"Well, he would've definitely filled his plate from the buffet of meats and those egg-looking things. And he probably wouldn't have been able to decide between a croissant and a cinnamon bun so he more than likely would've gone for both."

"Gotcha. That's what I figured. With a person of your dad's stature, the kinds of abdominal pains he is currently being bothered by aren't uncommon."

'A person of your dad's stature' is a nice way of saying my dad is fat. But Dr. Payne isn't being mean by stating this, he's merely stating a fact while politely dancing around it.

"What usually causes something like this?" I ask, not entirely confident I'll receive a response.

"We're still waiting on the test results, Rod, so this is not my diagnosis, but a lot of times with someone of your dad's stature—"

A fat guy...got it.

"—whose diet isn't the healthiest, they form gallstones, which can cause excruciating discomfort in the abdomen leading to vomiting and, in extreme cases, can cause the person's skin to appear yellow."

"Holy crap, I'm not crazy. I totally thought my dad's skin was turning yellow last night before we came in. Certainly more yellow than what they're trying to pass off as eggs over there at the buffet."

"You've got a good eye and a good sense of humor, Rod. Did your dad have an especially heavy meal last night, by any chance?"

"If your definition of heavy is devouring two entire pizzas by himself, minus the half a slice that my mom nibbled on, then yes, I'd say so."

"That makes sense."

"So if it is gallstones, what does that mean?" I ask.

"Again, we're not sure that we're dealing with gallstones. We won't be ready to make a diagnosis until we get the test results back. That said, when a person develops gallstones that block their bile ducts, bile builds up in the gallbladder, causing a gallbladder attack, which could be what happened with your dad."

As Dr. Payne is telling me incredibly important information about the status of my dad's health, his mention of bile thrusts me into a daydream of Joanne Jones and her cats. Most days that I go over there to scoop the litter boxes, I end up cleaning up vomit. I have no idea what's up with cats and throwing up so much. Mittens and Co. have made a full-time job out of puking. It's not hard to clean up, a few damp paper towels will do the trick, but Mrs. Jones always has me inspect the throw up and tell her whether it's chunky or just bile. I really need to find a new way to make money.

The daydream must have put a look of concern on my face because Dr. Payne's tone changes and he begins speaking in a higher voice, like you would to a child or a dog.

"There's nothing to worry about, Rod. If this is, in fact, a gallbladder attack that we're dealing with, it can be rectified with a very routine surgery and we can have your dad back home in a few days."

Oh crap, my dad has work today. Definitely at Wawa; not sure about Lowe's. I've got to get back up to his room to make sure he calls and lets them know that he's not going to make it. Being out for a few days is going to stress him out because money is always tight. I thank Dr. Payne for the information, discard the rest of my day-old bagel, and make my way back up to my dad's room.

* * * * * * * * *

His name may not be ideal for the profession but his knowledge sure makes him the right guy for the job. Dr. Payne was correct; my dad had a gallbladder attack and needs to have surgery. He tells my dad all about what's involved, that laparoscopic surgery is preferred over traditional open surgery because it's less invasive and usually has a shorter recovery time. However, certain complications can make open surgery a better choice, such as when the gallbladder is severely diseased. A severely diseased gallbladder can be more difficult to remove because it may have affected surrounding areas, which makes a laparoscopic procedure more difficult. Hospital stays are typically longer after an open procedure.

My dad's case is the more severe of the two. He's going to need the open surgery, which means he's going to be in the hospital for three to five days and it could be up to six to eight weeks until he is fully recovered and can return to his normal activities. Being that he's going to be out of work for *at least* a week, he's completely stressing about money. My mom doesn't drive and hasn't worked in nearly twenty years and I'm just a dumb teenager with no license and no job prospects. My dad keeps saying he doesn't want me to worry, that he can worry enough for the both of us. He wants me to go home, get some rest, and make sure everything is good there. I'm exhausted and my back hurts from trying to sleep in the chair next to my dad's hospital bed so I don't put up much of a fight, as I could definitely go for a few hours of sleep in my own bed.

chapter 13

*

hitchin' a ride

When he walks into my dad's hospital room wearing a Mets t-shirt, athletic shorts, and flip flops, it takes me a second to realize who it is. My dad greeting him as Bill also threw me off as I've only ever known him as Officer Stewart. As I set aside my copy of *Lyrics*, I notice for the first time that Officer Stewart has tattoos covering his arms, which look super cool. All the other times I've seen him he's been in uniform, which explains why I was unaware of his tattoos because they'd have been covered by long sleeves. He gives me his customary wink (which somehow gets cooler every time he flashes it) and then checks on my dad, asking him how he's feeling. They chat for a few minutes and then my dad asks if he'd mind giving me a ride home, which embarrasses me to no end.

"Give Rod a ride home? No problem. How much money have you got on you?" he asks, catching me off guard.

"Oh...uhh...I spent the ten bucks I had in the cafeteria but I've got some litter box money at home."

"Rod, I'm messing with you. Of course I'll give you a ride home and I don't want your money. Especially not litter box money, whatever that is. Where's Lynn? Will she be joining us on the ride?"

"She's around here somewhere," my dad says. "Probably walking around the hospital so she may be gone for a while. This has been pretty stressful on her, so she's going to stay here with me. Rod, you'll be on your own at home. No wild parties or I'll have Bill here throw you in the clink."

Officer Stewart chuckles, most likely out of politeness. Who says the word clink, anyway? My dad tells him that his surgery is scheduled for tomorrow, which he's relieved about because he just wants to get it out of the way. As they're talking and as I'm staring at Officer Stewart's tattoo-covered arms it hits me that he's off today, otherwise he'd be in uniform. He came in to check on my dad on his day off and now he's stuck giving me a ride home. I wonder if he would've still come to visit if he knew he'd have to drive home a useless teenager.

"You're a real good guy, I don't expect that from a Mets fan," I hear my dad say, snapping me from my reverie. Like a lot of things my dad says, this humiliates me to no end but he and Officer Stewart share a good laugh.

Officer Stewart has to be the coolest guy I've ever met. He's not quite Sting-level of cool, but I haven't met Sting (yet) so he doesn't qualify. That's no disrespect to my dad. My dad is a super nice guy and I love him but **1.)** he's my dad and **2.)** he is definitely a sweet guy, but he's not a cool guy. By the time we said goodbye to my dad and mom (who returned from her hospital walk just before we headed off), it was already 3 p.m. It's hard to believe I've been at the hospital for nearly twelve hours. It took us a decent amount of time to make our way to the parking lot because people kept stopping Officer Stewart to chat with him. Even though he's not in uniform, people still recognize him. He says that it comes with the territory of his job because he has to come to the hospital quite often with people he has in custody or to see people who are involved in a case he's investigating. What I witnessed, though, clearly goes much deeper than extending professional courtesy. It was easy to see that the doctors, nurses, and even maintenance people that stopped to say hello really seemed to care for him and vice versa. That's partly why it took so long to get out the door. It wasn't people just quickly saying hi as they passed by Officer Stewart in the hall; these people were genuinely happy to see him and wanted to know how he was doing and what was new with him. Officer Stewart downplayed it when I brought it up but this was more than just surface small talk. Something else I noticed while he was in conversation with members of the hospital staff is that his legs are also covered in tattoos. He looks completely different out of his police uniform.

"Driving," he says "like most things in life, is all about balance. Be aggressive enough not to let the other drivers on the road control what you do. If you show fear or hesitation, they will eat you alive. But be careful not to be too aggressive, because then you're the problem and we're all in this together."

Who thinks of stuff like that?! Certainly not me. It sounds like advice that Sting would impart. I wonder if Officer Stewart likes The Police. He's talking to me about driving because he enquired as to whether I'd be getting my license soon and I told him it doesn't look to be in the cards for me, at least not anytime soon. I can't blame it all on my mom's fear, because honestly, I've got some apprehensions about it, too.

Officer Stewart knows more about my mom than most people. Since the day he stopped on River Road when I was four, he's always checked in with my family. He knows my dad pretty well from Wawa because he stops there to get coffee during just about every one of his shifts. He tells me that my dad never charges him for his coffee and refuses to accept a tip, something I didn't know but doesn't surprise me one bit. Officer Stewart always waves to my mom when he passes her on her walks but never stops to chat because he knows it would make her uncomfortable.

"Hey, are you hungry?"

"Famished."

"Me too, and I could really go for a cup of coffee. Let's pop in here, my treat," he says, pulling up in front of The Store.

"Oh, you know what? I'm actually not that hungry. I should probably be getting home anyway," I say, beginning to panic, as I've never stepped foot inside this place and know my parents would be less than thrilled if I did.

"Wow, a chip off the old block, huh? Don't worry, I'm still loyal to Wawa, your dad's got nothing to worry about. The only thing worse than the coffee here is the customer service. The owner is a total slacker; forty years old, moved a whopping two blocks from the house he grew up in, and technically never failed in life because he never took a risk. But bad as it may be, the coffee has got caffeine in it and works in a pinch. Come on, I won't tell your dad you supported the competition."

chapter 14

*

englishman in neshanic

Officer Stewart, or Bill, which he insists I call him when he's not wearing his uniform, walks in first and I follow apprehensively behind. I definitely don't feel right about being inside The Store as I know it would bother my parents big time. It's not as if I have much of a choice though. Officer Stew...Bill has been so kind to me and now he just wants to enjoy a cup of coffee, so coming in with him is the least I can do to repay his kindness. Upon entering, we are hit with the smell of cigarettes and perhaps it's the lighting but it even looks hazy in here.

"Don't you know that smoking inside an establishment that serves food is illegal? I can call the Board of Health right now and have you shut down by the end of the day."

Holy crap. I didn't realize it but I think I might be in the middle of a sting operation. I think Officer Stewart is going to arrest the owner of this place!

"Go ahead, you'd be doing me a favor," says the guy behind the deli counter toward the back of The Store, cigarette dangling from his lips. "Here, you can even use my phone."

Nope, I was wrong. They're joking. I'm an idiot. I follow Bill toward the back of The Store. I presume the smoking man to be the owner Bill described as a total slacker. His attire gives off the vibe of a gas station attendant rather than a deli owner. He has on a white t-shirt with the word RANCID scrawled across it in red lettering, which is hopefully not an indication of the food being served. His jeans have a rather large chain wallet attached and up top he's wearing a solid black baseball cap, pledging no allegiance to a team nor sport.

We take seats at the counter next to the only other customer in the place, an old man hovering over a bowl of soup.

"How are ya, Mike?" Bill asks, offering a fist bump to the presumed owner.

"Living the dream. Off-duty today?"

"Yep, it's my day off. Just hanging out with my friend here. Let me introduce you. Mike, this is Rod. Rod, Mike."

I mimic what Bill did and stick out my fist to bump Mike's. He stares at me for a second then concedes, knocking my fist with his.

"You a part of the Big Brother program or something?" he asks Bill.

"Too bad you didn't have a big brother that would slap you around every time something sarcastic came out of your mouth," Bill replies.

"I do have a big brother. He's a total goon. Him slapping me around is the reason I'm sarcastic. My ex-therapist called it a defense mechanism. You guys want something to eat? I'm whipping up a Dolly's Special for Mr. B. over here," he says, turning his back to us as he fires up the grill.

"Any chance you can put that cigarette out and start me off with a cup of coffee?"

"You non-smokers make me sick."

"Me too," chimes in the old man, apparently named Mr. B., as he dabs out his own cigarette into an overfilled ash tray sitting beside his bowl of soup.

"How about you? Coffee?" Mike asks, looking at me.

"I don't drink coffee, I take tea, my dear," I respond, immediately wishing I were dead.

All three of them look over at me, Bill with a wide smile and a raised eyebrow, Mike looking like he's seen a ghost rather than a teenager who is foolishly quoting Sting lyrics, and Mr. B. with a look of horror on his face, rather ghostly himself with his pale skin and near-toothless mouth.

"What the hell did he just say?" enquires Mr. B.

"Sorry, that was really stupid. Those are Sting lyrics. I don't know why I just said that."

Sure I do, because I'm a socially awkward moron, that's why. Sting also has a line in the same song, "Be yourself, no matter what they say." Unless, of course, you're me. Then be someone else. Anyone else.

"Well I can pour you a cup of tea but I'm going to have to charge you extra for being a fan of Sting. That guy is a pretentious windbag. Aren't you a little young to be a Sting fan anyway? Hell, Mr. B. is a little young to be a Sting fan."

"What's a Sting fan?" asks a confused Mr. B.

"So, tell me about this Dolly's Special you're making. I'm starving," Bill says, mercifully putting an end to my ill-advised ice breaker.

Mike tops off Mr. B.'s cup of coffee and pours Bill a fresh one and me a cup of tea while explaining to us that a Dolly's Special is pork roll, egg, and cheese served on a hard roll with salt, pepper, and ketchup. He explains that if missing a single one of these ingredients, it is no longer considered a Dolly's Special, therefore substitutions will not be tolerated.

"Well, I'm sold. Give me one of those. And what kind of fruit do you have to cancel out my bad decision? Rod, do you want some fruit too?"

"Fruit would be delightful."

Never before in my sixteen years on this Earth have I used the word delightful. Why the lamest stuff comes out of my mouth when I'm in the company of strangers, I'll never understand. Perhaps Mike's ex-therapist would call it a defense mechanism, defending me from ever making a new friend. As he comes out from behind the counter, Mike's chain wallet brushes my leg on his way to the center of The Store. When he returns he puts two small cans of fruit cocktail down in front of us, the kind you probably used to eat when you were a little kid. I used to be as good at eating fruit cups as Colin apparently was at baseball. Too bad that's not a sporting event.

"Here you go. Two fruit cups. Only the finest."

"Hey, where's my fruit cup?" asks Mr. B.

"Yours is over there on the shelf, old man. What do I look like, Uber Eats?"

"Uber whats?"

"Here you go, sir, you can have mine. I was thinking more along the lines of fresh fruit. Just the Dolly's Special for me," Bill says.

"Score!" says a delighted Mr. B.

Mr. B. and I sit and enjoy our fruit cups as Bill makes small talk and Mike hovers over the grill, flipping the meat and eggs so casually that it's clear he's done it so many times it has become instinctual. At some point, another lit cigarette appears in his mouth and as I look at Bill to see if he notices it too, I see another one burning in Mr. B.'s ash tray. It's not lost on me that I'm sitting here, far out of range of my mom, enjoying a cup of coffee (well, a hot beverage in a mug, anyway) with new friends (sort of). It's not quite *Friends* level of camaraderie, but so far it's the closest I've come.

chapter 15

*

know your enemy

My phone rings and while I don't recognize the number, I'm certain it's my mom calling from my dad's hospital room. It doesn't surprise me in the least that she's calling just half an hour after I last saw her at the hospital. What surprises me is that this is only the first time my mom has called me, and a full half hour after I last saw her at the hospital. I flash Officer Stewart (or Bill, which I'll never be comfortable calling him), Mike, and Mr. B. the universal sign for "I've got to take this outside," pointing to the phone while motioning with my head toward the door. None of them takes notice, as they're entrenched in debate about whether it should be called Taylor Ham or pork roll. It's a New Jersey thing. My mom doesn't have anything pressing to tell me, only that she's worried about me and needs to make sure that I'm okay. I remind her that I left the hospital with a police officer, that it does not get any safer than that. She seems pretty out of it, which makes me wonder if she's doubling up on her pills. Extra stress will cause her to do that. Between you and me, a lot of things will cause her to do that.

After assuring my mom that everything is fine and promising to call her the minute I get home (I told her that Officer Stewart and I were having lunch together, conveniently leaving out the part about that lunch taking place at The Store), I find myself behind The Store, as I had unknowingly wandered while chatting. There's nothing of interest back here: an old detached garage that's seen better days, a couple of cars parked in front of it, and a dumpster. For some reason I decide to walk around the other side of the building to get back to The Store and, okay, there's no sense in lying about it: the reason I walked this way is that I was hoping to see Cat.

While I'm glad to see that she's not all alone again, wiping the tears from her eyes against the side of the building, I'm disappointed that she's not around. As I step out to the curb to take a peek at the library, I hear a voice call out to me.

"If I didn't know any better, I'd say you were looking for me."

I recognize Cat's voice but when I turn back to face The Store, I don't see her, or anyone for that matter.

"Rodney, up here," she says. I look up and see Cat standing on the roof of Follow the Sun Yoga. The first thing I notice is that she's got wings fastened to her back and before I can figure out why, my fear gets the best of me.

"Hang on, I'll be right down," she says, sending me into a full-on panic.

"NO! THOSE AREN'T GOING TO WORK! DON'T JU—"

Before I can get the last word out of my mouth, I see her step three feet to her left as she starts down the fire escape.

"You're hilarious," she says when meets me on the sidewalk. "For a second it seemed like you really thought I was going to jump."

I'm a real riot.

"So what's with the wings, anyway?" I ask while trying to coax my heart to slow down to an acceptable rate and share some of the blood with the rest of my body before I end up face down on the pavement.

"They're part of a cosplay costume I'm making."

"You're into cosplay, huh?"

"You could say that. You could also say that it saved my life. Well, it's one of two things that did."

As I go to enquire about the other thing that saved her life, my phone rings again. Guess who?

"Hey, Mom, what's up? No, I'm not home yet. I'm still having lunch with Officer Stewart. Yes, I'll call you when I get home. Okay. I love you too."

"No walkie-talkie today?" Cat asks.

"My dad is in the hospital and my mom is there with him so we're out of range. Too bad my phone number isn't unlisted."

"Oh my gosh, I'm sorry to hear that. I hope he won't be there long."

"He's having his gallbladder removed. His doctor said it's pretty routine and he should be home in a few days. My mom is staying there with him until he gets discharged. It'll be the longest she's been away from my house since I was born."

"That's going to be really tough for both of them, though especially for her, I imagine, being out of range and all. If you need a ride to the hospital to visit her, I'd be happy to take you."

She must recognize the puzzled look on my face as I try to recall whether I told her my age or that I don't have a car as she continues, "I don't mean to presume, but the only two interactions I've had with you ended with you jogging away and since you weren't exactly dressed for working out, I just figured you don't drive."

"Well, I'll be. You're quite intuitive." *And I hang around librarians and old cat ladies so much that I'm starting to speak like them. Excuse me while I barf.*

"Not to bring up a sore subject but—"

"But you will," I say, interrupting.

"Huh?"

"That's one of those phrases that states the exact opposite of its intention. Every time someone says 'not to bring up a sore subject,' a sore subject immediately follows. It's akin to people saying 'no offense.' The moment you hear those words you can be assured you're about to be offended."

"Fair point. Okay, so...*to* bring up a sore subject, care to tell me more about Green Day destroying your family?" Cat asks. "You lobbed that out there the other day but had to take off before you got to the details. I've been curious ever since."

I already told you she holds a power over me that makes me feel comfortable opening up and telling her things that I wouldn't tell most people, especially people I hardly know at all.

"They killed my brother, they're responsible for my entire high school calling me Nimrod, and there's a strong possibility they prevented me from meeting Sting, which likely would have mended my mom's broken heart and solved all of my problems."

"Your brother died? That's horrible. I'm so sorry."

"Yeah, it is, but it's okay. I didn't even know him. He died before I was born. Colin was only twenty when he died. He was home from college on summer break and he went to see his favorite band play in Asbury Park. Any guesses as to who that would be?"

"Green Day?"

"Ding ding! He was killed in a car accident on his way home."

As I say this, I recognize the familiar inquisitive look appear on Cat's face. I know it because it's the same look everyone gets, so I provide her with an answer without making her ask the question.

"And no, he wasn't drunk. It was an accident, plain and simple. No one else was involved. His car hit a tree. They think he fell asleep at the wheel. After Colin died, my mom gave up on two things: music and driving. To her, Green Day is the devilish face of rock 'n roll. They're the enemy that stole her son from her. Colin was a star baseball player; he still holds a bunch of school records at Somerville High. There are plaques with his name hanging outside the gym. He was playing baseball in college with all signs pointing toward the major leagues to become a big star. Then he discovered Green Day, lost his way, and now he's dead. My parents had me in an attempt to fill the void Colin left which, as it turns out, is a task I'm remarkably unsuited for and now my mom is putting the over in overprotective so that the same thing that happened to her Golden Child doesn't happen to me."

I sense that I'm rambling but, as usual, once I get going I find myself unable to stop.

"So to summarize, I'm living in the shadow of my dead brother and Green Day is the nightmarish soundtrack to the movie of my sad, unremarkable life. And now you probably think I'm crazy."

"Not at all. I think you're the most interesting person I've met since coming to this godforsaken town," she says with what seems like sincerity.

Wanting to keep this perfect moment just the way it is, I tell Cat that I should be getting back inside before my mom calls again. I ask her if she'd like to come in and meet Officer Stewart, who's a police officer and is just about the only friend I've got. She politely declines, telling me that she doesn't want to be subjected to seeing the Grouch again until she has to be back there for work in a couple hours.

"You work at The Store?"

"Sadly. I'm helping Aunt Amy get Follow the Sun Yoga on its feet but it's brand new so she's not making much money yet. I got a job at The Store to put gas in the tank. It's pretty terrible but at least the commute is good. And just so you know, we're friends now so I don't want to hear any of this 'Officer Stewart is my only friend' garbage anymore."

chapter 16

*

so lonely

My parents and I live in a three-bedroom house on a cul-de-sac. It's a nice house; gray with blue shutters that my dad painted himself (both the house and the shutters) back when he was still in good enough shape to carry out such an undertaking. My parents have the master bedroom, mine is across the hall, and then there's Colin's room, which sits between the two. Similar to what I'm sure you've seen in movies, Colin's room has remained largely untouched since he died. Turns out this type of thing shows up a lot in books and movies because it really happens. I imagine that one of the most difficult parts of death is for the family to have to get rid of the belongings of the deceased. After dispersing some of it to friends and family and holding onto a good deal of it for themselves, there's still always leftover stuff and most of it is just that: stuff. Stuff that needs to be thrown out. Many families, though, can't bring themselves to do this, mine included—especially my mom—and the room ends up becoming somewhat of a shrine.

Colin's old baseball trophies sit atop shelves that my dad built and hung on the wall years before I was born. There is an abundance of trophies. Hanging on the wall over his old bed are a Philadelphia Phillies pennant and a Scott Rolen poster (who was the Phillies star third baseman back when Colin was alive). In New Jersey, the majority of people are Yankees or Mets fans, but from Neshanic Station it takes the same amount of time to drive to a Phillies game as it does to

Yankees Stadium and my dad preferred driving to Philly, so that's how he and Colin became Phillies fans. Also in his room is his old Sega Genesis (which still works, by the way, and anytime you're up for it I will gladly challenge you to a game of NHLPA '93), which sits beside a bookcase that's filled to the max with books. There's an old TV whose screen is massive and heavy-looking, like a microwave. Flat screens didn't exist in Colin's day. It's got a VHS player built into it, which is how people watched movies back before streaming came along. The TV sits on top of a shelf that holds Colin's old VHS tapes, all movies from the 1990s. I've watched them all. Some are pretty good, like *Good Will Hunting*, *The Crow*, *Dumb and Dumber*, and *Reality Bites*. My mom still washes and changes the sheets on his bed every ten days even though no one ever sleeps in them except for her, occasionally, on particularly emotional nights.

His room is pretty much the same as it was before he died, but not exactly. What seems to have been scrubbed from his room, like in a television crime scene, is music. The only thing in there that's even music-related is Colin's old stereo, the one on which my mom played *Synchronicity* by The Police when I was young, but his old CDs are nowhere to be found. They must've gotten thrown out because I've searched high and low for them.

It's incredibly lonely and almost eerie being in my house with nobody else here. Technically, it's not the first time I've been alone in my house. There have been plenty of times when my dad was at work and my mom was out on one of her walks during which I was home alone. It is, however, the first time I'll ever be spending an entire night home alone. My parents never go anywhere. They don't go on trips or to the movies or to visit friends. My dad goes to work, then comes home and plops down in front of the TV. Except when she's out on her walks, my mom is home virtually all the time either obsessively cleaning the house or watching TV herself. She refuses to drive so it's not as if she can go anywhere anyway. My dad does all the grocery shopping (I go along too but he always has to drive), he picks up my mom's prescriptions, and he schleps me around whenever I need to go somewhere, which I try not to do too often because I don't want to be a burden. I imagine our helplessness is exhausting, what with his age, weight, and the fact that he works all the time. I've tried making a case for how helpful it'd be for me to learn to drive and get my license when I turn seventeen and I can tell my dad agrees, but he always says the same thing: "I'll talk to your mother, bud, but you know how she is." He's right—I do. The world took Colin away from her; she's not going to let anyone or anything take me. In a heartbeat, I'd trade her protection for a mere fraction of the love she has reserved for Colin.

Despite the fact that I've gotten little to no sleep in the past twenty-four hours, I'm not the least bit tired. After devouring the leftover chickpea tuna I found in the fridge (which tastes extraordinarily like tuna fish but will keep in the fridge for a few days without the fear of eating bad/stinky fish), I'm filled with energy and find myself bouncing off the walls. I cannot get Cat out of my head. She's not like girls from my school. There's something different about her. And she doesn't know me from Adam, so if I channel Sting and play it smooth she might not look right past me the way people from my school are conditioned to. It's clear that I need to do something romantic for her. The problem is I'm not romantic. While I don't know the first thing about romance, the thing I do know about is Sting, who is romance personified. To be like Sting, I need to think like Sting. What would he do if he met Cat and wanted to impress her? I open up *Lyrics* and after painstakingly reading through song after song, I've got my plan and get to work on my romantic gesture. At the risk of bragging, when my project is complete, I'm rather impressed with what I've come up with. Maybe there's a bit of Sting inside me after all.

chapter 17

*

every breath you take

Ever wake up completely unaware of where you are? What a bizarre feeling. I wouldn't call it terrifying because it comes and goes too quickly to register as terror. I guess disorienting is the best word to describe the feeling. It happens to me every now and again which is baffling, being that I never wake up anywhere but in my own house. I haven't had a sleepover in years. There was a time when I'd go to Frankie's house for sleepovers, but more often than not, I'd end up calling my dad in the middle of the night, at which point he'd meet me halfway across the street to walk me home. This was after I could no longer take any more of Frankie's barbs and would rather face the humiliation of being a baby (his words) and going home, tail between my legs, in the middle of the night.

This morning, jarred by the sound of the doorbell, my mind has reason to be confused. I open my eyes and it takes me a second to realize that I must have fallen asleep in Colin's room. One mystery solved; my mind turns to focus on who is ringing my doorbell at such an ungodly hour. *Holy crap, it's 11:30 a.m.* I've been asleep for nearly twelve hours. Apparently I was more exhausted than I'd thought. A kaleidoscope of butterflies gathers in my stomach and begins to perform a synchronized dance routine as I realize that it must be Cat at the door, coming to embrace me and tell me I'm the most romantic person she's ever met. I take the stairs two at a time and am stunned to see that it's Officer Stewart standing at my door.

"Morning, Romeo. Mind if I come in?"

One person's romantic gesture is another person's worst fear. This morning, Cat's Aunt Amy found the note I left taped to the front window of Follow the Sun Yoga. At first she thought it was an ad from a local politician "counting on her support," or perhaps a menu from a local restaurant. As she investigated further, the words on the paper gave her pause. At this point she showed it to Cat in an attempt to figure out if this was some kind of a threat, wondering if Cat knew of anyone who might leave such a thing. They racked their brains and although Cat had a hunch that it could be her recent ex-boyfriend back in Holmdel, she didn't think he was devious enough to do something this sinister (her words), nor did he know where she was staying in Neshanic Station. Confused and alarmed, they called the police. They were so close—if only they had called upon rock 'n roll's The Police instead of Neshanic Station's actual law enforcement.

In addition to being a cool and super nice guy, Officer Stewart is an excellent police officer. He said it didn't take him long to decipher the code and figure out what was going on. He admitted that upon first setting eyes on the note he thought they were dealing with a real creep and that it might be a stalking situation. But as he read the words over a few times, the melody to a song he didn't necessarily like but couldn't help but recognize, popped into his head:

Every breath you take, every move you make
Every bond you break, every step you take
I'll be watching you
Every single day, every word you say
Every game you play, every night you stay
I'll be watching you
Every move you make, every vow you break
Every smile you fake, every claim you stake
I'll be watching you

"That's when I thought to myself, who around here likes The Police enough to copy down their lyrics and leave it for the new punk rock girl in town?"

"Oh my god. I am such an idiot. Do they know it was me?" I ask.

"I didn't tell them it was you. I said I had a hunch as to who may be behind this misguided act and assured them I would get to the bottom of it; that I was quite confident they had nothing to worry about. What were you thinking?"

"*Every Breath You Take* is literally the most-played radio song ever. And I don't mean literally in the incorrect way that everyone uses it these days, like 'this is literally the most boring class ever,' as if something like that could even be measured. I mean that it's a fact that *Every Breath You Take* has been played on the radio more times than any other song in history. On top of that, it's super smooth. So I copied down some of the lyrics and left them where I knew Cat would see them. I tried to channel my inner Sting and do something romantic."

"Instead of trying to be like Sting, why don't you just be like Rod instead?"

"Cat isn't from around here. She doesn't go to my school so she doesn't know anything about me. Not that anyone from my school knows anything about me either. I'm the Invisible Man. I figured I had a clean slate and wanted to sweep her off her feet. Instead, I scared her out of her boots."

"That's a pretty good line," he says, chuckling. "You're a funny kid, Rod. If you're gonna try to be like someone else, she's not going to know who you are. No one is smooth like Sting. Isn't he the dude that does yoga and has sex for like six hours straight?"

"He said that in an interview once but he was being sarcastic. That's followed him around for years," I say looking at my shoes, too ashamed to meet his eyes.

"I guess there could be worse rumors to follow you. Though six hours of anything other than sleep sounds pretty miserable to me.

All right, so here's what we're going to do. We're going to head over there together and explain to them that this is a big misunderstanding."

"Are you crazy?!" I shout, immediately apologetic for the outburst. "I can't face them. I can never see Cat again. Heck, I'm never leaving the house again. How did everything get so messed up? My dad is trying to kill himself with junk food as me and my mom sit idly by and do nothing to stop him. And then you're kind enough to take my messed-up family to the hospital because only one of us can drive and then we drag you back to the hospital on your day off so you can drive me home and I meet a girl who is mysterious and interesting and beautiful and who knows nothing about me and then I tape a note to her window and lead her and her poor aunt to believe that there's a psychopath in town who's after them."

At this point I'm crying uncontrollably. The weight of everything that's happened over the past few days—over the entirety of my life—is being purged through my tear ducts. While boiling a kettle of water for tea, Officer Stewart is trying to help and offer me encouragement by telling me that I should be myself and stop trying to be like my hero, Sting. But how am I supposed to be myself when my own parents don't want me to be myself? They wanted Colin and Colin died, so they wanted another son just like him and instead got stuck with me. I'm nothing like Colin and because of that my dad uses food as a drug and my mom uses drugs as a drug. If I was just good at baseball and was a normal kid who fit in at school, I'm not saying they'd be happy and all their sadness would be washed away but they wouldn't be so goddamn miserable, that's for sure.

It's no wonder I spend all my free time in the library. My only friends are authors of books who create fictional worlds that look nothing like my own. The way Matthew Quick can help me feel less alone with his stories that are filled with flawed characters is the closest thing to solace that I've come across in life. To escape for a few hours within the pages of *Boy 21*, my favorite of his novels, with the main character, Finley, who uses basketball as an escape gives me hope that there's an escape out there for me—even if I've yet to find mine. I've never left the tri-state area but thanks to *The Good Thief* by Hannah Tinti, I've lived a life as an orphan missing a hand and have had run ins with scam artists, grave robbers, and petty thieves while on a whirlwind adventure with Benjamin, the man who rescued me from the orphanage. After reading my favorite books numerous times, if I close my eyes tight enough, their realities begin to bleed into my own.

Back in my own reality, it takes me a long time to gather myself. So long, in fact, that the tea that Officer Stewart made has already steeped and cooled down enough to drink. We sit for a while without saying anything. I know that I should say something, that Officer Stewart should be out on patrol keeping our town safe, not wasting his time sitting here with a confused (and crying) teenager, but my mind and mouth will not get on the same page so I'm unable to get anything out.

"Every move you make, every step you take, I'll be watching you. You didn't find that the least bit creepy as you were writing it?"

"I've perfected the science of the idiot," I say, shaking my head as we both begin to laugh.

chapter 18

*

peacemaker

Cat's Aunt Amy has a face that is both kind and attractive. Her long, curly brown hair bounces off her shoulders and although she is a yoga teacher by trade, she also clearly spends a good amount of time outside; her golden tan proof of this. Unlike Cat, Amy is dressed in a colorful outfit, a light green Follow the Sun Yoga tank top and maroon yoga pants. My mind has plenty of time to process these thoughts while Officer Stewart mercifully handles the majority of the talking, as it didn't take long for him to realize that my brain would need some time to work up to formulating coherent sentences.

I'm far too nervous to look at Cat. I attempted to but she has somehow become even more beautiful and twice as intimidating than she was just yesterday. Instead, I spend most of my time looking at her Aunt Amy, which has brought me to two conclusions: **1.)** she looks at me with no judgement in her eyes, despite her first impression of me being a psychopathic stalker, leading me to believe there really is something to this yoga stuff, and **2.)** that she appears to be around the same age as Officer Stewart and although we only just met, I get a really good feeling about her. At that moment, I decide that my life's mission is to get the two of them together, knowing with all my heart that they are destined to fall in love and get married.

"Terribly sorry," Officer Stewart says, holding up his phone, "but my wife is calling so I have to grab this."

Well, there goes that idea.

With Officer Stewart talking to his wife, the one who put the brakes on my future as a matchmaker, the conversation comes to a screeching halt and I've never met a silence I did not want to fill. I notice that Cat is not wearing her black jean jacket today. Being that it's a sweltering ninety-six degrees, it makes complete sense that she's gone with just a t-shirt (white this time), but the heat hasn't stopped her before. Because I cannot help myself, I launch into a rant and forget all about that little thing called breathing.

"Cool shirt. Fratellis. Great pizza. I used to go there with my dad. That's the place on Route 202 by the karate studio, right? I took karate for a few months when I was a kid but my dad and the sensei got into a big argument. Apparently it's insulting to call him anything but Sensei, which my dad thought was silly and insisted on calling him by his real name, John. That was the end of my karate career. Haven't been back to Fratelli's since."

"I can't tell if you're kidding or not."

"True story, I swear. My dad isn't a hothead or anything. He said he understood that the kids had to call him Sensei but couldn't understand why the parents couldn't just call him by his name. He's pretty much forgotten about it now but he used to bring it up all the time."

"Wow. I've got to say, I'm picturing little Rod in a karate outfit and I. Am. Loving. It," she says, putting an emphasis on each of the last words. "I'm actually a fan of *the band* The Fratellis, not the pizza place, though it does sound like quite a place."

Why do I ever open my big, dumb mouth?!

"You've never heard of The Fratellis? Man, you're missing out. They're brilliant. They're no Sting, but who is?"

The way she refers to them as brilliant makes me want to hold her and never let her go. The way I mistook a band for a pizza place makes me want someone to hold my mouth shut until I'm able to control it enough to stop saying stupid things.

Officer Stewart returns to the conversation and asks if everyone is comfortable calling this a misunderstanding and putting it behind them. Cat and her Aunt Amy take me at my word, accepting that this was an act of misguided romance rather than some kind of threat, thank goodness. Officer Stewart heads back to work but not before making me realize that being the world's least romantic person is not even the height of my ineptitude as a human being.

"Rod, please wish your dad luck in his surgery today and tell him I'll pop by the hospital to check on him the first chance I get," he says, bidding us farewell.

Holy crap, I haven't even called my dad yet today. *Worst son ever.* Come to think of it, I haven't heard from my mom, either. That's when I realize I don't have my phone on me. Oh man, I can't imagine how many missed calls are waiting for me.

Amy offers her sympathy then excuses herself, saying she has to get set up for her heated vinyasa class that's coming in shortly. She kisses Cat on the forehead and tells me it was nice to meet me.

"Wow," I say after Amy has disappeared inside Follow the Sun Yoga. "She might be the kindest person I've ever met."

"Told ya. She's my Sting."

chapter 19

*

bang bang

Stockholm Syndrome is defined as an emotional attachment to a captor formed by a hostage as a result of continuous stress, dependence, and a need to cooperate for survival. Perhaps that's a bit strong for describing my relationship with Frankie, but it's as close as I can get to making sense of why I once again find myself back at the scene of the crime, staring blankly at his TV screen. He called a little while after I returned home; must've seen me walk past as his bedroom window (one of them, anyway) faces the street. He wanted me to come over and check out his new VR device for his FPS game. Despite the fact that he was speaking in a code that I could not decipher, I accepted his invitation. What can I say? My house feels so empty with no one there, both literally and figuratively. Either that or I'm a glutton for punishment. The truth, I'm sure, lies somewhere in the middle.

Did you know that FPS stands for First Person Shooter? I sure didn't, which apparently makes me a friggin' idiot who is killing his flow with all of my stupid questions (his words). Frankie is decked out in his virtual reality gear. This is what he was so intent on sharing with me: massive headphones on his head with goggles the size of a small loaf of bread attached to his face—virtual reality's version of headgear. That happens to be the least disturbing part of his setup. In his arms he's holding a machine gun the length of one of my arms that I'm told recoils, providing the most immersive VR shooting experience. I know this description came straight from the box as there's no way Frankie would've used the word immersive correctly on his own. The battery pack is made to look like the clip of the rifle, proving to me that Frankie and I have very different definitions of "SO SICK!"

Before coming over, I found my phone in Colin's room and returned my mom's call while I made lunch. Technically, I had nine missed calls from her, which is actually fewer than I'd anticipated. Once I talked her off the proverbial ledge of believing something terrible had happened to me, she informed me that my dad's surgery went well. The way she spoke of it, you'd have thought *she* was the one who went under the knife: how stressful it was for *her*, how she can't get *her* heart rate down, etc. She then insisted that I come to visit *her* at the hospital, at which point I reminded her that I don't have a license and that the hospital is at least an hour away by bike. Hearing what she wants to hear, my mom told me that biking was a great idea and that she'd see me soon.

I travel to Somerville every day during the school year, which takes around twenty minutes via school bus. One of the many negatives about living in a small, forgotten town like Neshanic Station (so small that it doesn't even have its own high school) is that there is no public transportation available. There's no city bus, no passenger train (we have train tracks that pass behind The Store but they're for freight trains), and an Uber is out of the question because I don't have a credit card. Part of my reason for coming over to Frankie's is that I figured I could see if he'd be willing to give me a lift to the hospital but Frankie is far too immersed in his new toy that I don't even bother asking. I offer him one of the portobello mushroom wraps that I whipped up at my house and plan on bringing to the hospital for my parents, since what they're serving in the cafeteria is only a small step above Wawa.

"Are they vegan?"

When I tell him that they are, he so eloquently states that he "would never be high enough to eat that crap," before sticking his hand into a bag of Doritos, half of which end up in his mouth, the other half on the floor.

"What about an apple?" I ask.

"What *about* an apple?"

"Apples are vegan-friendly. Would you eat one of those?"

This query doesn't garner a response as I've lost his attention to his preferred reality. It's strange to me that he even wants me here. Seldom do I play the games with him and on the rare occasions that I do, he berates me for my novice skills. He doesn't engage in much conversation unless he's asking something to the effect of "Did you see that? I just shot that dude right in the face!" It must be the warm body factor. It's better to have someone around, even if you don't necessarily enjoy that person's company, than having no one at all. I'll admit to being guilty of feeling this way myself, which is why I find myself here in the first place.

Instead of trying to figure out my next step, my mind keeps going back to Cat. She's the kind of person Sting would write a song about. Unlike Frankie, she makes me feel good about myself. Even when I say dumb things, like mistaking a rock 'n roll band for a pizza place, she doesn't make me feel small. When I'm around her my heart beats twice as fast, at the rate of a squirrel's while running for his life from the neighborhood dog. Cat is different from the people at my school. She doesn't seem concerned with fitting in; she's like a fully-formed person already while the rest of us are all still trying to figure out where we belong and which lunch table is safe to sit down at without getting asked to leave, whether verbally or with an unwelcoming glare. I wonder if she takes yoga classes, leading me to ponder what she looks like in yoga pants.

"Hey, NIMROD!" I hear, feeling something pressing against my temple. From the corner of my eye I can see that Frankie is holding his virtual reality gun up to my head. "Are you even listening to me?!"

"No, I wasn't. You're boring. I'm outta here. It's been real."

chapter 20

*

king for a day

A church parking lot on a weekday afternoon seems like the perfect place to stop for a water break. I find a stoop in the back of the deserted parking lot to sit on while chugging water as if I were a contestant on a game show on which the challenge is to…well, chug water. It's safe to say that along with matchmaker, we can officially scratch game show creator off the Future Careers list. The suffocating heat causes me to sweat profusely, transforming my t-shirt from heather gray to charcoal.

A car pulls into the parking lot. My first instinct tells me that it could be the priest or whatever the head honcho is called here at the South Branch Reformed Church (we're not a religious family; my parents are Catholic on Christmas and Easter but take the rest of the year off, so I'm not up on the lingo) but upon hearing the struggle between the deafening music escaping from inside the car and the squealing that I assume is coming from under the hood, I'm leaning away from it being a person of the cloth. I just hope it's not someone I know from school; that's the last thing I need right now.

"You training for a marathon or something? Are they called marathons when people are riding bikes or is that just for running?"

Cat informs me that she followed me here all the way from town. She saw me load the gallon of water that I had purchased from The Store into my backpack and was intrigued by where I might be going on my bike that would necessitate so much h2o (her word). Cat's surprise about how I couldn't hear her car behind me, considering that the engine sounds like one thousand trapped crickets screaming to get out, prompts my own admission of an act of deviousness.

"I didn't hear the crickets, as you call them, because of these," I tell her, pulling from my pocket the noise-cancelling earbuds that I "borrowed" from Frankie. "Now, I must tell you that Frankie doesn't exactly know that I borrowed these per se but, while it doesn't make it right, he has so many gadgets that I guarantee he won't know these are gone. Even if he somehow did notice they're missing, which he won't, he'll whine to his dad and a new pair will magically appear on his doorstep before the sun sets. Amazon seems to move even faster for the wealthy."

"Rodney, you klepto. What would your police officer friend say about you stealing?"

"Is this before or after I told him that Frankie held his virtual reality machine gun up to my temple in an effort to exert power over me?"

"I don't know him, but I think I hate him. What a chump," she says. "So, where are you headed, anyway?"

"I'm riding to Somerville to visit my mom in the hospital."

"I thought your dad was the one who got surgery."

"Oh, he is. But my mom is the one who requires thoughts and prayers."

Cat offers me a deal. She says she's going thrifting today and (as I pretend to know what that means) if I'd be willing to accompany her on her excursion, she'd be happy to take me to the hospital afterward. Being that it would take me at least another forty minutes to get to the hospital by bike, I've got time until my mom sends a search party out to look for me, so I graciously accept her offer. As I mull over her question of whether there's a thrift store anywhere near the hospital, Cat pulls up the location of one on her smartphone.

"You really should get one of these. On second thought, everyone has a smartphone but you're the only person I know with a flip phone. Yours is way more original."

"Wait a sec—why were you following me, anyway?" I ask.

"Because every time I see you, you become more interesting to me," she says, which is the nicest thing anyone has ever said to me.

* * * * * * * *

Cat and I decide that hiding my bike behind the church is a safe bet, which is likely true, but based on the fact that neither of us had any idea as to what else to do with it, and the fact that her car (rightfully) doesn't have a bike rack affixed to it, there wasn't really any other option.

"Sorry about the temperature in here. You might want to roll down your window. No A.C."

"Works for me. I'm a windows kind of guy anyway. Where's the button?" I ask, searching the door panel for the window control.

"You gotta do it manually in this hunk of junk. The crank is on the door," Cat informs me.

"No A.C. and no power windows in the Catmobile, huh? Old school. I like it."

"The Catmobile?"

"That was stupid, wasn't it? It's as if I have to say at least five dumb things per day. I don't know what the count is today but hopefully I'm nearing my quota."

"I've got to say, I friggin' love the name Catmobile and I'm pissed at myself for not thinking of it first."

This is one of those times in which I have no idea if she's being sarcastic but, like Sting, I'm choosing to remain optimistic and I'm taking her words at face value.

Calling what Cat has over me a power is too strong, or maybe too sinister, a word for how she makes me feel. She's just so easy to talk to, so non-judgemental, that I can't help but open up to her with complete honesty. Even though I've never spoken to a therapist, and the one my mom sees seems intent on prescribing pills then moving onto the next customer, the disarming quality Cat possesses makes it seem like she would be a good fit for the profession. So when she asks me what's on my mind as I stare out the window at the wooded estate that once belonged to Doris Duke, I share with her that I'm a bit anxious, wondering what it's going to be like seeing my mom—if she'll read me like a book, knowing that I didn't ride my bike all the way here, perhaps using her Overbearing Mom Radar to know that I am with a girl, which would surely send her into cardiac arrest, shifting her role from visitor to patient. I tell her that I'm in a constant state of unease around my mom, feeling that she can hardly look me in the eyes because I'm not Colin, the son she once had and clearly still wants. Cat talks about her own mom for a bit, saying she can definitely relate to my feelings of inadequacy.

"All a kid wants is a parent's approval, and to be denied that through no fault of your own is wrong. I've harbored feelings of resentment toward my mom for most of my life—still do. But I've also come to realize that as much as we want to believe that our parents are these people who've got it all figured out, that's not the case. They're people like you and me, just with more years of experience and more scars to show for it. Your mom, although I've never met her, shows her love by being overprotective, feeling the need to keep you in range which she believes will keep you safe. My mom is the opposite; the less she sees of me, the better off she is."

* * * * * * * * *

The weight of our conversation centered around our moms is instantly lifted as Cat steps inside Incogneeto, this vintage wonderland, proclaiming that she's arrived at Mecca. Boasting over 250,000 unique, one-of-a-kind pieces (according to the sign on the door, anyway), Incogneeto is unlike any store I've ever been inside. I didn't even know stores like this existed, let alone a mere five minutes from the school in which I spend one hundred and eighty days of my year. Admittedly, despite having spent the past three school years just a few blocks over, I'm not familiar with the majority of the stores in downtown Somerville. I get bussed in from Neshanic Station, serve my time inside the brick walls of Somerville High, and get schlepped right back home. It makes me simultaneously happy and sad to know that such glorious places like this exist at arm's length.

Cat spins around with a smile so wide it threatens to swallow her ears, taking in the jewelry, suits, jackets, perfume, pearls, feather boas, vintage gloves, etc. She tells me this place is a cosplayers dream. She happens to be creating her own character—well, sort of (her words)—but lots of people dress as the hero of their favorite movies. Cat pulls a crown off the rack, placing it upon my head and telling me that through cosplay and amazing stores like this one, I can be anything I want to be—a king, perhaps. She hits it off with the owner, Stacy, immediately. I thought her requests were far-fetched but when Cat tells Stacy that she's looking for a red tie, preferably with a question mark on it but if not she can add that later, and a Lone Ranger mask, Stacy grabs her by the hand and assures her she came to the right place.

With Cat and Stacy off on their quest, I wander the crowded aisles of Incogneeto, crown on head, and fantasize about what character I would become if I were to take her up on her offer to tag along to Cosplay Con in Asbury Park at the end of the summer. Being that Asbury Park is far out of range, coupled with the fact that it's the place Colin went to see Green Day, having never returned, there's no possible way in hell I could ever make that happen, but there are no restrictions on daydreaming. As for cosplay costumes, the possibilities are endless, as the selection here offers fashions from every time period imaginable. I could go as Amory Blaine, the protagonist from my favorite book, *This Side of Paradise* (which is F. Scott Fitzgerald's finest work, despite popular opinion that it's *The Great Gatsby*). Sitting on the rack in front of me is a three-piece suit, white with black pinstripes, that would put me right back in the Roaring Twenties. I'm certain that Stacy, once she's finished helping Cat, could help me find a wide-brimmed fedora to tie the outfit together. Or perhaps I could transport myself to a more recent era and go with something more flashy, like the outfits The Police wore in their music videos in the 1980s. A pair of aviator sunglasses, a black-and-white-striped long sleeve shirt, and a pair of parachute pants would do the trick. If I dig deep enough through the overflowing racks, maybe I'll get lucky and find an olive green jumpsuit like Sting was known to wear on stage in those days. Recalling Cat's statement that many people dress as the hero of their favorite movies, an outfit in the kid's section catches my eye and I am instantly transported to Cosplay Con…

"So you're a…bumblebee?" Cat asks upon my arrival, with more than a hint of regret for inviting the person outfitted in a nine-year-old's Halloween costume.

"Not just any bumblebee—I'm Barry from *Bee Movie*," I say, as if that'll make this horrendous decision any better. "And look, I fashioned a sparkler to my behind as a stinger. When it gets dark I thought we could light it."

"Tell you what, Rodney—"

"Please, call me Barry. I want to stay in character."

"Okay…Barry. You wait out here…outside of the convention. I'll go inside and get us situated with the tickets and then I'll come back out to get you," Cat says, which would turn out to be the last words she ever spoke to me.

"Rodney, where are you?" Cat asks, mercifully ending my daymare, landing me back in the aisles of Incogneeto.

"My real name isn't Rod—it's Barry, just like the bee from *Bee Movie*. I assure you that I will never show up to a cosplay convention dressed in a bumblebee costume, but for the first time in my life, I feel like myself and I think I'm finally ready to leave the hive."

chapter 21

*

if you love somebody, set them free

Part of what drew me to *Bee Movie* was that I shared a name with the main character. I'd never met anyone else named Barry before and even though I couldn't meet the fictitious animated bee from the movie, this felt like a win. It didn't hurt that Barry the Bee was super cool. He didn't want to be just another worker bee like everyone else, stuck in a crappy job for the rest of his life simply because that's what bees were supposed to do. He wanted something more, even if he did not yet know what that something was. He made a decision to leave the hive. Against the advice and wishes of his best friend and parents, Barry went off on an adventure to see what else the world had to offer. Even as a little kid, I related to Barry in a big way. I felt as if I were living the life of a worker bee, stuck in a hive taking care of the queen day and night. I knew that there had to be more to life. I admired his desire to leave the hive, yet I did not possess the same courage as Barry, who actually left his.

I'm not proud of the fact that I'm embarrassed by my name. It was my dad's father's name, and although he died long before I was born, from everything I'm told he was a great guy. I've seen pictures of him, even some of him with Colin. It's bizarre that we share the same grandfather but Colin actually got to know him and I never will—nor will I ever know Colin, for that matter.

After I reveal my true identity to Cat and ask her to continue calling me Rod, as I've grown quite fond of the moniker over the years and feel more like a Rod than a Barry, she shares a secret of her own with me.

"Cat isn't my real name either," she confesses.

"Well, yeah, it's short for Catherine, right?"

"Nope, not even close. Oh look, we're here," she says, navigating the Catmobile into a spot in the visitor lot of Robert Wood Johnson University Hospital. The name may lead you to believe there is a university in Somerville called Robert Wood Johnson, but I assure you there is not.

Once inside, Cat insists on hanging in the waiting room, which comes as a major relief, and tells me to take all the time I need. She accepts and starts in on the portobello wrap I offer her, telling me how wonderful it is (again, I remain optimistic that this compliment is sarcasm-free), asking where I learned to cook like this. While I inspect my backpack for a book to provide her with something to do while she waits, I tell her that I got the recipe from *Forks Over Knives the Cookbook*. After the impact the documentary made on me, I marched down to the library and borrowed the cookbook, which wasn't exactly a popular item amongst the residents of my podunk town so I continued renewing it for six months straight, at which point I had many of the recipes memorized. Soon I found confidence in the kitchen and began improvising here and there and experimenting with my own creations. But the portobello wrap is straight from the book and is a favorite of mine and my dad's (my mom isn't a big eater).

In true Rod fashion, all I have to offer is my copy of *Lyrics* by Sting. It takes Cat a second to realize what it is, but when she opens to the bookmarked page, and comes upon the lyrics for *Every Breath You Take*, my cover is blown.

"Rodney, is this what I think it is? Wait a second...is this considered evidence?"

"Not if you don't press charges."

"Fair enough. Okay, so you can hold onto this," she says, handing *Lyrics* back to me. "Any chance I can snag those wireless earbuds you *borrowed* from Frankie? I'm surprised they're compatible with that flip phone of yours."

"Bluetooth capabilities," I say, holding my antiquated phone up to my face like a commercial. "This ain't your grandma's flip phone."

"Go see your dad before I change my mind about sitting in this waiting room."

* * * * * * * * *

It takes my dad a few seconds to realize that I'm standing in his room, in front of his hospital bed, as he's got his nose buried in Sting's memoir.

"Did you know that Sting's dad was a milkman and as a kid Sting, who was just little Gordon back then, used to go along on his route with him?" my dad asks, matter-of-factly as if we were already in the middle of a conversation.

"No, I had no idea. So you're enjoying the book?" I ask, placing the container of portobello wraps (minus one) on the side table.

"My dad, who you're named after, drove a bread truck. Used to wake up at 4 a.m. to start his deliveries. On my breaks from school I'd go along with him. God, those winter mornings were brutal. But I sucked it up because my dad never complained and I wanted him to think I was tough like he was. Sting did the same thing. Man, this book is bringing back some memories I haven't thought about in years."

As my dad talks more about *Broken Music*, his eyes glisten with hope and he looks not at all like a man who has just had his gallbladder removed, which I share with him. He thanks me for leaving this book behind, saying it's really helping to put things in perspective. He tells me that he's going to make some big changes once he gets out of the hospital.

My mom is here too but she's asleep. She has her photo album clutched like a football in one hand and her pill bottle in a jaws of life grip in the other. My dad tells me that she's been out for a bit so she should be up soon. We chat for a while about his surgery, how he's feeling, who the Phillies are playing tonight, etc. He asks how things are at the house and then asks if I've gotten to have any fun at all, in no way imagining my answer was going to be anything but an emphatic no. At that moment, the muscles that control my lips stage a mutiny and pull everything back in their best effort to make me smile like a buffoon. I resist with all my might but my dad catches on and begins to reel me in.

"I'm not going to ask questions, I know teenagers hate that. But if you want to go out with friends—a group or just one person maybe—I think I've got some money you can borrow if you need it."

That's the kind of guy my dad is. Money was an issue *before* he landed in the hospital. Now he'll be out of work for who knows how long, yet still he's offering me whatever he's got in his wallet. I tell him that there is a new girl in town who seems pretty cool but that I think it's best to hang at the house and make sure everything is in order there.

"Here's what you're going to do," my dad whispers. "You're going to leave before your mom wakes up and you're gonna ask the new girl in town to hang out with you."

"I can't leave before Mom wakes up. She was urgent on the phone. She really needs to see me."

"Rod, I love your mother. I do. But when is she not urgent on the phone? Get out of here. I'll tell her you stayed as long as you could but had to ride home before it started to get dark."

"I wouldn't even know what to do with her if she did want to hang out."

"Don't overthink it. Stay out of that analytical head of yours and keep it simple. Go and get some coffee."

"I don't even drink coffee, Dad."

"Well now is as good a time as any to start. Times may have changed and I may be out of touch with a lot of things, but getting a cup of coffee with a girl is timeless. We live in New Jersey, land of the twenty-four-hour diner. Many a great night has been spent between two people and a cup of coffee at a diner. You're a good kid. Scratch that—you're a great kid. Go do something wild for once. Go be free."

chapter 22

*

american idiot(s)

I've got to hand it to my dad—getting coffee does seem to be a timeless tradition. As Cat and I cautiously sip from our scorching cups while leaning against the back of the Catmobile in the parking lot of 7-Eleven, my instinct is to share with her a random fact about how hot liquid actually cools down your body on a sweltering day. My dad and I watched a show on PBS about an army in a country that I can't for the life of me recall that drank hot coffee while marching in full uniform in 110 degree heat, as it helped to regulate their body temperature. But it seems that I may be turning over a new leaf as I manage to keep this insipid anecdote to myself. I'm out of the hive, drinking coffee for the first time, hanging out with a girl who's way out of my league. Perhaps this is the emergence of New Rod.

"So, what's the second thing?"

"What?"

"The other day you said cosplay is one of two things that saved your life. What's the other?"

After a thoughtful pause, Cat asks, "What are your plans for the rest of the night?"

"Trying to make sure my heart doesn't beat out of my chest. How much caffeine is in here, anyway?!"

"Don't worry, Mr. Green Tea, you'll be fine. I promise. Tell you what, I'll share with you the second thing that changed my life if you come to a basement show in New Brunswick with me. Some friends of mine will be there and I want you to meet them. What do you say?"

"That depends."

"Depends on what?"

"On what exactly a basement show is."

* * * * * * * *

New Brunswick is the college town where Rutgers University is located, about twenty minutes from the 7-Eleven in Somerville. When I was young I went to a football game there with Frankie and his dad. Penn State beat Rutgers 64-10. Frankie's dad is a Rutgers alumnus and went crazy the entire time as if Rutgers losing a football game was a personal affront. I look over to see the wind sneaking in through the window of the Catmobile has caught Cat's jet-black hair perfectly, assuring me that my second trip to New Brunswick is going to be more enjoyable.

It's a perfect summer evening. The sun isn't going anywhere for quite a while because it doesn't get dark until nearly 9 p.m. on summer nights in New Jersey. As we make our way through Somerville, toward Route 287, I begin to wonder if I'm dressed properly for a basement show in my camouflage shorts and gray t-shirt, which has dried out and returned to its natural shade of heather. Cat assures me that I'll fit right in. I ask her again about the second thing that changed her life and she answers my question with a question.

"So, you've never heard Green Day before? Like, ever?"

"Perhaps in passing or without knowing it was them, but never by choice. I really haven't heard much music other than The Police and Sting's solo stuff."

"Surely you're aware that *American Idiot* is one of the most famous albums of all time. It changed the world."

"Funny you should mention that. You know how everyone knows a few famous people that were born on their birthday, causing them to feel a connection with these otherwise perfect strangers?"

"Of course. Mine's April 15th and since we're close friends now, I'll totally be expecting a card. I share a birthday with Emma Watson and Maisie Williams, both of whom have played characters who I've portrayed in cosplay: Emma Watson's Hermione Granger from *Harry Potter* and Maisie Williams's Arya Stark from *Game of Thrones*."

"Well, I was born on September 20th, the same day *American Idiot* was released. I've never heard it out of principle, but from what everyone says, including you just now, it's genius, which rubs salt in the wound of Green Day being the black cloud constantly looming over my head. So I can't help but feel like *I* am the American Idiot."

"That album is the second thing that saved my life and that's not hyperbole. I was a certain way before hearing it and a completely different person afterward. So I guess I'm the American Idiot, too."

With that, Cat instructs me to (manually) roll down my window, explaining the importance of listening to music with the volume turned up and the windows rolled down. She asks me if I trust her and when I nod she puts in Green Day's *American Idiot* on CD.

"No bluetooth capabilities in the Catmobile," she says, flashing a smile that melts me.

Before the sense of dread has a chance to set in, knowing what my listening to Green Day would do to my mom who by now is probably just figuring out that I've come and gone without seeing her at the hospital, the opening chords of their punk rock opera kick in, blasting me back into my seat like a passenger on a plane during takeoff. Seconds later, upon hearing the first words sung—"Don't wanna be an American idiot"—I know that my life, just like Cat's when she first heard this, will never be the same. For better or worse, though, remains to be seen.

As Cat spots a place to park, I implore her to play the song *American Idiot* one more time before getting out of the car, but she tells me that five times was plenty and that there are other songs on the album, which I *will* be hearing later. We park a few blocks away and walk to Baldwin Street, where the show is taking place. Cat tells me that's what you do in case the cops come; you never want to be parked right out front because then it's easy for them to bust you. My mind begins to get the better of me wondering exactly what goes on at these basement shows that would entice the police to shut them down and also what the punishment is for getting caught at one. Before my brain gets too carried away, we arrive at the house, pay the $5 admission, and head down into the basement.

Ellie is the first of Cat's friends to spot us, and she greets Cat with an ear-to-ear smile and a wave. She gives Cat a welcoming hug, doing the same to me when we're introduced. It turns out she lives in Hillsborough, which is where Colin's memorial tree is located, a fact that I, uncharacteristically, am able to keep to myself. *Hello again, New Rod.*

Ellie waves over two guys from the side of the room, one about my size and the other a massive human being I wouldn't be surprised to hear is a member of the Rutgers football team. The smaller of the two introduces himself as Wheels but the others throw him under the bus, saying that no one calls him Wheels and that his real name is Adam.

I smile and tell Adam that I'll call him Wheels, that my first name isn't actually Rod but that's what everyone calls me.

"No way! What's your real name?" Wheels asks.

I look over to Cat to see if she's going to give me up to her friends but instead she flashes me the universal sign for "my lips are sealed."

"Is it cool if we just stick with Rod?" I ask nervously, to which Wheels responds, "Absolutely," while offering a fist bump in solidarity.

Will is the other friend, the one towering over the rest of the people in this New Brunswick basement. He may be the size of a football player but his baby face makes him look no older than twelve.

Soft spoken and noticeably uncomfortable, Will is preoccupied with not wanting to block anyone's view when the band begins and insists on going back to lean against the wall from which they came. His friends oblige and move back to the wall so that he won't feel uncomfortable, as good friends should. But when the band begins getting ready to play, Cat grabs me by the hand and weaves her way through the crowd so that we are front and center. This is an unfinished basement with exposed cinder-block walls and a dusty concrete floor, so there is no stage or barrier separating the band from the audience. A swarm of anxiety jolts through my body as the feedback grows louder and louder. I look back and want nothing more than to be back up against the wall with Ellie, Wheels, and Will, my new friends. The band looks just like the rest of us (one of them is even sporting camouflage shorts, like me) with nothing discernable to set them apart from the audience (no stage clothes, no makeup, etc.) except the instruments in their hands. Behind the drum kit, a hand-painted banner hangs on the cinder-block wall that reads NO DRINKING, NO DRUGS, NO BULLSHIT. The singer, a foot and a half from my face, shouts into the microphone, "We're Preexisting Condition, let's have some fucking fun!" before the band erupts into a violent burst of flailing body parts. The music is loud and incredibly distorted, bouncing off the cinder-block walls of the cramped basement, while the singer screams bloody murder into the microphone. He spends half his time rolling on the ground like a worm searching for mud and the other half standing inches away from the audience members' faces, holding direct and lengthy eye contact. Although I'm unable to make out a word that he is saying, I love every waking second of it. The power of the music and the ferocity with which it's being played by people not much older than me, is eye-opening and inspiring. Sure, Preexisting Condition's songs may lack the accessibility of, say, *Can't Stand Losing You* by The Police, which would have you humming along to Sting's bassline for the rest of the day, but these are not rock stars. These are young adults just like me who feel extremely passionate about whatever it is they're screaming about, and for the first time in my life, I do not feel alone in a crowded room.

They couldn't have been playing for longer than twenty (perfect) minutes when the singer announces that this is their last song. At first I thought I heard him wrong. *How could it be over already? They just started.*

"This last one is a cover and I'm gonna need some help singing it as my voice is shot. It's called *American Idiot*. Who wants to help me sing it?"

Admittedly, I'm not a strong kid. I've never lifted a weight in my life. But the force with which I'm thrusted into the singer's personal space, by a push from behind I'm assuming (and hoping) is from Cat, is downright pathetic. The singer smiles and places the microphone in my shaking hand. I whisper into his ear like a scared child that I don't know the words to which he replies, "No one gives a shit. Just scream your brains out."

Cat hands me her phone, which has the lyrics to *American Idiot* pulled up on the screen, and before I'm able to think of a way out, the opening chords kick in and we're off to the races. I flub the very first line, singing "My name is Rod, I'm the American Idiot," surprisingly in time with the band, and the next two and a half minutes are amongst the best of my life as I sing, bounce, and smile like I never have before. Too scared to look up, I fix my gaze on the lyrics on Cat's phone. When I begin to gyrate too much to focus on the words, I take the singer of Preexisting Condition's advice and shout random words into the ether and, as promised, no one seems to notice or care.

Like Preexisting Condition's entire set, the moment is over far too quickly, but that's probably not a bad thing as the caffeine and adrenaline have mixed in my blood and I worry that my feet are no longer touching the ground. In fact, the entire show ends prematurely as the cops come down to break things up shortly after my performance ends, before the second band even gets a chance to play. I find it odd that the police would bother to shut down the show as there are no drugs or alcohol to be found, just kids having a good time playing admittedly abrasive music. Even if the style isn't to your liking, it still seems like a much more positive and productive outlet than what goes on at other parties. The last part (about what goes on at other parties) is purely speculative, of course, as I have never actually attended a party (not since Frankie Friel's eighth-grade graduation party, that is, and even that I left early).

Despite the fact that they were shutting down the show, I must say that the cops were far more polite than I was expecting. In my paranoid mind I was thinking it would be like a raid: cops busting in with guns drawn, telling everyone to HIT THE DECK. Instead, they calmly usher us out, saying things like, "You don't have to go home but you can't stay here." While it's disappointing not to be able to spend more time getting to know Cat's friends, I am elated that as we are whisked away in different directions, Ellie calls out, "It was nice meeting you, Rod! You're a total rockstar! Get my Instagram handle from Cat so we can stay in touch!"

"Get mine, too. Later, dude!" Will shouts in a voice far too soft to match his lumbering body.

I make a mental note to create an Instagram account when I get back to my computer. *Stupid flip phone.*

"Same here. Peace, Rod!"

"Peace, Wheels," I shout back, conjuring a genuine smile of gratitude from one nicknamed friend to another.

"Come on, Rodman," which was enunciated to rhyme with Robin, "to the Catmobile!" Cat says, again taking me by the hand, which feels even better than the first time.

* * * * * * * * *

On the car ride back to Neshanic, I am unable to stop talking. I confess to Cat that being at the show was a bit terrifying but in an exhilarating way. I tell her that tonight was one of the first times that I didn't feel alone in a crowded room. Instead of laughing at me, which would've been justified, Cat tells me I'm awesome.

"And your friends, they seem like such great people. Where do you all know each other from?"

"We're all connected through Green Day, actually. I met Ellie at my first Green Day concert, where we hit it off. She's super into cosplay too so we go to conventions together. I met Adam, a.k.a. Wheels, in a Green Day subreddit and he and Will have been best friends since they were kids, so that's how Ellie and I met that gentle giant. We're all spread out geographically but we meet up at shows or record stores or just hang out somewhere and listen to music."

This matter-of-fact statement blows me away, because at home I've only known music to tear people apart. I share this with Cat and she tells me that music is healing, that it's always there for you when you need it, and that she hopes this experience begins to change my mind about it. She tells me that when she first discovered the album *American Idiot*, it did for her exactly what this basement show did for me: it made her feel less alone.

"I still can't believe everything that happened in the past few hours. All my life Green Day has been tormenting me and then all of a sudden the girl of my dreams plays me their song, which I can't get enough of, and then end up singing it in front of a room full of strangers. This is not real life. Things like this don't happen to me."

"Good things happen when you leave the hive. Don't ever forget that, Rodney."

I am elated that Cat doesn't mention me referring to her as the girl of my dreams. Either she missed it or purposely let it slide, perhaps knowing I'd die of embarrassment if she acknowledged those words had managed to escape my lips.

"And now, without further ado, you've got the rest of *American Idiot* to experience. I will take the long way home so that you get to hear every perfect note of the greatest album of all time."

We roll our windows down, Cat turns the stereo up, and I let the music travel from the speakers directly into my soul.

chapter 23

*

voices inside my head

I'm not someone who drinks coffee. I'm also not someone who rides in cars with people I hardly know. And I'm definitely not someone who listens to music—*especially* not Green Day. In short, I'm not someone who leaves the hive. People who are capable of doing these things, as trivial as they may seem, do not screw them up as royally as I did last night.

The voice of my conscience sounds eerily similar to that of my mom's and last night that voice inside my head won out in a battle against sleep. It's a wonder I remember what my mom's voice sounds like at all being that I didn't speak to her once yesterday, a fact that hit me as I laid down in my bed. Feeling that I had just experienced the most incredible day of my life, guilt simultaneously reared its ugly head, reminding me that **1.)** I forgot to pick up my bike from the church, and **2.)** I hadn't heard from my mom at all, so something must have been wrong. Well, something was wrong, all right. I had sixteen missed calls from my dad's hospital room before I realized that my phone had been paired to Frankie's "borrowed" earbuds the entire night, preventing me from hearing any of the missed calls. I guess it's true what they say: karma is a bitch.

This morning, the first thing I do is call my mom to make sure she hasn't thrown herself out the window of my dad's hospital room. While speaking to her, it's clear to me that she's having a difficult time.

This whole ordeal has been rough on her, both my dad being in the hospital and me being out of range. As silly as it may seem, the walkie-talkies that feel like tethers to me provide her with a sense of comfort, so I decide to be a good son and get myself to the hospital as soon as possible and spend the day there, making sure to bring our walkie-talkies along. Even though we'll still be out of range and won't be able to communicate with them once I leave, I think being able to hold one will bring a sense of familiarity that I hope will provide her with some relief.

Despite it being early and that a pre-8 a.m. text likely betrays proper flirting etiquette, I send Cat a message, telling her about my forgotten bike in hopes that she's awake and will offer a ride to retrieve it so that I don't have to come out and ask. Much to my delight, she texts right back telling me to meet her at The Store, that coffee is on her. Over coffee and small talk, I tell her about my sleepless night and that during my bout of insomnia I made banana-almond granola and a macaroni salad to bring along to the hospital. Once the caffeine gets into my bloodstream and begins doing its work, I realize that we're the only two people in The Store.

"Wait...are you working right now?"

"I am. I guess technically that means coffee is on the Grouch, but I won't tell if you don't. Refill?"

"Please," I say, sliding my cup over to her side of the deli counter.

Cat tells me about her work arrangement at The Store. Most days she comes in and opens up at 7 a.m. It's her job to make coffee and handle all the customers (of which she says there aren't many) until around 11 a.m. when Mike (or the Grouch, as she refers to him) has fought off his hangover enough to come down and take over. She then goes and does her own thing for the afternoon, coming back around 5 or 6 p.m., which is when the Grouch disappears to his apartment upstairs and drinks himself into a stupor (her words). She tells me that she doesn't mind the unconventional nature of her schedule because the less time she spends around the Grouch, the better.

Being that it's just after 8 a.m., I begin to wonder if I'll have to wait three hours until she goes on her midday break when the bell on the front door rings, signaling the morning's first customer.

"Hey, Rod! I hear you need a lift."

I turn to see Cat's Aunt Amy, again clad in a Follow the Sun Yoga tank top, though this time it's sky blue. It hits me that Cat has prearranged a ride for me with her aunt. She didn't inform me of this, knowing that I would've declined, not wanting to put her out having met her all of once, and would've opted to walk instead. I glance back at Cat and her sly (and intoxicating) smile confirms my assessment.

It's a short seven-minute drive to the church but still I feel incredibly awkward. Prior to this, the only time I'd been in Amy's company a police officer had to be present to mediate and explain that I am not, in fact, a threat. Despite my pleas, Amy insists on throwing my bike on the rack attached to the back of her car and driving me the rest of the way to the hospital. The icing on the cake is when she grabs my trusty Huffy out of my hands as I struggle to get it up on the rack, lifting it with ease and placing it on the rack herself.

"So, Rod, let me ask you, have you ever considered taking a yoga class?"

"Oh, I, uhh...I'm not really a morning person. I totally could've gotten the bike up on the rack myself, I, uhh...it's just that my shoulder is a little tender."

"No, no...it's not that," she says with a smile. "I'm in the process of starting a teen yoga class. I remember the stress I was under when I was a teenager, and now with social media and the added pressures teens face, I believe that practicing yoga would help to alleviate some of that stress. It's done so much for me and I only wish I had found it sooner in life, so that's what gave me the idea."

I tell Amy that it's a good idea, one that I'll consider. Then I lie to her, telling her I'll mention it to some of my friends. The lie isn't that I *would* mention it to my friends, because I surely would. The lie is that I have friends to whom I could spread the word. There is one person that I know would benefit from some stress relief, but I'd have an easier time making a whole bunch of friends than getting her to a yoga class.

chapter 24

*

nuclear family

My mom suffers from a fear of abandonment and one doesn't have to be Carl Jung to figure out why. On multiple nights every week, I wake up to see her standing in my doorway watching me sleep. It used to scare the crap out of me and it would take forever to fall back asleep if I was able to at all. Eventually I got used to seeing her standing there and would sometimes ask if everything was all right. She would never respond or even acknowledge the question; she always just continued staring. So it comes as no surprise that when I enter the hospital, she hugs me with such force that I make a mental note to ask Dr. Payne to x-ray my ribs next time I run into him.

Despite being sore, my dad says he feels better than he has in a long time. It's hard to be sure since he's lying down but he looks to have lost some weight. When I tell him so he makes one of his patented dad jokes—"that's what hospital food will do to ya"—which reminds me to take the granola and macaroni salad out of my backpack. Apparently throughout the course of the night in the hospital, nurses come into the room periodically to check their patients' vitals and make sure the IV is full, so my dad is beat. My mom suggests letting him rest and that we go down to the cafeteria.

"You drink coffee now?" my mom asks as I start in on my third cup of the day. Perhaps it's the caffeine altering my perception but she seems more energized than usual.

"Nasty habit, trying to quit," I joke, holding up my cup, which generates a sideways but not unpleasant glance from my mom, almost like she doesn't quite recognize me. "So, Mom, I'm really sorry about yesterday—not sticking around to see you and missing all of your calls. I can explain."

"I think it's my turn to explain for once, sweetheart. These past couple days have been rough for me. Heck, these past couple decades have been rough for me. But being out of range has forced me to do some self-reflection, which is something I usually try to avoid."

Although my mom has yet to say anything specific, this is the most open I can recall her being in some time, maybe ever. She's also working on a bagel, against my advice to avoid them, which is another rare occurrence: seeing her eat. Most times when we have meals together at home, I don't see her eat more than two or three bites total; instead, she spends the entirety of the meal moving her food around with her fork, staring vacantly out the window or at the photo album in her lap. My dad will then end up finishing what's left on her plate, calling himself the Human Garbage Can. It used to worry me, especially when I was younger, thinking she was starving herself to death. But she always stayed around the same weight, never getting super skinny or anything, so I just figured her body needed less than mine and *far* less than my dad's. Now, with her halfway through a bagel within five minutes of sitting down, I can't help but think that this hospital stay is doing her some good, too.

"I don't know exactly how many times I called you last night but I imagine it was a lot."

Sixteen...but who's counting?

"I know that I can be a bit overbearing at times, but I want you to know that I wasn't always this way. Back when your brother was alive, there were cell phones but not like today. He had one but it was mainly for emergencies so it would sit in his car turned off and was only something you'd turn on if you really needed to. Anyway, I can't help but feel that if it was as easy to keep in touch back then as it is today, then maybe I could've done my job as a mother and kept my Colin safe, kept him alive."

For a moment, these words sting. Even in a heart-to-heart with me, she has to go and throw in *MY* Colin. My brain also jumps to the fact that if Colin hadn't died then I wouldn't be alive today, wondering if that's a wish she would cash in. Quickly, I catch my brain in this moment of selfishness and realize that this isn't at all what my mom is implying. For the first time in god knows how long, she's sharing her pain and talking to me like I'm her son, not her employee, so I snap out of my self-indulgence and tell her she can call me as many times as she wants and I'll do a better job of making sure my phone is working properly.

"You're a good boy and I want you to know that I trust you. I know you have a lot less freedom than most sixteen-year olds and I apologize for that. I only meant to call once, just to check in because I didn't get to see you at all yesterday. But when I didn't hear back, my emotions got the better of me, telling me something bad happened to you, compelling me to call again...and again...and again. I ended up having to take five pills last night because I was in the midst of a full-on panic attack."

"Wow, Mom, that's a lot."

"The good news is I haven't taken a single pill today."

My mom takes a long pause here before asking, "Do you ever wonder if crazy people know they're crazy?" I don't answer because I can't, not without crying anyway, so I sit and hope the question is rhetorical but then she continues.

"Well, we do."

The sound of my phone buzzing on the table stops my heart from completely breaking. It's a text from Cat: *Take me to meet the Cat Lady with the hard toenails or she doesn't exist.*

"I'm glad to see your phone is working better today."

"Oh, yeah," I say, holding it up with a nervous smile. *Ever the wordsmith.*

"Sweetheart, you're blushing. Who was that? Did you make a new friend?"

"That? I don't know. Oh, that's no one."

"Well, this 'no one' really knows how to make you smile," she says, going back to the sideways glance, this time with a touch of suspicion thrown into the mix.

* * * * * * * *

Luck is on our side and we catch two episodes of *Man with a Plan* on the TV in my dad's room. Even though Matt Leblanc's name in the show is Adam, my mom still refers to him as Joey, his character's name on *Friends*, which I find endearing. The show is hilarious and I imagine if I had a therapist he'd surmise that part of the appeal is that it's about a happy family, much like the kind I've always wanted to be a part of. For the moment, that's exactly what we are. As much as an afternoon spent in a cramped hospital room can be, it's nice.

My dad's nurse, Roxanne, has been exceptional in her care according to my dad. She made up a cot for my mom right next to my dad's bed, against hospital rules, and also lets my mom order off the room service menu even though it's supposed to be for patients only. Between Dr. Payne and Roxanne, they've got a good thing going here, so the cafeteria gets a pass on its embarrassingly unhealthy selection. Hearing that my dad's nurse shares a name with the character in one of Sting's most famous songs comforts me like a warm blanket.

Apparently Sting's best friend and bandmate in his pre-Police band, Last Exit, is named Gerry, spelled the right way (my dad's words). Sting's memoir has my dad thoroughly hooked, so after *Man With a Plan* is over, he loses himself within its pages. My mom and I flip channels through the sorry selection of daytime television. We catch only the tail end of the segment but the guest on *The Dr. Oz Show* is a doctor discussing the benefits of a vegan diet. After it's over, my mom lands on *Judge Judy* and I excuse myself to use the bathroom.

"Are you feeling okay, honey?" my mom enquires. "This must

be the fourth time you've gone to the bathroom."

"Oh, yeah...I'm good. Coffee goes right through me," I say, hoping to throw her off the trail that I've actually been disappearing into the bathroom to text with Cat. She's bored at work and has been texting me, which I know would make my mom uncomfortable (to put it lightly) so I've been keeping my phone in my pocket and trying to keep my heart from beating out of my chest each time I feel it vibrate in my pocket. Sure, I feel guilty not being fully present while I'm here with my parents but nothing like this has ever happened to me before. I'm not saying Cat's my girlfriend or anything like that. She's going back to Holmdel after the summer anyway so I'm not even sure how that would work. It's just nice to have someone around my age who seems to enjoy talking to me.

"You must be Rod," is the first thing I hear when I step out of the bathroom and before I can process what's happening my dad's nurse envelopes me in a hug fit for an old friend. My dad pops his head out from his book with a huge smile on his face as I remain embraced in one of the lengthier hugs I can remember receiving. "I've heard so much about you. But Gerry, you didn't tell me he was *this* good-looking," she says with a smile and then pulls me back into her chest, where I feel like I'm being smothered by two oversized pillows.

My mom is nowhere to be seen. My dad informs me that she needed to stretch her legs, which is when I realize that she's onto me and knows coffee isn't solely to blame for my frequent bathroom visits. Roxanne, my dad, and I chat for a bit and she's as kind as my dad made her out to be. She's one of those people you can imagine insisting you come to Thanksgiving dinner after only knowing you for five minutes but, unlike most people, actually makes you want to jump at the invitation because you know you'll have a wonderful time. While she doesn't invite me over for Thanksgiving (which is a relief because nothing will bum out a group of people like inviting a vegan to Thanksgiving dinner), she does tell me all about her three kids, Ricky, Nadine, and little Tommy (who's 26 but he'll always be little to her, much to his chagrin), and makes sure to show me pictures of her grandbabies (yes, she's a grandma, but those babies know better than to be calling her Granny, it's Maw Maw, which her son's wife wasn't thrilled about but she knew better than to go making a big deal about it because it was not up for debate). Roxanne has such an affable way about her; I can see why my dad likes her so much. She's kind and entertaining and, for a guy like me who can never quite find the right words to say, she's a breath of fresh air because she handles most of the talking.

"Wait a sec!" my dad exclaims. "What happened with the girl?"

"What girl?" my mom says, entering the room at the most inopportune time.

I look at my dad in a panic. After an awkward pause, he does his best to backpedal.

"Not girl, hun—squirrel. There was a squirrel up on the roof of the house last night that was driving Rod crazy."

My mom, clutching her photo album like a distraught nun holding a rosary, walks over to the end table next to her cot and reaches for her pill bottle.

"I guess that squirrel is to blame for you missing all of my calls," she says, melting my eyes with hers, which have been replaced with laser beams.

chapter 25

*

she

Convinced that I must be embellishing the ailments and gross things that come out of Joanne Jones's mouth while I'm there scooping litter boxes, today on her mid-afternoon break from The Store, Cat meets me at Joanne's house. After successfully disarming the alarm (*phew*!), I introduce Cat as my cousin from California. I could've told Mrs. Jones that she was a serial killer who targets lonely old cat ladies and it wouldn't have made a difference. She saw Cat as a sounding board to which she could air her grievances about the evil nurse that works for her, the one she believes is poisoning her food. She even attempts to get Cat to test the food to see if it's been poisoned! Fortunately, Cat is quick on her feet and swiftly changes the subject, enquiring about the framed pictures on the wall. If there's anything Joanne Jones can talk about more than her spring-loaded intestines or her distrust of nurses, it's her grandsons, the Triplets. Cat stands and listens to their life stories while I quickly but proficiently scoop the litter boxes. Upon finishing, I run out, grab Cat by the arm and yell over my shoulder to Mrs. Jones that we're going to be late for her flight back to California.

"Still think I was exaggerating?" I say as we begin our walk toward The Store.

"I'll never doubt you again, Cousin Rodney."

"At least you heard that. Miss Jones couldn't have cared less. For some reason, once we got in there, I got it in my head that you needed an alias. It must be all the *Law and Order: SVU* I watch with my dad."

Cat's phone chimes. The text she receives places the most radiant smile across her face, causing my heart to beat twice as fast. She tells me it's from her Aunt Amy, a random text telling Cat how happy she is that Cat's here with her for the summer.

"How amazing is my Aunt Amy?" she asks, no doubt rhetorically, but I've never met a question I didn't feel the need to answer.

"She does seem great. Why isn't she married, anyway?" As the words come out of my mouth, I realize that I've hopped over a few boundaries and wish that I had a keylock for my mouth like Cat's smartphone does, one that would force me to think before speaking while typing in the code to unlock my lips.

"I'm sorry, that's none of my business," I quickly add.

"Well, I couldn't agree more with your assessment of her being great. She is the most wonderful, caring, ambitious person I've ever met. It's impossible for me to believe that she is in any way related to my mother, who is none of those things. Aunt Amy was actually engaged. She had a wedding date and venue booked; the whole deal. I was even going to be a bridesmaid. But then it all fell apart," she tells me.

"Oh, man, that's terrible. What happened?"

"She was with her fiancé, Joe, for about five years. He was a great guy. From the outside looking in, everything seemed perfect. They owned a house in Keyport, which is less than ten minutes from Holmdel. The best thing about Holmdel, in fact, probably the only thing that got me through my first year of living there was knowing that Aunt Amy was just ten minutes away. All I had to do was get through the school day and then I could head over to her place, have dinner with her and Joe, and watch TV or play board games with them. They never made me feel like I was intruding."

"That all sounds pretty great to me," I add.

"It was. So when Aunt Amy called the whole thing off, left

Joe, and moved to Neshanic Station, forty-five minutes away, it was all too much for me to wrap my head around. To me, it was a betrayal. How could she just pick up and leave? I was so mad at her and the only reason she would give me is that 'Joe is a great guy, he's just not ready to get married.' And yet *she* was the one who called it off, not Joe. This all happened around the same time that this prick from my school, Derek Sanders, started spreading nasty rumors about me, so it was a really difficult time. Then one day my mother, being the nurturing person she is, says 'If you're going to be so sensitive about everything, you're going to end up just like Amy, broken-hearted all because a man likes his beer more than he likes her. Welcome to the real world, honey.'"

"Ouch."

"She's always had a way with words. The worst part is that after she said it, all the pieces started to fall into place in my head. I thought about how Joe totally didn't mind when Aunt Amy and I would have our girls' nights. He was always more than happy to walk to the pub down the street, giving us a full run of the house. I would smile, whereas Aunt Amy would shoot him a look of concern. I assumed she was worried that he was bummed to have to leave his own house but that he was too nice to say anything. I didn't realize that he had a drinking problem. Sure, he always had a beer in his hand when I was around him but in every commercial you see on TV, people are hanging out at a party, all holding beer bottles, smiling and having a good old time. I started going through the images of him in my mind and I couldn't find a single memory of him without a drink in his hand. Then it all made sense and I hated myself for being so hard on Aunt Amy for leaving him, realizing it had to be infinitely harder on her yet she's too good of a person to disparage him and share his problems with others."

With this admission, Cat begins to cry and I feel like a jackass for asking a question about what is none of my business.

"I'm sorry I asked. That was way too personal a question and I really didn't mean to upset you."

"Not at all, Rodney. It's just that men are so frustrating. Why the hell would Joe choose beer over my Aunt Amy? I've had beer and Aunt Amy is *way* better. And why would Derek Sanders make up outright lies and ruin my chance of a fresh start at a new high school?"

I want to tell Cat that not all men are like that and promise her I'll never do anything to hurt her. I want to tell her that she makes me feel the way I've always wanted to feel, that her lips are perfect and I'd like nothing more than to kiss them. Above all else, I want to tell her to run as fast as she can when I see the black BMW pull up beside us.

"Hey there, Nimrod."

"Hey, man," I respond rather unenthusiastically. I cannot think of a worse representation of the male race to insert himself into this moment. And then he proves me right.

"So, who's she?" he asks, giving Cat a not-so-subtle once over.

"She is Cat. You must be Frankie," she says, answering for herself.

"Cat, huh? Not from around here, I assume?"

"And what leads you to that assumption?"

"Because if you were, you wouldn't be caught dead hanging around with this Nimrod," he says, cracking himself up.

"You're right, dude, I'm not from around here, which is why I'm having so much trouble finding an out-of-the-way place where I can make out with Rod. And I really need to find one soon before I rip his clothes off right here out in the open. Now if you'll excuse us, you're making me lose my boner."

She then pulls me in and kisses me like I've never been kissed before. Truth be told, I never have been kissed before, but that's beside the point. Cat's lips are the softest surface I have ever felt and she smells like a mixture of strawberries and clean clothes fresh out of a dryer. I'm not exactly sure what a blackout is but her kiss transports me to somewhere I've never been. A kaleidoscope swirls around my brain projecting the most vibrant colors I've ever seen while the bassline to Sting's *Walking on the Moon* plays on a loop.

As we walk away from Frankie, who is left slack-jawed and uncharacteristically speechless, I fear that my knees will give out and prompt Cat to have to assist me back to my feet. Fortunately they function as they should, but my brain fails to communicate with my mouth, rendering me speechless for at least a block.

"I hope that was okay," Cat says, breaking the deafening silence.

"You're amazing."

"You're sweet but I don't want you to think that I did that just for show. I mean, I did want to put that red-headed prick in his place but I wanted to kiss you even before he showed up. His little weasel face made me see red."

"It was perfect. That kiss was the best thing I have ever felt in my life. And the way you shot Frankie down back there—you are amazing in every way. I love the way you speak and how quick-witted you are and that you don't take crap from anybody. You wear a jacket in the summer and make it seem totally natural. I wish I had an ounce of your confidence. I truly admire you."

"First off, that was the best thing anyone's ever said to me. Ever. Now, allow me to let you in on a little secret, Rodney. Ever hear the phrase 'fake it 'til you make it?'"

"Sure."

"That's all confidence is. I'm sure there are outliers who are born with confidence. Your buddy, Sting, seems to be one of those lucky few. But the rest of us? Not so much. We're all just pretending. At least at first. We put on a little front, when in reality we're all scared shitless inside because, despite what anyone tells you, no one has this mystery that is life figured out. Even with that though, I'm not as confident as you think."

"You're being modest. You are the most confident person I've ever met," I tell her as we continue walking toward The Store.

"What are you doing right now?" she asks.

"Talking to you," I (idiotically) reply.

"You're hilarious," she laughs.

Only when I'm not trying to be.

"Let's go on an adventure. I want to be the person that you think I am."

chapter 26

*

fire, ready, aim

When I hop into the Catmobile, which is parked behind Follow the Sun Yoga, Cat has a confused look on her face and understandably so. She sent me into The Store to buy a dozen eggs and instead I arrive with a handful of tomatoes. Her plan is to drive to Holmdel to egg Derek Sanders's car. Derek is the ex-boyfriend who spread some nasty rumors about her. She couldn't go into The Store herself because she was supposed to be back at work in a few hours but sent Mike a text saying she was having "woman issues" and wouldn't be able to come back for her second shift. When he responded simply with "EWWW," she sent me in for the eggs.

I try to justify the tomatoes to Cat by telling her that back in the old days, before television was even a thing, crowds used to throw tomatoes at performers when they stunk. It was the audience's way of getting them off the stage. Vaudeville, I think it was called. My dad loves watching old movies, especially those with Laurel and Hardy, who are actually super funny, so he told me about the tomato thing once while we watched one of their early silent movies. Judging by her response, it's clear she's not buying my excuse.

"I suppose it's my fault for sending in the vegan to buy eggs. No matter, they're round and can be thrown, so tomatoes will do," she sighs.

Cat isn't *from* Holmdel; she currently *resides* there. She's

131

adamant about the distinction. Since she was a kid, it's just been Cat, her mom, and a whole slew of boyfriends who stick around anywhere from six months to a year before her mom moves onto someone else, at which point Cat and her mom pack up their things and move to another town. All in all, she's lived in nine different places in her seventeen years. Another thing Cat loves about cosplay, she says, is that it provides her with a sense of community. Events like Cosplay Con give her somewhere to go to meet like-minded people. Changing schools so often makes it difficult to hang onto the few friends she's been able to make in school but Cat's cosplay friends come from all over; the events at which they meet are the nucleus, so it doesn't matter that they don't live in the same town or go to the same school.

"He's not so bad," she tells me, referring to her mom's current boyfriend, who's been one of the longer relationships. "He doesn't know what to do with me because he doesn't have any kids of his own, so starting off with a teenager is no easy task. His biggest problem is that he works all the time, but he seems to really like my mom for whatever reason."

Holmdel is a wealthy town. She and her mom live in the boyfriend's house, which Cat refers to as a McMansion. I'm not entirely sure what that means but I smile and nod because there isn't much room to get a word in even if I wanted to, which I don't. I like hearing her talk. She's animated and passionate.

"My mom has had a lot of boyfriends, which I don't say in judgement because I've had a lot of boyfriends too, and anyone who calls me a slut, like Derek Sanders, can suck it. The irony of Derek telling people that I'm a slut is that I refused to go all the way with him. He got bent out of shape and told people otherwise, making up some real detailed stuff that we supposedly did. Stuff that he'd have no idea how to do in real life. I didn't deny the rumors because that would have made me seem like I was lying so I just let him talk. Eventually he stopped and moved on to bother someone else but the rumors lived on and morphed into others. That's the thing about rumors—there's really no good way to squash them. If you deny them, you appear guilty. If you don't acknowledge them, you appear guilty. And once they're out there, they take on lives of their own, making it nearly impossible to get them to disappear. I guess that's one of the benefits of changing schools so much. You can outrun rumors. But, of course, this one got started not long after I started at Holmdel High School. This past year marked my second there, which is a new Cat record for consecutive years at the same school. Everything in Holmdel is so screwed up now. I had a chance to start over and Derek messed that up for me."

We sit there in the Catmobile, its engine off, for a few minutes before I enquire about why we aren't moving. Cat reminds me about the orchestra of crickets that will make their presence known as soon as she turns the key. If Mike hears that, and he undoubtedly would, we'll be busted and he'll make her finish her shift so that he can get to work on his nightly buzz.

"All we have to do is wait for a train to go past. Since the tracks are right there above us," she says, looking up toward the freight train tracks that run atop the hill overlooking The Store, "it makes enough noise to drown out the crickets."

"Great plan, Rosie."

"Rosie?"

Cat's wearing a red banana in her hair fastened as a headband (that looks amazing, by the way) like Rosie the Riveter from those old-time ads. You know, the one where the woman is rolling up her sleeve and flexing her muscle with the speech bubble that reads, "We Can Do It!" This led Rosie to pop out of my mouth, my subtle attempt at guessing her real name. I share this with Cat, which makes her laugh.

"She *was* a total badass and based on her motto, she's all about being optimistic, just like you. But we've got a different one today. Our mantra is: fire, ready, aim. Got that?"

"Isn't the phrase ready, aim, fire?"

"Not according to Billie Joe Armstrong," she says.

As a train rolls past high above The Store, Cat starts up the

Catmobile, pulls out of the driveway, and puts on the Green Day song *Fire, Ready, Aim* the way it's meant to be listened to: with the volume turned up and the windows rolled down.

* * * * * * * *

We sit parked outside Derek Sanders's house for some time without saying a word. The Catmobile is turned off so that the crickets don't announce our presence. Cat and I were silent for the majority of the forty-five minute drive from Neshanic Station to Holmdel, as well. She's quite passionate about her love of music so other than a few rhetorical questions along the lines of "Isn't this great?" and "How good is this song?", Green Day handled the sound on the journey here. Being comfortable with someone in silence is such a rarity, at least for me. I spend a lot of time alone so I'm fine with silence—in theory. When I get around people, I become uncomfortable and my instinct is to fill the space, usually with mindless babble that I regret moments after it leaves my mouth. With Cat it's different. As we sit here together, staring at the McMansion inhabited by the Sanders family (after looking it up on her phone, I now know a McMansion is a large and pretentious house, usually of shoddy construction, typical of upscale suburban developments in the late 20th and early 21st centuries), I feel for Cat. She's biting at her nails as if they're covered in delicious maple syrup but surprisingly I don't feel the need to say anything.

"Holy shit, there he is," Cat says, shifting down in her seat to stay out of sight.

Derek lives on a cul-de-sac which is surrounded by only four houses, each one at least double the size of the homes in my neighborhood. It's broad daylight and there are no other cars on the street. It's only a matter of time before he spots us. If I didn't believe her earlier about being more confident in Neshanic Station, where no one knows her, than she is in Holmdel, I sure do now. A piece of garbage like Derek (or Frankie) will do that to a person. They'll dismiss morals and the social contract, using whatever ammo they can find to cut a person down in hopes of making themselves feel less small. What gives people like this the right to do such a thing? This rich jerk can walk around feeling good about himself while ruining another person's high school experience by saying things that aren't even true.

I'm flushed with emotion, thinking of Frankie announcing to the entire school that my mom is the Woman in White without facing any consequences. Before I know what's happening, I hop out of the car, wind up, and launch a tomato like I'm a pitcher for my dad's beloved Philadelphia Phillies and, much to the surprise of all parties present, it wallops Derek Sanders on the side of the head. Perhaps Colin wasn't the only one with a good arm in the family after all. It's still likely that Colin possessed better reflexes than I, as I'm far less successful in attempting to evade the running haymaker Derek throws in retaliation.

They say that during a fight, adrenaline takes control and you don't feel the pain of the punches landing against your skull until afterward. They are full of shit. I feel the first one, which lands square in my eye and it hurts. Bad. His second punch catches me in the ear, which causes even more pain than the first. I'd like to say I purposely dodge Derek's third punch but my head is only out of the way because I turn back to look when Cat screams "Take this, you bastard!", which is when a tomato surely meant for Derek's face hits me square between the eyes. I lose my balance and hit the deck. Cat shouts a few choice words at Derek but I'm too busy picking tomato seeds out of my eyeballs to catch most of them, and before I know it, we're back in the Catmobile heading toward Neshanic Station.

Cat apologizes profusely for what transpired, saying that we'll head straight to The Store to get some ice on my eye, which is already starting to show signs of turning black. I bite into one of the remaining tomatoes as if it were an apple, just like my dad showed me how to do when I was a kid. It's a bit of an atypical way to eat a tomato, I'll admit, and causes Cat to believe that I've been concussed, but I assure her that I feel better than I have in a long time. It's not often, I imagine, that someone experiences his first kiss and his first black eye on the very same day. As I sit and think about how much my life has changed for the better in just a few short days, all due to meeting Cat, I ask her if she'd mind putting Green Day back on and (of course) turning it up loud.

chapter 27

*

hungry for you

We drive back to Neshanic Station in record time. The Catmobile is deceptively speedy when it needs to be. As we enter The Store, seemingly its only patrons, Mike is in the back behind the deli counter, smoking a cigarette. I don't think I've ever seen him without a lit cigarette in his hand. Barely looking up, not yet noticing my blackening eye, he tells Cat that "tampons are on the bottom shelf, underneath the paper towels," adding that he "doesn't know if those things expire but she'd do well to check the date because most of the ladies that frequent this place are a few years past their prime, if you know what I mean." I don't know what he means, but I also know I don't want him to elaborate. Cat informs him that she's feeling much better and can close The Store tonight after all. She walks behind the deli counter, pointing me to a stool next to Mr. B., who is working on a cigarette of his own. She begins to stuff ice cubes into a Ziploc bag. Mike swigs from an energy drink and as our eyes meet, his double take confirms my suspicion that my throbbing eye looks as bad as it feels.

"What happened to you?" he asks, smiling ear to ear. I realize this is perhaps the first time I've ever seen him smile. "Let me guess, someone called Sting a stuck-up douchebag and you risked your pretty little face to defend his honor?"

"Rod did defend someone's honor, but it wasn't Sting's," Cat interjects. "I still can't believe you did that," she says, looking at me with equal parts worry and gratitude.

"Wow, man, you got in a fight for your girl? Too bad she's on the rag or you would totally be getting some tonight," Mike says, leading Cat to peg him in the head with an ice cube.

"Technically, I'm not sure if being punched in the face twice and then pelted with a tomato, friendly fire or otherwise, counts as a fight," I add, smiling in Cat's direction.

"Well, her aim seems to be improving," Mike rebuts, holding the ice-cold Monster Energy can up to his head where the ice cube struck.

Cat puts on a pot of coffee while I hold the ice pack to my eye, drinking in the banter between Mike and his elderly compatriot, Mr. B. I can see why Cat refers to him behind his back as the Grouch, as he does display a gruff demeanor. That's not to say he's entirely unpleasant. Perhaps it's a defense mechanism and deep down he's a nice guy. Once he gets talking he's actually quite animated and engaging. You just have to be willing to sift through a lot of sarcasm to get to the good stuff.

"If I drink one more cup of coffee without eating something, I'm going to shit my pants," Mr. B. says, seemingly out of nowhere, prompting Cat to swiftly remove the full cup she just placed in front of him.

"Well that paints a disturbing picture, but I do agree that we need some food. Today, we're changing things up," Mike declares. "If I eat another goddamn Dolly's Special I'm going to stick this fork directly into my eye."

"Me too," Mr. B. concurs.

"You'll eat what I give you and you'll like it," Mike snaps. "I've got it, let's order Domino's!" Mike says, eyes widened as if he just won the lottery.

Mr. B. does a little shimmy with his arms while still hunched over the deli counter in his usual crooked posture, making me wish someone had recorded the moment as it would surely guarantee us the

$10,000 grand prize from *AFV* (which, if you don't know, stands for *America's Funniest Videos*. And if you don't...what rock have you been living under?)

"I've got a better idea," Cat says. "Why don't you have Rod make pizza instead? He's an excellent cook and I'm sure there's a recipe for pizza in the *Forks Over Knives* cookbook, isn't there, Rod?"

In usual Rod form, I stare blankly ahead, trying to recall a single word of the English language.

It takes a bit of convincing on Cat's part, as Mike had his heart set on Domino's (which is confusing since he keeps referring to it as Regret in a Box as if that's a positive), but they agree that Cat will drive me to my house so I can grab the necessary ingredients. In fear, I attempt to weasel out of the deal (the one which I had no part in making) and tell them that as much as I would love to make them pizza, I have to get to the hospital to visit my parents. Cat offers to drive me there after our meal, at which point Mike reminds her that she volunteered to close The Store, so he would drive me, as long as my pizza lives up to Domino's standards (which actually makes me feel better as it removes 90% of the pressure).

* * * * * * * * *

As I cut, chop, and prepare the ingredients, Cat is in the front of The Store taking an old woman's very long and very specific lottery order. "I said straight and box. Did you get that? And that's a 3-way box, not a 6-way!" Mr. B. seems to have dozed off sitting upright on his stool.

My vegan deep-dish pizza is a recipe I came up with years ago and is something I could make in my sleep at this point. This comes in handy when Mike asks me the dreaded question that always feels like an interrogation: "So...no meat?"

The worst part about being vegan, for me anyway, is the initial reaction that people have upon learning that you don't eat meat or dairy products. In my experience, this is how it typically goes:

• First, they are shocked. "You don't eat meat? *Any* meat? What about fish? Well at least you can still eat pizza. I couldn't live without pizza! You don't eat cheese either? Where do you get your protein from?" *Enough already with the protein.*

• Next, they feel as if your dietary choice is a personal attack on their ethics. "I love animals too! Just because I eat meat doesn't mean I don't love animals. I would never eat a dog or anything. I wouldn't eat meat either if I thought about it, but I just love bacon so much that I block it out, the killing and all."

• Lastly, the taunting. "You don't know what you're missing! This is soooo good. You're missing out, man. You sure you don't want some? Your loss!"

If it were up to me, eating would be something we do in private. No cafeterias, no dinner parties, no going out to a diner with friends (quite a popular pastime here in good old New Jersey). Instead, when it's time to eat, everyone should go to their own little nooks, eat their food, and reconvene afterwards. This way, if I don't want to eat animal products, it doesn't stir anything up in you, and if you want to enjoy your PB&J sandwich, you don't have to worry about killing someone afflicted with a severe nut allergy who happens to be nearby.

I already told you that my favorite movie of all time is *Bee Movie* and that's not just because it's where I first discovered Sting. It's also the reason I stopped eating meat. Don't worry, there is no vegetarian agenda within *Bee Movie*. It's an animated movie about a society of bees, each with his or her own life, hopes, and dreams. After watching it a few times, I started thinking that maybe that's how it really is. God, I must sound like such an idiot, but hear me out. It's not that I think bees speak English, wear sweaters, and drink coffee like they do in the movie. But how are we to know that they don't interact with each other, much like we do but in a way that we can't understand? Maybe they have names and friends and personalities and if one of them dies, another one is sad about his friend's passing. That got me thinking about more than bees. What about cows and pigs and chickens? Who's to say that they don't have little societies and their own little personalities? *Bee Movie* inadvertently planted the seed in me that animals are more than just things. Whether those are cute things that we pet at petting zoos, or annoying things that buzz around our faces, or massive things that we like to look at in books about far-off places—to themselves, they are more than just things, so why shouldn't they be more than things to me? It could be *Bee Movie* or it could be any of those movies in which animals are the main characters. I always end up feeling the same way: that these animals are just like me. They have families and they're just trying to survive and find their niche in the world. Why would I want to eat them?

In large part due to *Bee Movie*, at nine years old I decided that I was going to stop eating meat. My parents chuckled when I first told them, probably thinking it was cute so they went along with it. I could tell they were patronizing me and didn't think it would last so that's why they didn't bother trying to talk me out of it. After I had abstained from meat for a few days, my parents were pretty surprised. Each night at dinner they'd say, "Are you sure you don't want any of this steak? It's really good," and each time that I answered, "No, thank you," they giggled a little less and became more impressed with my will power (their words). But it wasn't will power at all. Calling it will power suggests that I wanted to eat it but was restraining myself. I simply didn't want it anymore. I saw that steak as something that was previously a cow that had a name and friends and I just wasn't into it.

On my seventh day of not eating meat, my one-week anniversary, if you will, we went to my Uncle Andy's house for his annual 4th of July BBQ. My Uncle Andy is my dad's brother. He lives out in Pennsylvania and his house is basically on top of a mountain. His driveway is a super steep rock hill that always gives my dad's little car trouble, which causes my Uncle Andy to playfully bust on him about it when we eventually reach the top. He says things like, "If that little Tic-Tac of yours ever gets stuck I'll come down with Betsy and will give you a tow." Betsy is one of his pickup trucks. My Uncle Andy is the kind of guy who owns multiple pickup trucks and gives them names. He's not a bad guy. He's just loud and he likes trucks and guns and meat. Lots of meat. In fact, I don't think I've ever seen him eat anything but meat. Every summer, he invites us over for his annual BBQ, where he roasts a pig and rents a beer truck that parks in his yard. My mom always drinks a lot of wine while we're there, causing her to fall asleep before we even get to the bottom of his driveway and snore for the entire hour-and-a-half ride home.

The parties at my Uncle Andy's house aren't terrible, it's just that I'm usually the only kid there so I end up getting bored quickly. He's got video games and always makes a point to get me set up inside so I can play them, which is kind of him. But he doesn't have *Mario Kart* or any baseball games, which are the only kinds I can even partially play—just shooter games that I could never get into, so I always sneak a book in my cargo shorts and read it once he returns to the party. That particular year I was dreading going to the party more than usual. Not because I thought I'd be tempted by any of the meat. The cause of my anxiety was seeing the pig. I had never eaten it before; I always stuck to hot dogs and hamburgers because it always seemed too real to me, its face looking at me with an apple sticking out of its mouth. Why do they do that with the apple, anyway? The poor pig's face was all I could think of and we weren't even there yet. Along with seeing the pig, I was afraid my Uncle Andy would ridicule me when he found out that I was no longer eating meat. He and his friends drink lots of beer and shoot guns off the deck of his house and bust on each other in a way that goes beyond trying to be funny and just seems mean after a while. The last thing I wanted was my Uncle Andy or any of his friends finding out I wasn't eating meat, causing them to set their sights on me.

The night was nearly over and I was doing pretty well avoiding the meat issue. My plan was to always have a bowl of chips in my hand, figuring that if I was eating *something*, no one would feel the need to offer me more food. Since my Uncle Andy was hosting the party, he knew everyone there and was doing a lot of mingling. As my mom and I stood on the deck listening to some drunk guy tell us a never ending story about how he met his ex-wife, I was hoping for some kind of escape from the conversation. With Budweiser Breath in the middle of his saga, my Uncle Andy made a beeline for me, armed with a hot dog in each hand.

"Bubba!" Did I mention that my Uncle Andy's nickname for me is Bubba? No idea where it came from but when I was nine it actually made me feel cool (if nothing else, it was a welcome respite from being referred to as Stinky). "You can't just eat chips all night. You're a growing boy and a growing boy needs protein." *Again with the protein.* "Here you go, partner. One for you and one for me," he said, taking a massive bite out of his hot dog.

"Oh, that's okay, Uncle Andy. I filled up on all of these chips. I'm not even hungry anymore. These are so good that I couldn't control myself."

"Nonsense, there's always room for a hot dog!"

"He doesn't eat meat anymore," my mom slurred, clearly tipsy from the wine. "He's a vegetarian," elongating the word vegetarian as if she were saying it to someone who had never heard the word before.

You know those moments in movies when the music at a loud party stops on a dime, leading everyone in attendance to zero in on a single conversation? I always thought they were played-out but there is simply no better way to describe what transpired at that moment. I'm not saying that the terribly loud country music playing out of my Uncle Andy's speakers actually stopped, but it sure did seem like everyone within a ten-foot radius heard the word vegetarian and turned their heads to see who let the freak into the party. At that moment, if I'd had one wish it would've been for Budweiser Breath to loudly resume the story that moments ago I wanted so desperately to end. Half of that wish came true. Budweiser Breath did speak up, but unfortunately he didn't miss my mom's declaration that a vegetarian was on the premises.

"A vegetarian? What's the matter with you, boy? Don't you know that meat puts hair on your chest!"

"Yeah, and what kind of meat did you eat to get all that hair that covers your back?" Uncle Andy snapped back at him.

"Don't tell me you're one of those people that thinks shooting animals and eating their dead bodies is wrong!" he continued, ignoring my Uncle Andy. "That's not gonna go over too well in the schoolyard!"

I had my doubts that Budweiser Breath had spent much time at school, but I also didn't think he was wrong, which is why I wasn't planning on announcing to the kids at school, or the people at this party, that I was no longer eating meat.

"All right, Ronny, that's enough. Why don't you go grab us a couple beers?"

Ronny wasn't done and now he was being loud enough that people were watching.

"Look here, little boy," he said as he took the apple from the pig's mouth and tossed it on the ground. He began moving the pig's mouth with his hand, talking in a high-pitched voice. "My name is Porky and I'm just a dumb old pig. You don't have to be afraid to eat me, that's what I'm—"

Budweiser Breath crashed down onto the deck like a sack of potatoes, then Porky fell on top of him. My Uncle Andy had picked up the apple and thrown a strike right between Ronny's eyes.

"That's my nephew and he's a lot cooler than you are. If he doesn't want to eat meat, that's his choice. Maybe you should take a cue from him, you fat piece of shit," my Uncle shouted.

That was the first time someone had ever stuck up for me like that and it's something I'll never forget. I had very little, if anything at all, in common with my Uncle Andy. He was an older man who lived on a mountain in Pennsylvania. He liked guns, four-wheelers, beer, and country music. I assumed he thought I was just some dumb little kid who ate chips and wore a Phillies hat and, if I'm being truthful, I thought he and his friends were rednecks (even though I probably didn't know the term redneck back when I was nine). I thought we were different and that we shared no common ground. But something inside of him compelled him to stick up for me in front of all his friends, who probably thought vegetarians were aliens from a different planet, and that made me not only see my Uncle Andy in an entirely different light but also made me think twice about assuming that I know who people really are and what they stand for just based on the food they eat, the music they listen to, or the hobbies they keep.

I finish telling Mike this story just as my vegan deep-dish comes out of the oven (which, unlike the other night, I've successfully avoided burning). It's the most I've ever shared about myself with him and I'm feeling self-conscious. There isn't more than ten seconds of silence as he processes my tale, looking from me to the steaming hot pizza, but it feels like years pass and all I want is for him to say something—to validate me, my story, and the dietary choice that seems foreign to so many but more natural to me than anything else I've ever found in life.

"Thanks for sharing, man. I was actually asking if you forgot to cut up meat to put on the pizza or if you were leaving it off on purpose. But it was a hell of a story nonetheless."

chapter 28

*

whatsername

It's said that after you've had sex, you give off a glow that is a dead giveaway because there's no other glow quite like it. Well, I didn't have sex, but apparently there's a first kiss glow as well. My dad recognizes it the moment I step foot into his hospital room and shoots me a proud smirk. For a moment I think that perhaps it's my black eye that catches his attention, but Cat took care of that before I left The Store. Like a kiss-sniffing dog, my mom must also sense my elation because she moves in to mark her territory.

She pulls me in for a smothering hug that lacks any of the comfort of Roxanne's. When I'm finally released to come up for air, on the shoulder of her white walking blouse is a splotch of the skin-tone makeup that had previously been on my cheekbone covering up the burgeoning shiner Derek Sanders gifted me earlier. I catch it a split second before my mom does but before I'm able to react, my mom launches into full-on panic mode. Rapid-fire questions come hurling at me one after another: "How did this happen?" "Who did this to you?" "Did you call the police?"

Although no answer would've calmed her hysteria, providing *any* answer would've been better than what I did, which was look at my phone to see who was texting me.

Cat: Clear your schedule. Tomorrow, you're mine.

Another way in which Cat is different from all of the kids in my school: she punctuates and uses proper grammar in her texts. My eyes give away my reverence, which sends my mom into more of a frenzy.

"Who is that? Someone more important than your mother? I'd love to meet this mystery person. Perhaps he…or she can tell me how you got this black eye. Is it a she?"

"Lynn, why don't you tell Rod the good news?" my dad interjects, clearly trying to keep her from completely flipping her lid.

"Yeah, what's the good news?" I ask. My mom ignores the words coming out of my mouth, choosing instead to inspect my eye as if she were a mechanic trying to figure out the cause of an engine's failure to start.

"Dr. Payne says I'll be heading home within the next two days," my dad shares.

Maybe if I paid more attention in biology class instead of spending all of my time trying to come up with a way to meet Sting, I'd understand how the human brain can process such a wealth of information in such a short amount of time while simultaneously producing conflicting emotions. When the words first leave my dad's mouth, I'm elated that he'll be coming home, as it's tough seeing him stuck in a hospital room for all this time. Not half a second later, the sense of dread hits as I realize that my adventures with Cat will be coming to an end. Sure, she'll still be in Neshanic Station for the remainder of the summer, but things won't be as they have these past few days—the best days of my life. Under my mom's watchful eye it's going to be challenging enough finding ways to make it the half-mile to see Cat at work. There's no way I'll be going on any more adventures with her—no more basement shows, no more throwing tomatoes at (extremely strong) ex-boyfriends in Holmdel, no more listening to Green Day at ear-splitting volumes. I do my best to hide my dismay.

"That's great, Dad. Home just isn't the same without you."

* * * * * * * *

My mom again suggests we go to the cafeteria as she needs some time with her baby (her words). Knowing I'm on a time limit with Mike in the waiting room (who I imagine is far less patient than Cat), I negotiate to stay in the room, reasoning that I want to visit with both her *and* my dad (the guy who actually needs to be in the hospital). She turns up the guilt machine to ten and I have no choice but to join her in the ~~interrogation room~~ cafeteria.

Unlike last time, my mom passes on food but I've got a hunch that the day-old bagels aren't to blame for her loss of appetite. Joining her at the table, I bring over hot tea for both of us (in an attempt to avoid the suspicious look coffee garnered me during our last meal) and two packets of cashews. They're not even good cashews, they're the kind that come in those skinny sleeves that contain more salt than they do nuts. But they're two for a dollar and in this place I'll take what I can get. The moment I stupidly set my phone on the table, it vibrates with another text.

Cat: Your life is going to change tomorrow and you're totally going to fall in love with me!

One step ahead of her.

"So, Mr. Popular. I hope you can pull yourself away from that thing long enough to fill me in on your life. We've been out of range for so long that I'm just not myself. And now seeing you like this, in this condition—I just feel like I don't even know you anymore."

My mom is melodramatic, that's nothing new. But for her this is surprisingly calm. We've been apart, aside from my quick visits, for four days, which is four days longer than we've ever been apart before. She's here at the hospital, unable to take the long walks around town that serve some kind of therapeutic purpose to her, and then I show up with my phone vibrating (which it never does) and my eye black and throbbing like a lovesick heart. I know this is killing her so I try to think of some comforting words.

"Well, Dad said you guys would be coming home hopefully within—" and then, like the idiot I am, I again look at my vibrating phone. Before I can flip it open to see what Cat has written this time, my mom swats my phone off the table as if it were a mosquito on a blood hunt.

"Mom, what the hell?"

"Watch your language!"

"What the hell" is the closest I've ever come to cursing at my mom. She detests swearing, almost to the degree of her disdain for Green Day. The only person more surprised that it came from my mouth than I am is my mom.

"I guess whoever is incessantly buzzing your phone is more important than me. You may have the black eye but I'm the one who's been beaten up," she says, pushing away from her untouched tea and exiting the cafeteria.

* * * * * * * *

The rest of my visit is awkward, as you'd probably imagine. When I get back to his room, my dad is out of bed, which is great to see and now it's clear that he's definitely lost weight. He hands me Sting's memoir, telling me that he finished reading it and thanking me for lending it to him. He tells me that Dr. Payne suggested my dad begin making his own meals and that I and my avoidance of meat would be a good influence on him. My dad asks if I'd be up for showing him some of my favorite recipes, saying that he's taking this surgery as a wake-up call and is determined to change his ways. This is a proclamation that I've been hoping to hear my entire life but I'm too distracted to fully process it as the bulk of my attention is on my mom, who is in the corner of the room with a crazed look in her eye. My dad can clearly feel the tension in the room and has taken over my role as the space-filler, trying in vain to keep things light. He's now talking about the Phillies and how much they stink again this year. Like the pin being pulled from a hand grenade, me sneaking a glance at my vibrating phone sets off the explosion that comes out of my mom's mouth, a roar that quite possibly shakes the entire floor of the hospital.

"**WHATSERNAME?!**"

Before I'm able to react to my mom's detonation, Mike's patience has expired and he strolls through my dad's hospital door.

"Rod?" he asks, peering in.

"Mike?" my dad asks, confused.

"Gerry? Lynn?" Mike gasps, scanning the room, looking as if he's seen two ghosts. Our eyes lock. "Holy shit."

chapter 29

*

she's too good for me

Since two things Cat loves are adventures and surprises, she refuses to tell me where we're going. Under normal circumstances, this would stress me out to no end but when she showed up at my house at 9 a.m., my mind was still hazy from the bizarre events of last night so I now find myself sitting in the Catmobile, rehashing the surreal scene.

"He somehow knows my parents. But they never go into The Store, they never go *anywhere,* so I don't know how Mike would know them."

"What did he say when you asked him? You did ask him, didn't you, Rodney?"

"He didn't utter a single word on the ride home. It's like he was in a daze. I, of course, filled the space with awkward small talk because that's what I do. He offered a few grunts here and there but other than that he chain-smoked and stared straight ahead through the windshield. It's clear he knows my parents, though. He dropped me off right in front of my house without me even telling him where I live. It was super weird."

"He's the Grouch. He oozes weirdness. It would only be weird if he wasn't being weird," she reasons.

Cat may have a point. She certainly knows him better than I do. Heck, I hardly know the guy at all. But it still doesn't explain how Mike knows my parents. Between my mind trying to solve that riddle and reading Cat's texts promising that my life was about to forever change, that I was going to fall (more) in love with her, I once again got hardly any sleep last night.

She informs me that something must have been in the air last night as I'm not the only one who had a peculiar episode involving parents. Not long after Mike and I left for the hospital, Cat's mom and boyfriend showed up at The Store unannounced. Her mom was insistent on taking her out to dinner, but since Cat had to stay to close The Store, she instead made them dinner and they all ate together at the deli counter.

"You would have been proud of me, Rodney. They wanted Dolly's Specials but instead I made them your vegan deep-dish pizza since there were plenty of ingredients leftover from when you made it earlier. It wasn't nearly as delicious as yours, but I think it came out pretty good."

"That's great! If there's any leftover I'd love to try some. So, what did your mom want, anyway?"

"The same thing she always wants—to complicate my life. But I'm doing my best to remain optimistic, like a certain someone taught me, and as painstaking as it was to sit through a dinner with my spiteful mother, without their visit we wouldn't be going on this life-altering adventure today," she says as we pull into Raritan Station, the closest passenger train station to Neshanic.

"Where are we going?" I ask again, my voice audibly quivering with trepidation.

* * * * * * * * *

I already told you that science is not my strongest subject so I don't know whether freaking out qualifies as a hereditary trait, but I am my mother's son (even if I'm not the one she wants) and I can freak out with the best of them, which is exactly what I do when Cat tells me that her plan is to go into New York City. Like a machine gun, I begin firing off reasons I can't go into the city today, or any other day for that matter. I remind Cat of the time I ruined the sixth-grade field trip when I broke off from the class in a failed attempt to meet Sting. There's also the issue that I forgot to charge my phone last night and there's no way that half a battery is going to last all the way to New York and back, which leads to my final and most important reason for not getting on a train today: that I have to go to the hospital to visit my parents, *especially* after leaving on such weird terms last night.

Cat does her best to settle my nerves. Little does she know, she's dealing with a professional when it comes to anxiety and I swat away her attempts at logic like flies. When she reminds me of Dr. Payne's assessment that my dad would be released in two days, I bring my old friend, semantics, into the conversation and point out that his actual words were "within the next two days," which means it could be today or tomorrow.

"Nice try, but if your dad was getting released today, the doctor would've said so. Doctors are trained in the art of bedside manner and that's a classic case of letting someone down easy."

She makes a valiant point, but I'm not budging.

"Get on this train with me and before we pull out of the station, I'll tell you my real name."

Enticing, I'll give her that. But not enough to get me to go into New York City. Not with the history between myself and The Big Apple. Then she brings out the big guns.

"Rodney, these past few days have been amazing for me and I believe you feel the same way. At least I hope you do. But we both know that once your parents come home, things are going to change. I'm hoping your mom will come around and let us see each other but there's no way we're going to go on these daily adventures together anymore. This is our greatest adventure yet and I swear to god it's going to change your life. I know you had a bad experience in New York but that was a long time ago. There are amazing things happening in the world outside of Neshanic Station. Channel your inner Barry.

Pretend I'm Vanessa and come with me to the Tournament of Roses Parade. Spread your wings and fly! Good things happen when you leave the hive."

"Tournament of Roses Parade? Did you watch *Bee Movie*?"

"Yep! Aunt Amy and I were endlessly scrolling last night and it popped up, so I took it as synchronicity and hit play. Great movie! And I must say, even in animated form, Sting is a total hunk. Aunt Amy was gaga over him."

Damn, she's good. After delivering her closing argument, Cat exits the car, walking toward the train station as I watch her from the passenger seat of the Catmobile, my head spinning like a carousel. I'm at a total loss as to what to do. Cat's right; these past few days have been nothing short of incredible, and with my parents' imminent return tomorrow, my time with Cat, at least the way it's been, is coming to an end. She's also right that good things happened to Barry when he left the hive. But where she's wrong is in thinking that I possess the courage Barry had. The one time I went into New York City, I believed that the title of Sting's album was a clue on a treasure map, that I was a pirate destined to retrieve my gold, letting down my entire class of peers in the process. Not only am I not like Barry, but I'm not who Cat wants to see me as, either. Cat and her friends have free will and act on their impulses like actual teenagers do. I'm a small-town nimrod forced to carry around a walkie-talkie, a child who needs to be escorted by the secret service just to visit the local library. By chance, she happened to get stuck in the crappy little town of Neshanic Station where I'm the only option. Once she goes back to Holmdel at the end of the summer, she'll realize that she's too good for me and I will likely never hear from her again. Cat's adventures are amazing; I will treasure every one of them for as long as I live. I'm certain she's right, that something good lies ahead in New York City. The sad reality is that there is nothing good enough to overpower the debilitating fear that has me glued to the seat of the Catmobile, unable to get on that train with her.

Cat is standing a hundred feet away, surely wondering why

she's wasted this past week hanging out with a coward like me. She gives the universal sign for "roll down the window," which I do even though I'm quite certain I don't want to hear what's coming.

"We're going to meet Sting, goddammit! Now get on this train before you miss your chance!"

chapter 30

*

viva la gloria (little girl)

Cat purchases two round-trip tickets to New York Penn Station, insisting that because this was her idea, the tickets are on her. She promises that we'll go Dutch on everything else. I reluctantly agree, making a mental note to figure out what it means to "go Dutch" in the meantime. As usual, she looks super cool. She's wearing a plain white t-shirt with the sleeves cut off, tight black jeans, and black boots that have yellow stitching around them. I'm of course wearing my signature camouflage cut-off shorts and I'm also sporting a white shirt though mine is not blank. The t-shirt I'm wearing has the design straight off the album *Synchronicity* on it: the classic blue, yellow, and red rows of stripes laid overtop the black and white pictures of the members of The Police. It was a gift from my dad for Christmas two years ago, one of the few shirts I own that did not previously belong to Colin. It hits me then that I will be wearing his band's shirt when I meet my hero. Talk about synchronicity.

"I can't believe you've lived less than an hour away from New York City your entire life and you've only ever been there once."

"I know, it's weird. I'm more of a Philly guy though," I utter like the poser that I am.

"That's cool! There are some awesome spots in Center City. And there's this beautiful tattoo shop in Fishtown that Aunt Amy brought me to once because she knows the owner. It used to be a church that they converted into a tattoo studio. True Hand Society, I think it's called. I'm totally going to get tattooed there one day. Fishtown used to be a dump but now it's got great shops. I bet there's a vegan restaurant there, too."

"A vegan restaurant in Fishtown? That'd be something," I say, channeling my dad.

"Very funny. So, Mr. Dad Jokes, what's your favorite spot to hit in Philly?"

"Oh...uhh...I'd have to say...Citizens Bank."

"You go all the way to Philadelphia to go to a bank? What am I missing? Do you go and watch people skateboard there? Wait...do you skate?"

"No, it's not really a bank. Well, Citizens Bank is, I suppose. But I meant Citizens Bank Park. It's where the Phillies play. My dad and I try to go once a year to catch a game together. And I don't know if they have them in Fishtown, but at the stadium they sell these vegan hot dogs that are delicious. It took an entire inning of convincing but eventually I wore him down and got my dad to take a bite. He complained and said it tasted like sneakers, which I thought was weird because how would he know what sneakers taste like? But then when he was finished with his beef hot dog he picked up my second vegan dog by mistake and ate the entire thing without realizing it."

"Apparently your dad enjoys the taste of sneakers," Cat adds.

"As long as they're not vegan sneakers."

I'm trying my best to be optimistic and believe that we're actually going to meet Sting today. Still, I can't help but think it's a bit far-fetched. Cat knows something is up and pulls it out of me. I share with her my apprehension, suggesting that if Sting was doing an appearance, I'd know about it, being that I'm on his email list and I also check his website daily. This leads her to fill me in on the family dinner she had at The Store last night. As usual, Cat's mom got on her nerves early in the conversation so once they were in a speaking stalemate, her mom's boyfriend took over. She tells me that the nice thing about her mom's boyfriend is that he really does make an effort to talk to her, even though she doesn't feel like they share anything in common.

"Here's where it gets crazy," she tells me as her eyes widen like saucers. "As I'm telling them about you and how much you love Sting—"

"Wait a second," I say, cutting her off. "You were talking about me?"

"Okay, story time is over."

"No, please! I really want to hear this. Here, I'm gonna zip it, lock it, and put it in my pocket."

"You are *so* not smooth. But I like you anyway. Now, where was I?" she asks.

"At the part where you were telling your mom and her boyfriend of my affinity for Sting, the smoothest man in the world—my polar opposite."

"Right! My mom's boyfriend tells me that he loves Sting too. Not only that, but that Sting is going to be in New York City doing a signing tomorrow, which is now today. At first I thought he was messing with me because you know everything about Sting, you basically stalk him, so if he were going to be anywhere near us you would know about it."

"Stalk might be a bit strong, but otherwise I agree," I add.

"He tells me that it's a fan-club-exclusive event and that he's a member and was totally planning on attending until he got booked for a last-minute work trip to San Francisco, which is part of the reason they took me out to dinner because he's going to be gone for a few weeks and wanted to see me before he left."

"Your mom's boyfriend sounds like a pretty sweet guy," I say. "A sweet guy with impeccable taste."

"Yeah, he's not so bad. He told me that we can get into the event if we use his name and he even sent me his fan club ID number, which I have right here," she says, waving her phone around in the air.

It begins to make perfect sense that Sting would be doing a signing. For one, he's not currently on tour. He has one coming up that starts in Atlantic City but not for a few more weeks. Not much tour information gets posted on his Facebook page until after the fact when the person who runs his social media accounts puts up pictures from the previous night's show. But I just happen to check his website religiously to keep up on such things, so despite not being able to afford a ticket to his concert, I always know when he's out on tour. There's a comfort in knowing, I suppose. Anyway, being that he's not on tour, there's a good chance he's in New York City since he has a home there (sure, he has multiple homes around the world, but I do know that he spends quite a bit of time in NYC. And yes, now I sound like a stalker but I assure you that I am not. I'm merely a big fan). While I cannot afford a membership to his official fan club, I follow the Sting subreddit and lately what's been discussed in there is his new line of trademarked yoga mats that are set to be released any day now. The mat itself has his customary "Sting" signature across it but the real perk is that it has a built-in mini music player that plays meditative versions of his songs, dubbed *Mat Songs*. Like the fanatic I am, I put two and two together and conclude that his line of yoga mats is officially being released and he must be doing a signing in New York City to celebrate, exclusive to fan club members. It all makes perfect sense and after I tell this to Cat, she agrees.

"This is like a dream," I share with her, emotions taking over. "Not just the fact that we are mere hours away from meeting my hero. Being with you this past week has been incredible. I was a different person a week ago and I like who I am so much better now. I owe this all to you."

"As much as I'd love to take credit, you owe this to you, Rodney."

"Last week I was a guy who couldn't venture further than the range of a walkie-talkie in case his mom paged him to come home and fetch her a glass of juice. Now I'm on a train heading into New York City with the coolest girl I've ever met, about to realize my dream of meeting Sting, who I'm sure holds the key to helping my mom."

Like in a movie, at that exact moment, my phone rings.

I'm able to justify not answering my mom's call for two reasons: **1.)** my phone is only halfway charged so I need to conserve every last bit of battery in case it's needed for an emergency, and **2.)**

if I don't speak to my mom, I don't have to lie to her about where I'm heading, knowing she would disapprove and would guilt me into turning back and heading straight to the hospital to be with her. The irony is that I'm venturing into the city *for* her. I've been wrong about synchronicity in NYC before, but not this time. I can feel it.

* * * * * * * * *

The train is louder and bumpier than I had imagined. The man who goes around from seat to seat, checking and punching people's tickets, informs us that the trip to New York Penn Station will take us eighty-eight minutes including a quick transfer at Newark Penn Station. I must look confused because Cat whispers that when we transfer in Newark, we'll hop onto a connecting train that will then take us the rest of the way to New York. This clears part of my confusion but still I wonder why they would name two stations Penn Station when Newark and New York already sound nearly identical. Sometimes I feel that the cause of so many of the world's problems comes down to human beings' insistence on complicating matters. One of those stations had to come first; for argument's sake, let's say it was New York Penn Station. While brainstorming a name for the new train station in nearby Newark, no one at the table foresaw the confusion that these similar names were going to cause? I drift further into my daydream as I watch the ticket-taker continue down the aisle, taking people's tickets, punching them with his special hole-punch, and repeating the upcoming stops on the line as if he were a robot, not hearing a single question he hasn't been asked one thousand times before. It reminds me of *Bee Movie* and the jobs people fall into because "that's just what we do"—go to school, graduate, get a job, retire. There's got to be more to life than that. I don't know what it is that I'm looking for out of life but at least I know what I'm *not* looking for and that is working a job that I don't enjoy for a boss I don't like, only to make just enough money to afford to live in a house with a fence and a couple of kids who hate me all because "that's just what we do."

I look at Cat, wondering how I ended up here, and then I realize I still don't even know her real name.

"I'll tell you, Rodney, but this isn't one of those things you can tease me about. I mean it! You have to promise me."

"Hey, you've kept my real name a secret, as far as I know anyway, so you can trust me. And that's not the only reason I'm keeping your secret. It's not a tit-for-tat situation. God, I can't believe I just said tit. That's a real phrase. Anyway, I promise your secret is safe with me. And I promise not to say tit again. And if you don't want to tell me—"

"It's Gloria," she says, mercifully cutting off my ramble.

"Gloria? Wow, that's really pretty. You don't look like a Gloria," I say for reasons unknown.

"I actually do and that's the scary part. My mom named me after her mom, my grandma. If you were to see a picture of her when she was young, you'd see I look exactly like her."

"Oh, that's really nice."

"I see why you'd think that and, yeah, it would be nice if my mother's evil motives weren't behind it."

"What do you mean?"

"It's a nice tribute to name one's child after one's parent, right? Well, my mom hated her mom. She only named me Gloria to stick it to her mom. If that makes absolutely no sense to you, you're not alone. But somehow in my mother's spiteful mind it did. She despised her mother, Gloria, then she had a kid that she didn't want who she decided to name Gloria. Then, every time she called her kid by the name she gave her, it reminded her of her mother and those ill-natured feelings would get directed at the innocent little girl—me," Cat tells me, tears welling up in her eyes.

"Wow, I don't know what to say."

"It's okay, Rodney, you don't have to say a thing. I'm fine

with it. Gloria is an old lady name so I'm good with Cat."

"How did you get the nickname Cat?" I ask.

"When I was young we moved around a lot so I was always switching schools and didn't have many friends. One day in fourth grade we were learning about odes and our assignment was to write an ode to our best friend. I wrote mine to my cat, Otis. Every other kid in class wrote theirs to an actual human and made fun of me for my best friend being a cat."

"So they started calling you Cat?"

"No, that was all me. It was my 'fuck you.' I called myself Cat, put up a wall, and pretended to be the thick-skinned person I wanted to be. And then one day I actually was that person."

With that, something comes over me. Never have I met anyone like Cat, nor have I felt the connection I do to her; even her nickname story is something to which I can relate. Perhaps some of Sting's smoothness has rubbed off on me via osmosis as I put one hand on her waist, the other on her cheek, and lean in to kiss her. Before I can, my phone rings. Guess who?

* * * * * * * *

"Do you know what you're going to say?" Cat asks, the first words spoken since my failed attempt at a kiss.

"When I get to the hospital tonight, I'm going to tell them the truth. About everything. This amazing surprise of yours is actually going to make it much easier to tell them everything. Meeting Sting is going to change my entire life and I feel like I'll have all the answers I've been searching for and will no longer be at a loss for words. I'll just know," I say confidently.

"I think that's an excellent plan," Cat responds. "Really, though, I was asking if you know what you're going to say to Sting.

I'm assuming there's going to be throngs of soccer moms waiting to meet him, god willing not wearing thongs, so actual face time with Sting is going to be limited. Summing up your years of fanaticism isn't an easy task. Do you have something in mind to ask The Stinger?"

My mind is too full at the moment to point out to Cat that no one refers to him as The Stinger. After all, how can I focus on that when I am so royally screwed? For years I've daydreamed about many scenarios in which I met Sting: hanging out with him at Lake House, his 16th-century English estate; Sting asking me to come backstage and shoot the breeze after I somehow scored front-row seats to his concert in Atlantic City; even having him over to my house as an unlikely Thanksgiving guest (hey, I said these were fantasies, didn't I?). But never did I imagine, let alone plan for, a succinct two-minute conversation with him. All of my fantasies involved relaxed, casual hang sessions where neither of us had anywhere else to be, each of us without a care in the world. How was I going to roll everything up into one quick conversation? With only two minutes of face time, I'm in a panic wondering how I'm going to be able to sum up my entire life to him, or at least all of the parts that involve him. I'll start with Green Day killing my brother, because that's really the catalyst for everything; I'll explain that they ruined my mom's life, then along came Baby Rod, who was supposed to save the day but failed and made things even worse. That part alone will easily eat up thirty seconds. *A minute and thirty seconds left. Ugh.* Next, I'll have to get to the synchronicity we share, starting with *Bee Movie* when he got my mom to dance, then in *Friends* when he got her to sing. I'll have to explain that while these may sound like small events, they featured emotions I'd never seen my mom display before. I'm down to a minute of face time left, tops. How do I quickly sum up that he's got something—a power, a gift? I don't know what to call it—that he's the only one who can pull these emotions out of my mom so he's the only one that can help her be happy again, like she was in those old pictures with Colin. She and my dad had me for that purpose, to make her smile again, but I couldn't do it; only Sting can. I'm way over my time limit. The buzzer has sounded, Sting's security guard is escorting me out of line, and man, is he strong. There's too much to tell Sting to even know where to begin, I think, as I begin sweating profusely.

"Is it hot on this train?" I ask, my mind racing. I can hear my heartbeat inside my skull. It's as if my heart is sitting on that bump above my earlobe, its little heart-legs dangling as its heels bop back and forth against my lobe to the rhythm of its breakneck pulse.

The conductor's voice over the loudspeaker startles me so much that I physically lift up out of my seat and may or may not let out one of my high-pitched yelps (I don't stop to ask Cat for confirmation of whether that happened or if I imagined it. Fingers crossed for the latter). His distorted loudspeaker voice informs us that we have reached Newark Penn Station and if we are continuing to New York Penn Station, to exit the train and look for Track 2, from where our connecting train will depart in five minutes to bring us to our final destination. Cat grabs hold of my embarrassingly clammy hand, leading us off the train as I attempt to gather every fiber of my being to hold myself together even though I know it's no use, as my mind and body have already conspired to unravel.

chapter 31

*

macy's day parade

We are in New York City and I am a zombie, unable to take in this experience the way I would have liked. How can I when I am within arm's reach of meeting my hero and haven't the faintest idea of what I'm going to say to him? My world has been upended by my inability to think clearly and come up with something concise to say. Brevity is not my strong suit. I'm not sure that I have a defined strong suit but I do know that concision it is not.

Being in the City That Never Sleeps on a class trip is worlds away from being here with the most divine person I have ever come in contact with. Cat navigates the city streets like a pro. She weaves us through a myriad of people in Penn Station as if she were Arnold Schwarzenegger dodging bullets in a 1980s action movie (Arnold was a favorite of Colin's. He had a bunch of his movies on VHS and I've watched them all). On the street, people of all shapes and sizes move rapidly, coming from all directions but they look like nothing more than flashes of color as my mind struggles to focus. I clutch Cat's hand, unwilling to let go, having put all of my trust into her sense of direction. Mere feet from the sidewalks that we shuffle along, the city streets are a cacophony of honks, sirens, and whistles. These avenues and alleyways are the roadway equivalent of a panic attack but the commotion doesn't seem to register with any of the pedestrians that Cat and I have fallen in line with.

Cat ducks into a cafe and I follow subserviently behind. She tells me to take a seat while she waits online to get us some coffee. Perhaps she's right—a jolt of caffeine may do me some good.

"Here, drink this," she says, putting a cup of black coffee in front of me. "Where are you?"

The concern in Cat's voice is evident and justified. I need to snap out of this. She's handing me the greatest gift I will ever receive. My wildest dream is about to come true and it's all because of her. I cannot turn this into a babysitting situation. I am not my mother. I have left the hive. Time to act accordingly.

"I'm walking on the moon," I respond. Nothing says "I'm back" like a Sting reference.

"Oh good, you're still in there. I thought I lost you for a while. I totally get that you're nervous. What is it specifically—the phone call from your mom, being in New York City, or that you're about to meet Sting?"

"Yes," I say as I take a sip of my coffee and try to hide the fact that it burned the bejesus out of my lip. "So where are we going to meet Sting anyway?"

"Macy's in Herald Square," she says.

"Macy's? Why would Sting be at a random department store in New York City?"

"I wouldn't call it a random department store. It's one of the most famous stores in the world. The thing takes up an entire city block. Ever heard of the Macy's Thanksgiving Day Parade?"

My blank stare gives away the fact that I have not.

"As a kid, it's amazing. The streets are filled with giant floats of all of your favorite characters. Don't laugh but I used to be obsessed with Ariel from *The Little Mermaid*. I wanted to be her more than anything. One of the few nice things my mom ever did for me was take me to the parade so that I could see the Ariel float. I wore my Ariel dress and a wig that made me look just like her. Not to brag but I was cosplaying before I even knew what it was. We came into the city super early and got hot chocolate and made our way up near the front because I was small and didn't want anyone standing in front of me, blocking my view. All these floats passed by— SpongeBob SquarePants, Dora the Explorer, Buzz Lightyear—and they all looked amazing. But it was taking forever and Ariel still hadn't come yet. I had to pee so bad but my mom refused to take me to find a bathroom because she said we'd lose our spot in line, and she was probably right but what was I supposed to do? I'd guzzled a large hot chocolate and I was just a little girl with a tiny bladder and I started to cry, which made my mom upset. She told me I was an ungrateful crybaby, which only made me cry harder. Then I couldn't hold it anymore and I peed myself and totally ruined my Ariel costume. My own mom wouldn't hold my hand as we left because she said I smelled like pee and that I was too old to do this and there was a sea of people because it was Thanksgiving Day in New York City. She made me feel so small. What was I supposed to do? I was only seven, how was I supposed to hold it in for the entire day?"

I look straight ahead, not knowing what to say. My heart is broken for young Cat.

"I forgot how bad that day turned out to be but despite my awful memory of it, the Macy's Parade is super famous and people travel from all over the world to come to it. I can't believe you haven't heard of it! You'd be lost without me."

"But it's not Thanksgiving. I mean, it'd be awesome if Sting had his own float and I think he totally deserves such an honor, but it's July and just because there's a parade here once a year doesn't explain why he'd be at Macy's today."

"Trust me, this place is a landmark. Macy's totally strengthens your yoga mat theory as it would make sense to have the signing in the sporting goods section of New York City's most famous department store," Cat says.

"Speaking of which," I say, "I've decided that I'm going to buy one of his yoga mats and I want you to keep it. As a thank you for doing all this for me."

"You don't have to do that. You keep it. Or give it to your

mom instead. Maybe it'll get her into yoga and that's part of the healing process Sting has planned for her. What were his yoga songs called again?"

"*Mat Songs*. Sting is super clever," I say, loving Cat even more for believing in my (and my mom's) Sting-chronicity.

Cat and I sip our coffee in this authentic New York City cafe while we commence some good old-fashioned people watching. To some folks we give nicknames, for others we try to put together backstories. This is just what I needed. This being the coffee. This also being an adventure to meet my hero. And most of all, this being Cat, because she is everything.

* * * * * * * * *

We take our time finishing our coffee, perhaps as a way of tricking our (okay, my) brains into believing that once we leave this cafe, it's really no big deal, just another day in the life. It's not as if my life's meaning is riding on this one encounter with you-know-who. Nah, we're just strolling through the city on our way to a department store. Because my brain is a bastard who will not shut up, I cannot stand the silence and feel a primal need to fill the space.

"Do you think Mike is doing okay at The Store? With you being here with me that probably means he has to work there all day by himself, right?"

"We were having such a nice day and you had to go and bring up the Grouch. Why would you do that, Rodney?" Cat asks, flashing that sly smile of hers.

"You really don't like him, huh?"

"Maybe it's unfair of me, though I really don't think so, but he just reminds me of so many guys I know. My mom has dated guys like him. Hell, I've dated guys like him. Guys that think the world owes them something. Guys that have taken a few lumps and instead of getting better, they get bitter. Guys like the Grouch don't take anything seriously. He's cynical, therefore he's never disappointed when things go wrong. He expects it. Plus, he flicks his disgusting cigarette butts in front of the yoga studio and we get stuck sweeping them up. He makes me physically ill. I can't get inside that guy's head. That's far too dark a place for me. Now, we've only got another ten blocks to go, let's talk about something more positive before we get there."

She's right. We need all the optimism we can get. I've pushed down my anxiety as far as it will go and resolved not to think about what I'm going to say once I'm face to face with Sting. I believe that there's a synchronicity between us and I am trusting that connection to provide me with what needs to be said. Now, though, as I count down the blocks left to Macy's, I feel the anxiety crawling up my body, doing its best to infiltrate my brain. *Need to keep talking.*

"Maybe on the way home we can stop and get a thank-you card. I feel like I should send one to your mom's boyfriend. I need to let him know how much this means to me. I can't believe he's a fellow Sting fan!" I say.

"You and me both. All this time that I've been living with him, I've never once heard him mention Sting nor have I ever heard him listen to music for that matter. The only time music is on is when he's watching wrestling and bad heavy metal is blasting through his obnoxiously loud surround-sound speakers."

"If I were a professional wrestler, I would definitely walk out to *American Idiot*. Actually *Fire, Ready, Aim* would be perfect, too. Either one would totally get me pumped," I state.

"Oh yeah, and what would your wrestling name be?"

"I could be called Rod Man. Or...Ram Rod. That sounds pretty tough. Or even Nimrod if I wanted to be a goofy character."

"If you were a goofy character I wouldn't suggest coming out to Green Day. Maybe circus music instead," she adds, stopping abruptly. "We're here. Are you ready?"

chapter 32

*

truth hits everybody

Cat and I maneuver our way through Macy's in search of the sporting goods section or a crowd of middle-aged soccer moms, whichever we happen upon first. Every single hair on my body is standing at attention. That said, other than on my head I am virtually hairless, but all those I do have are standing tall. My nerves are back to firing on all cylinders and I can't help but envy Cat for her composed demeanor. Of course, Sting is not her hero so she really has nothing to be anxious about today. But in the admittedly short time that I've known her, I've only known her as cool, confident Cat. Triple C—a nickname that (I hope) will never leave my lips.

I attempt to implement the advice Cat gave me to "fake it 'til I make it." I puff out my chest, tip my nose back, and add a little swagger into my shoulders as I walk tall and proud.

"Why are you walking like that?" Cat asks.

"Meet Confident Rod. I'm faking it 'til I make it, just like you suggested."

"If I told you to walk like that, then I apologize. New plan—just be yourself. You are amazing, Rod. I truly mean that. You don't give yourself enough credit for how unique you are and how much you have to offer. Don't fake a thing—be Rod."

As my eyes well up and I come dangerously close to weeping,

we happen upon a life-size cardboard cutout of Sting practicing yoga atop one of his signature yoga mats.

"I'll say it again...for an old dude, he's super hot."

"Totally!" I agree far too emphatically.

The never-ending queue ahead of us, waiting for their moment to speak with the one and only Sting, is a bit discouraging but I remain optimistic and figure there's no one I'd rather stand in a long line with than Cat.

The line moves along slowly but surely. I'm not certain which of us took notice first but we agree that there are a whole lot fewer soccer moms here than either of us had envisioned. In fact, the line is mostly made up of middle-aged men. This makes sense being that many fans of The Police are probably in that age group. It's also striking how many of these men are clad in wrestling shirts. Apparently Cat's mom's boyfriend isn't the only one whose two favorite things are Sting and pro wrestling. Cat and I are quite amused by the personas represented on these wrestling t-shirts. Even to someone like me who was never a fan, some of the faces on these shirts are universally recognizable: Hulk Hogan, The Rock, and John Cena are three that stand out, as much (at least to me) for their movie roles as their wrestling pedigrees. What's curious to me is the number of shirts with a picture of Brandon Lee's character from *The Crow* but with Sting's name written in place of the title. *The Crow* is a movie from the 1990s that Colin had in his VHS collection. It's about a couple who were brutally murdered by a gang of hooligans and the main character comes back to life to avenge his and his fiancée's murder. He wears all black, paints his face white with black around his eyes and mouth like a tragic clown, and appears out of nowhere, taking out the gang members one by one. I must've watched this movie upwards of twenty times. One of the things that stands out to me about the movie is its music. The songs are ominous and fit the tone of the movie perfectly, complimenting the film's dark aesthetic.

I can't for the life of me think of what Sting has to do with *The Crow*, though. I'm certain he's not on the soundtrack. I don't put anything past his musical abilities but nothing I've heard of his (and I've heard it all) seems like it would fit on the soundtrack of *The Crow*. As I share this curiosity with Cat, she looks up from her phone with an expression I have never seen on her face before, one that can only be described as utter distress.

"Okay, don't freak out," she says, which of course causes every cell in my body to begin freaking out. "But you need to take a look at this."

* * * * * * * * *

Unbeknownst to both Cat and me but apparently well known by every single other person standing in this seemingly endless line of people, there is another Sting. This other Sting is a professional wrestler. Now it makes perfect sense why Cat's mom's boyfriend, the wrestling aficionado, is a member of Sting's fan club—because it's the fan club of the other Sting. The crowd of the men with receding hairlines and pizza-stained t-shirts suddenly seem perfectly fitting here, waiting for a meet-and-greet with a pro wrestler. I don't mean to sound disparaging in my assessment of the other Sting. I'm sure he's very good at what he does. He must be to have gathered such a crowd, all waiting for a photo op and a signature. But let's get one thing straight: as far as I'm concerned, there is only one Sting and that's the one who fronted The Police, the greatest rock 'n roll band ever to exist, who then went on to forge one of the most successful solo careers in music history, selling over one hundred million albums worldwide.

The worry over what to say to my hero has flown out the window. I now have an entirely new dilemma to focus on: the stabbing pain I feel in my heart. Our blunder is evident, though neither of us can bring ourselves to step out of line, having already waited all this time. Instead, we remain in line, trading looks of bewilderment and a few "uhhs" here and there, wondering what our next step should be, hoping the other will take the initiative and make the decision. Before we can come to an accord, it's our turn to meet Sting. The other Sting. We are face to face with him as he sits behind a stack of books which appear to be his memoir, a look of exhaustion on his face. His black hair is slicked back and tucked behind his ears, his face covered in white and black paint, and a black trench coat hangs across his broad shoulders, the shoulders of an aging athlete. All the t-shirts in the line that I mistook for *The Crow* now make perfect sense—the other Sting looks just like him.

"Hey there, you guys big wrestling fans?" he asks with a lack of enthusiasm matching those that are likely sprawled across our faces. I've been so anxious to meet my hero and have worried myself an ulcer about what to say to him but now, with the other Sting sitting in front of me, I'm at a complete loss for words and cannot get my mouth to work. Fortunately, Cat's works just fine.

"Not really," she says candidly.

Okay, perhaps it's unfortunate that Cat grabbed ahold of the situation. Insulting a gargantuan professional wrestler is not on today's to-do list.

"No?" Sting chuckles, smiling for what looks to be the first time today, as the white face paint around his mouth cracks ever so slightly. "Why'd you wait in this long line to meet me then? Is your dad a big wrestling fan? Please don't tell me your grandfather is. My ego can't take that kind of hit today."

"Not quite. We actually thought we were meeting Sting the musician. He's a bit of a hero to Rod," Cat says, nodding toward me, the voiceless moron standing beside her. "He put out a signature line of yoga mats and we thought he was here doing a signing. I'm sure you're great and all, my mom's boyfriend apparently thinks so, but it's a bit of a bummer to us, is all."

"Well, at least you're polite about it. His other fan that made the same mistake an hour ago was a real nutjob."

"Someone else thought you were the real Sting too?" Cat exclaims.

"First off...I am the REAL Sting, so let's get that straight," he says.

Some people claim that wrestling isn't real, but I bet they wouldn't say it to this guy's face. He is terrifying.

"But yeah, another fan of Sting the musician, as we will agree to call him, got up here all worked up and was hootin' and hollerin' about me not being the real Sting and she wanted her yoga mat signed and this, that, and the other thing. I told her that while it's true that I'm not *that* Sting, since she waited all this time in line I'd be happy to take a photo or sign the mat anyway; that it'd make a funny story to tell at a dinner party down the road. Well, she didn't like that idea one bit. Guess what she did?"

"Flipped you off?" Cat surmises.

"She threw the friggin' thing at me! I damn near put her in a headlock, but I controlled myself. You know why?"

"Because she was a lady?"

"No, because she had the crazy eyes. I had to have Bobby, my security guy, escort her out of here," he tells us, motioning toward a man in an all black suit who, impossibly, is even larger than the other Sting.

"Wow, that's wild! Well, at least you've got a good dinner party story to tell now," Cat adds.

"Yep, I suppose I do. Your friend doesn't say much, huh?" he says, giving me the once-over. "How'd you get that shiner, pal?" he asks, but I don't have it in me to respond.

"He's pretty bummed. Not 'throw a yoga mat at you' bummed, but bummed nonetheless."

"Well, dude, I'm sorry you didn't meet your hero today, but now it makes sense that you're wearing that shirt," the other Sting says, referencing my *Synchronicity* t-shirt. "You're welcome to take this yoga mat if you want it. I don't have any use for the thing. I never saw what the big deal was with that other Sting anyway. I mean, I liked The Police back in the day but his solo stuff sucks."

At that slight toward my hero, the *real* Sting, my mouth began working and there's a good chance I caught a case of the crazy eyes, too. It's all a bit of a blur but I remember telling the other Sting, rather loudly, that Sting does not, in fact, suck and that he's done more good in the world than some dude in face paint ever could. I'm not one for cursing but I do recall letting some expletives fly as well. The next thing I remember is being intimately introduced to Bobby the security guard and the underside of his arm as he dragged me away in a headlock, to the applause of a line full of wrestling fans waiting to meet their hero, the other Sting.

chapter 33

*

graffitia

Cat and I walk for a long time after meeting the other Sting. She's really good at reading a situation and not speaking when no words need to be said. Usually I'm a nervous talker, but on our walk I don't say anything for a good long while. What I want to say is that this isn't Cat's fault. That her heart is in the right place and she got me closer to meeting my hero than I have ever come before and most likely ever will again. Just because there's a professional wrestler also named Sting doesn't take away the fact that this is the nicest thing anyone has ever done for me. That's what I want to say. Instead, I say nothing.

Not meeting Sting is a bummer, especially after coming so close. But, truth be told, I only thought I was meeting him for about two hours. Before that, Cat kept the entire thing a secret and I didn't know what I was doing that was going to change my life (her words). Sure, I've wanted to meet Sting for a long time now but it was only a reality in my mind for a couple of hours so the letdown isn't as drastic as you might think. What's draining my optimism is that our adventure will be coming to an end shortly. I don't want to go back to my old life, to who I was before I met Cat. Most of the days of my life have been spent trying to fill the shoes of a brother I've never met, one who was better than me at everything. Colin had a plan for his life from an early age. He had goals that he was in the process of achieving and his existence was enough to make my parents smile, something I've rarely been able to do. When my parents get home tomorrow and I hit them with the truth about where I was today (cementing my standing as the crappy son), I will certainly be facing some type of punishment, but whatever it is won't be nearly as bad as Cat returning to her regular life in Holmdel at the end of the summer.

It's a gorgeous day and I've never roamed the streets of New York City the way Cat and I are doing now, so I'm trying my best to be present and take it all in. I have no idea what direction we're going or even what direction we're supposed to be heading in, but I do know that we've been walking far longer since leaving Macy's than it took us to get there from the train in the first place, even factoring in the time for our coffee stop.

"So...uhh...where are we heading?"

"Well, I had one more surprise planned for today but since the first one was such a monumental failure I suppose I should let the cat out of the bag on this one. We're going to the Organic Grill for lunch. It's kind of a far walk but I looked it up online and it's this cool vegan spot that has really great reviews," she says. "The food you make is incredible, Rodney. I don't know if anyone has ever told you this before, but you have a real talent and I wanted to show you that when you leave the hive there are places you can go, like the Organic Grill, where you will shine. I'm not suggesting you apply for a job, I just want you to see that there are options outside of Neshanic Station."

* * * * * * * * *

Our meals are exceptional. We share the kung pao cauliflower pops as an appetizer and for my meal I order the tofu rancheros off the Breakfast All Day menu. Both are amazing and I pocket a to-go menu so that I can attempt to recreate these meals at home. Cat has a veggie burger that is also incredible. I know because she made me taste it. It's called an Original OG and is a veggie burger with sunflower sour cream drizzle and buffalo sauce, cashew bleu cheese, lettuce, tomato, and sprouts. No matter how much I argue, Cat won't let me pay for our meal. After I cause quite a scene, she finally gives in and agrees to honor our original deal of going Dutch (which she reluctantly explains to me means splitting the bill).

Spent from the long walk from Macy's to the Organic Grill, we agree to take a cab back to Penn Station. I'd seen in movies and television shows that people simply walk to the curb, throw a hand up in the air, and within seconds they are seen getting into the back seat, informing the cab driver of their desired destination. Well, Hollywood is full of crap. Like an idiot, I stand with my hand up, waving at any and every car that drives past. Plenty of cabs drive by but not one of them bothers to stop. Finally, a sympathetic local informs us that we aren't going to have any luck flagging down a cab where we're standing and would be better off walking over a block and a half to Avenue A, so that's exactly what Cat and I do.

We had each ordered coffee to go from the Organic Grill, which was really nice to have on our short walk to Avenue A. There's something about its warmth that gives me comfort even in this massive and confusing city. I'm always more at ease when I have something to carry. I never know what to do with my hands when there's nothing in them. Do I put them in my pockets? Do I hold them together? Do I walk with them down by my side? Am I swinging them too much? Those are weird things to wonder, huh? But have you ever noticed that once you start thinking about something like what to do with your hands while you're walking, it becomes a completely unnatural act? As we walk, coffee in hand, we come across a mural that Cat falls in love with. It's a painting of a guy named Joe Strummer, which I only know because the spray paint tells me so. On the left it says "The future is unwritten" in orange and white spray paint. I don't know how they blended those colors together but whoever the artist is has a wealth of talent. In the middle is the painting of Joe in a leather jacket, wearing sunglasses and with really cool-looking slicked-back hair. Spray painted on the right is "Joe Strummer 1952-2002," and underneath, "Know your rights," all in the same orange and white graffiti lettering. His name sounds vaguely familiar but I'm not sure exactly who he is, which I keep to myself because I don't want Cat to think I'm not cool. She is super into art and wants me to take a picture of her in front of this mural, which I'm attempting to do when a passerby asks if we want him to take the picture so we can be in it together.

"How do we know you're not going to steal our phone?" Cat asks him.

I'm flushed with embarrassment when she poses the accusatory question to this seemingly well-meaning stranger, whose curly jet black hair snakes out from underneath a paperboy hat turned sideways. He's wearing a black leather jacket in which, similar to when Cat wears one, he doesn't look a bit out of place despite the oppressive July heat. Underneath is a white v-neck shirt and a black necklace around his neck. At first glance, he looks like an actor or maybe a poet.

"Wow, I wasn't expecting that," he replies, chuckling. "But I totally respect it. You never know who you can trust. See that guy on the wall there that you're trying to get a picture with? He's my hero. I would never do anything dishonest in front of Joe," he says, holding his hands to his heart.

He doesn't make fun of us for not knowing who Joe Strummer is. I couldn't even come up with a guess and Cat thought he was in The Ramones, which this hospitable shutterbug told her was close, but that he was actually the lead singer for a band called The Clash, a band which he tells us is essential listening.

His speech has a unique rhythm, a free-association wordplay quality that makes it seem as if he may not even know what's going to come out of his mouth next. During sophomore year we read *On the Road* by Jack Kerouac, another story of leaving the hive, and this guy seems like a character plucked straight from that novel. The more he speaks, the more fascinated I become.

With Cat still shooting him a wary stare, he offers to take a photo of us with his own phone and transfer it to Cat using Airdrop. I have no clue what this means but the suggestion satisfies Cat. As we pose in front of Joe, he asks what brings us into the city today. While I had been tongue-tied in front of the other Sting, leaving Cat to do all of the talking, now I'm unable to stop my tongue from moving (as in talking a lot, not that I'm standing here moving my tongue in front of his face. That would've been far worse than my inability to shut the heck up). I share the story of our mix-up with the other Sting and how crushing it was that I wasn't able to meet the real Sting. I tell him of the synchronicity I share with Sting and of my certainty that he held the key to unlocking my mother's happiness.

"There's no doubt about it, Sting is an amazing musician. His work with The Police was especially profound, mixing rock 'n roll with reggae in a way that had never been done before. It's not easy but try to keep a PMA. Do you know what that is?" he asks, filling us in without waiting for an answer. "That's a positive mental attitude. You're in New York City on a beautiful day with coffee and great company," he says, nodding toward Cat. "And you had a hilarious moment meeting a professional wrestler instead of the singer of The Police, so it sounds to me that, despite not meeting your hero, you had a pretty amazing day."

"Yeah, you're definitely right," I agree. "I'm trying to keep my PMA. I really am. It's just that, for the first time ever, my life was actually enjoyable and I felt like I was finally becoming who I really am. That lasted all of a week and tomorrow it's going to go back to being crap."

"Look behind you and tell me what you think Joe would say to that."

I look over at the mural of Joe Strummer. Other than his name there are only two sentences written on the wall. I have a 50-50 chance of getting the correct answer and while I'm sure I'll instinctively choose wrong, I sheepishly offer my answer.

"The future is unwritten?"

"That's right, doctor. The future is wide open, so keep a PMA and good things will come your way," he offers, humming *Can't Stand*

Losing You by The Police as he walks away.

* * * * * * * *

In the cab on the way to Penn Station, Cat shows me the photo of us in front of Joe Strummer, which is a great shot, and asks me the same question that I was thinking at that exact moment.

"Is it me or does PMA sound incredibly similar to Sting's ethos?"

"Yes! His long-standing strategy of optimism even in the face of some daunting realities. I must say, PMA is much catchier."

"Aunt Amy is super jealous that we met Jesse Malin," she says, reading a text.

"Who's Jesse Malin?"

"I have no idea, but look." Cat shows me that her Aunt Amy has sent a screenshot of a photo from Jesse Malin's Instagram account. It's the picture of us in front of Joe Strummer with the caption "Sunset Kids in NYC. Keep the PMA, doctors."

chapter 34

*

next to you

"Okay, I'm ready. Let's do it."

Holy hell. It's going to happen! But here? Now? I mean, in a way it makes sense. We just had an incredible afternoon together; certainly the best and most adventurous day of my life. We forged a bond that can never be broken, no matter what distance comes between us. And Cat is exactly the person I want to lose my virginity to, no doubt about that. I just never imagined it would be here, on a New Jersey Transit train, heading home from New York City. But who am I to argue? As I begin to remove my *Synchronicity* t-shirt, I am quickly blasted back into reality, reminded of what a complete idiot I am.

"What are you doing?"

"Oh...I don't know. Uhh...nothing."

"What did you think I meant by 'let's do it?' Jesus, Rodney. What kind of girl do you think I am? I mean, I like you a lot so that wouldn't be out of the question at some point. But here? Even just hygiene-wise, do you think I would ever do it on a train?"

"So what did you mean by 'let's do it'?" I ask, (semi-erect) tail between my legs.

"I meant that I want you to play Sting for me."

As mortifying as the situation is, thinking Cat wanted to fornicate with me right here on this dirty passenger train, what she actually wants to do is second on the list of Best Things I Could Ever Hope to Hear.

Number one is her actually wanting to have sex with me, of course.

You already know that my fascination with Sting began years ago, the first time I saw him in *Bee Movie*. He's been a constant in my life ever since. Despite knowing jack about music in general, I know a good amount about *his* music. I should, after all, being that I regularly scour it for clues as to why he has such an effect on my mom and the meaning of the synchronicity between us. While Cat is busy pulling up his discography on Spotify, I begin mentally checking off albums that won't work, because you've only got one chance to make a first impression. Although one of my favorite albums in Sting's entire catalog (both The Police and his solo work) is *Ten Summoner's Tales* (which I guarantee you know at least two songs from, those being *If I Ever Lose My Faith in You* and *Fields of Gold,* and heck, I bet you even know *Shape of My Heart,* too), Cat loves Green Day and needs to be introduced to Sting's badass side. No one writes a smooth song like Sting, but Cat is looking for raw power and he can do that as well. The first two albums by The Police contain their most aggressive work. Sure, there are smooth songs in there as well—*So Lonely*, *Roxanne*, and *Walking on the Moon*, to name a few. On the other end are *Peanuts, Truth Hits Everybody, It's Alright for You*—these are the songs that will sink their hooks into Cat. Plus, Jesse Malin (who Instagram informed us is a well-known rock musician as well) walked away humming *Can't Stand Losing You* which has been stuck in my head ever since, making the decision is an easy one: *Outlandos D'Amour*, the debut album by The Police. Ten songs of perfect rock 'n roll. What a way for a band to introduce itself to the world. What a way for me to introduce Cat to Sting's brilliant songs.

"Got it," I say, smiling at Cat. She plugs her earbuds into her phone, handing the left one to me and keeping the right one for herself. We sit on the train, linked by a thin, white cord, connected by so much more. This is the most romantic moment of my life and, for once, I don't screw it up with (too many) words.

"There's nowhere else in the world I'd rather be than right here," I say, giving her the thumbs-up to press play on the album's opener, *Next to You.*

chapter 35

*

coming clean

"What do you mean, he's been released? Who did he leave with?" I look over at Cat, stunned, as she mouths, "What the hell?"

The battery on my phone is completely dead but I know the hospital's number by heart, an unexpected benefit of my mom's persistent calling from there all week, so I made the call from Cat's phone. Finding out that my dad (and mom) has been released from the hospital this afternoon while I was off gallivanting in New York City, on another synchronicity mission gone awry, my heart and the Catmobile race to see which can get to overdrive faster.

I thank Cat for giving me the most wonderful afternoon I could ask for on what is likely to be my last day of freedom for the foreseeable future, since I plan on coming clean to my parents on the events of the past week. No more lies. I'm going to tell them everything: that I've been hanging around The Store, that I met Cat and of the positive effect she's had on my life in such a short amount of time, and also of the adventures we've gone on together, from the basement show in New Brunswick, to the tomato crusade in Holmdel, and even today's escapade into the city. The only thing I think I'll keep to myself is how much I've come to love Green Day. My dad is just getting out of the hospital; my mom doesn't need to be sent there next.

As I share my plans of candor with Cat, she begins to cry. I'm talking the bawling, blubbering kind of crying one does while reading

The Fault in Our Stars. She is crying so uncontrollably, in fact, that I begin to wonder if she knows something I don't, as if maybe there's a standard grounding sentence for running off to NYC whilst ignoring every last phone call. It's likely Cat knows better than I do, being that I've never actually been grounded before, which could be why she's taking this impending punishment so hard. I tell Cat to keep a PMA and I thank her for helping me leave the hive.

"I'm moving back to Holmdel on Saturday," she blurts out.

My heart feels like it's been stabbed with a knife, rendering me speechless. Surprisingly I'm still able to work out the math in my head that, since it's Wednesday, Cat has only two more days to spend in Neshanic Station. She was supposed to be staying with her Aunt Amy for the entire summer, so although I knew our time together was finite, I was under the impression that we still had the entire month of August to be together. She tells me that this was the motive behind her mom's unannounced dinner visit last night and that she attempted to tell me a handful of times throughout the day, that at first she was afraid the bad news would spoil my moment with Sting and then when he turned out to be the other Sting, she felt it would be piling it on.

We pull into my driveway and I am a disaster. No tears leave my eyes, mainly because my hyperventilating takes precedence. Cat holds my hand, telling me that she's going inside with me. My head shakes furiously from side to side in a resounding NO but she insists, reminding me that if anyone understands mom issues, it's her. She is coming in to be my rock, she says, just like I was for her in front of Derek Sanders. My overemphatic breathing is brought to a halt when the rickety garage door begins to open. At first I think my brain is playing tricks on me, but when it's clear that it's Frankie emerging from my house, I fear that my mind is on the verge of redlining, completely unable to process the events unfolding in front of me.

"Bout time you showed up," Frankie says as Cat and I exit the Catmobile.

"What the hell are you doing here? Are my parents inside?"

"Duh! Didn't you get my text? The one where I told you your

parents are stranded in the hospital with no way to get home and somehow I got stuck with having to pick them up?"

Suddenly, I'm jolted back in time to when Cat and I were walking away from our encounter with the other Sting, just moments before we happened upon Jesse Malin. My phone, on its last legs of battery, was being pinged back to back to back. Frankie is the kind of person who uses a separate text message for every (unpunctuated) sentence he writes. After scanning the first three he sent me—"Wut up nimrod," "wear u at," and finally "duuuude"—I could no longer be bothered to look, figuring these were a prolonged lead-up to asking me to come over and watch him play video games. Of course I would have responded had I known they would be followed by a "Your parents are being released from the hospital and their derelict son is off traipsing through the forbidden streets of New York City leaving them stranded so they called me to come and give them a ride home" (I'm paraphrasing, of course, as Frankie couldn't be bothered to write a coherent sentence if his life depended on it).

"Why do you break up every thought into a new message? Haven't you ever heard of a goddamn paragraph!" I yell, pushing past him.

"What the hell, Nimrod?! Your name should be NimRude instead."

chapter 36

*

every little thing she does is manic

When I get inside, my dad is on the couch watching TV. My mom is nowhere to be seen.

"Hey, Dad, watching the Phils?" I ask, trying (and failing) to act casual.

"Nope. *Forks Over Knives*," he responds, and it is confirmed that I have created a (health-conscious) monster as I peer at the screen to witness Dr. Matthew Lederman shopping with his patient in the produce section of the supermarket, a scene from the documentary that changed my life.

"Oh, I'm sorry, I didn't see you there. I'm Gerry, Rod's dad. Please forgive me for not getting up."

I turn to see that Cat, true to her word, followed me in. My rock. Wondering what's going to happen when my mom appears and sees that I brought a girl home with me, my heart is beating like a hummingbird's, rendering me incapable of introducing Cat to my dad. Fortunately, unlike yours truly, Cat has the brain of a functioning human being.

"I'm Cat, it's so nice to meet you. Please accept my apology for you getting stranded at the hospital. It was totally my fault."

My dad and Cat chat for a bit but I'm far too consumed listening for any sounds that indicate movement coming from outside of the den. If I can pinpoint my mom's whereabouts, maybe I can get

Cat out of the house before my worlds collide. Bats have the best hearing of any mammal on the planet. They use echolocation, emitting ultrasonic sounds enabling them to measure the length of time before the sounds echo back in order to locate prey. I do my best to channel my inner bat, but instead end up standing there tongue-tied, the voiceless nimrod that I am.

"So Rod, any chance you'd be up for teaching your old man how to make those delicious portobello wraps for dinner? Doctor's orders."

"I don't think we have the ingredients for portobello wraps but we can definitely cook something together. Maybe stuffed tomatoes? I think there are still a few left over."

"It's been a long time but I used to be pretty good in the kitchen back in my Navy days," he says, settling on an audience of one (Cat) as my eyes dart around the room like a junkie looking to score. "Cat, will you be joining us for—"

"Where's Mom?" I blurt out, unable to handle the suspense any longer.

After a pause, likely to process my rudeness, my dad informs me that Frankie's driving made her a little carsick so she went upstairs to catch a nap.

"A cat nap, if you will," he says, cracking himself up. He just can't help himself. "So, dinner?"

"Thanks so much for the offer, Mr. Williams, but I really should be going. I've kept Rod long enough. Before I go," she says turning to me, "would I be able to borrow that Police box set you were telling me about?"

The box set that Cat is referring to is *Message in a Box*, a four-CD set containing every single song ever recorded by The Police, including demos, rarities, etc. The icing on the cake is the 68-page booklet inside telling the story of The Police. The last thing I want to do is have my mom encounter Cat. Those worlds cannot collide. But to rob Cat of a proper introduction to the greatest rock 'n roll band ever to exist is unacceptable, so it's a risk worth taking.

* * * * * * * * *

My mission is simple: get *Message in a Box* into Cat's hands and get her out of my house in short order. There's a storm brewing behind my mom's bedroom door, one that not even the world's most revitalizing nap can abate. Being that she's my mom, I've weathered my share, but I need to make sure Cat does not get caught in the eye of her storm. As we make our way up the stairs, my bladder screams at me, reminding me that I have ignored it since we were in New York City and no longer will it accept this blatant neglect. As quietly as possible, I point my room out to Cat (first one on the right), tell her where she'll find the box set (bookshelf in corner, top row; books about Sting and The Police are on the left, CDs by Sting and The Police on the right, *Message in a Box,* which is a combination of both, smack dab in the middle), and encourage her to meet me back downstairs, since my dad is lonely and I'm sure would appreciate the company (a dirty trick, I know, but I'm desperate).

The euphoria my central nervous system experiences from uncorking my bladder is short-lived as I hear the familiar creak of my parents' bedroom door. Knowing full well what that sound means, I throw caution to the wind and attempt to cut off the flow of urine but am instantly scorned by my urethra as it sends a painful reminder to my body that once it is in motion, it will NOT be stopped. I change my course of action and push with all my might, trying to eject the pee from my body as fast as humanly possible. The sound is muffled but I can hear a voice in the other room which means my mom has encountered Cat and nothing, I repeat, *nothing* good can come of this. Without stopping to wash my hands I burst through the bathroom door, find my room empty and immediately realize that my mom and Cat are in Colin's room. I plant myself in the middle of the one-sided conversation just as my mom is accusing Cat of rifling through Colin's drawers, sounding like the crazy person the town locals assume the Woman in White to be.

"Mom, calm down, please. This is my friend, Cat."

"There are no girls allowed in this room!"

"She got turned around. She was looking for my room."

"This is my son's room!" she yells.

And then I turn into the monster that no one saw coming.

"I'M YOUR FUCKING SON!"

As the front door of my house flies open, my mom bursting off to the right, Cat heading left toward her car, I stand on my front steps at a fork in the road, trying to decide which direction to go, which of the only two women in my life to follow. Our lives are dictated by the decisions we make and, with my head hung low, I stand frozen like a coward and follow the path of indecision.

chapter 37

*

good riddance (time of your life)

Cat: This is a long shot, but will you meet me on the roof of the yoga studio? Please.

 Cat: I know I messed up and you have every right to be mad at me but please give me a chance to explain. Then, if you never want to speak to me again I'll respect your wishes and stop contacting you.

 Cat: Geez...now who's the stalker? I realize how creepy it must seem that I was in Colin's room but it's not what you think. I know your analytic brain, Rodney. Don't let it run wild. Come talk to me. I promise it'll all make sense. Please.

 Cat: This is the last text I'll send. Everyone knows that five unrequited texts = a restraining order and I don't need that on my record. Come talk to me, Rodney. Say the word, any word, and I'll stay up here all night waiting for you.

 Cat: For what it's worth, it was worth all the while...

* * * * * * * *

I received all of Cat's texts as they came through but I haven't responded. As much as my overactive brain is running in circles trying to figure out why she was in Colin's room and why one of his drawers was open (which I discovered after coming back inside after she and my mom had cleared out of the house), my mom has been gone for hours, longer than she's usually gone while out walking, and I'm beginning to worry, so I don't feel right texting with Cat when I should be focused on my mom. It is, after all, my fault that she's gone.

His stay in the hospital has done a number on my dad, who is more exhausted than he thought so we postpone our cooking lesson. Opting instead to keep it light, I make us an apple-carrot juice (so basic, yet so delicious) and a big salad. My mom still isn't back yet so I'm keeping hers cold in the fridge. As he starts to doze off in front of the Phillies game, I tell my dad I'm running over to Frankie's to thank him for giving my parents a lift home. *How the hell did that happen, anyway?* I stick *Message in a Box* into my cargo pocket, hop on my bike, and head straight for Follow the Sun Yoga.

I make it all the way to the back of the library before chickening out. This is the exact spot where the walkie-talkies go out of range. Even though I doubt my mom has hers with her since she rushed out of the house abruptly, I've caused enough anguish so instead of going any further, I decide to turn back home. If I'm not there when she returns there's no telling what she'll do.

"Mom, come in. Are you there?" I ask into the walkie-talkie with more than a touch of desperation.

No response.

Bad things happen when I leave the hive.

chapter 38

*

stray heart

It's 8:30 p.m. and I can no longer sit idly by.

"I think we should go look for her."

"So do I," my dad agrees, gingerly hoisting his ailing body from the couch. "But me...not *we*."

Before I'm able to protest, my dad continues, "You'll need to stay here in case your mom returns home before I find her. When that happens, you call me immediately so I can call off the search and come home. Sound like a plan?"

My dad is right. We need one man on the streets and one man here at home base, if you will. Feeling useless sitting on the couch, I make myself a cup of tea and set up shop on the front porch. It's a beautiful night, not a cloud to be seen. The sun has begun its slumber for the evening while the moon is hard at work illuminating the night sky. There's a bit of a breeze in the air, making for the perfect temperature—hoodie and a pair of shorts weather. Nothing like it. Despite the perfect weather, I'm all out of PMA. I can't even say that my heart is broken, as that would imply some feeling. It's more that my heart is gone, nowhere to be found. And I can't say I blame it. If I could run and hide until this is over and sorted, that's exactly what I'd do. Cat is gone and so is my mom, the difference being that in two days Cat will be gone forever. She'll be back to her life in Holmdel having forgotten all about me as I'll have become to her what I am to everyone in my high school: the Invisible Man. Best-case scenario, she comes back to Neshanic next summer to stay with her Aunt Amy. My mom, on the other hand, assuming that we are able to find her, is here to stay, making my decision an easy one; I need to focus on fixing that relationship and let Cat go. No more basement shows, no more (one-sided) fist fights, and, above all else, absolutely no more Green Day.

I'm kicking myself for second-guessing what I've known for years now, that Green Day is out to get me and has been sabotaging every part of my life from the get-go. I let my guard down, let them suck me in with their catchy songs, and look what happens—all hell breaks loose. I begin to wonder if I lived a past life during which I wronged one of the members and now they're using this one to get back at me. Even as a screenplay idea that seems far-fetched but you've seen the facts...what would you think?

In the war between logic and anxiety, logic never wins. I stare off past Frankie's house into the woods where, as a kid, I would spend time reading and enjoying being out of a house where I always felt like an outsider. I begin to wonder if my mom was right when she told me that it wasn't safe back there. Perhaps this is the final scene in the movie of my life. Green Day has my mom back there, ready to burn down the entire landscape, the trees, the wildlife, and my mom included. I inch my way back into the woods, following the smell of smoke, when suddenly I hear footsteps coming toward me out of the darkness and I'm sure my days are numbered. But then I hear my name called in an English accent and see his signature short blonde hair, and realize that this is the synchronicity my life has been building toward. Sting, single-handedly responsible for saving hundreds of thousands of acres of rainforest, will not let this happen on his watch, taking me as his sidekick to storm back and stop this massacre from going any further.

Just then a figure appears in front of me, snapping me out of one of my more bizarre daydreams yet. Butterflies fill my stomach; a split second of thinking it's Sting quickly shifts to the more realistic hope that it's my mom, but eventually I realize that the silhouette standing before me is, in fact, Frankie.

"Hey man, mind if I sit down?" he asks.

"Have at it," I say, immediately regretting my choice of phrase; it's one that has never before passed through my lips.

Frankie starts off with some awkward small talk, asking how I'm doing and why I'm sitting on the porch. I'm cordial but reserved as I have yet to decipher his motive. Rarely does Frankie ask how I'm doing unless he wants to tell me how *he's* doing. Perhaps I'm a pushover but something does seem different about him tonight.

"So, that Cat girl that I keep seeing you with. Is she your girlfriend?"

"I don't know. I mean, I thought she was. But that's over now. She's going back home in a couple days."

"Too bad, man. She's hot."

I'm not sure how I feel hearing Frankie refer to Cat as hot. She definitely is hot. She's more than hot; she's beautiful. While I agree with his assessment, I just don't know if I like hearing him say that. Geez, she's not even my girlfriend and here I am being territorial. Instead of saying anything, I simply nod.

"So, listen," he continues. "This isn't exactly easy for me but I owe you an apology. I've been super stressed out about some stuff going on and instead of dealing with my own problems, I end up lashing out at you. I'm sorry I've been such a jerk to you lately and, well, always."

I have no idea what to say. Frankie has never apologized to me. Ever. Even for little things that warranted an apology that would've been so easy to give, like when he'd step on my shoe by mistake, look at me, and then say something like "Why'd you put your foot there?" Caught completely off guard, all I'm able to muster is, "Oh, yeah...it's okay, I guess."

"You've always been nice to me and I haven't always reciprocated. Even me agreeing to pick up your parents from the hospital was an attempt at one-upping you."

"I appreciate the honesty. Do you mind if I ask where this is all coming from?" I ask, still trying to uncover a motive, not fully convinced that this isn't some kind of prank that he's secretly filming with plans of sending it around to the entire student body of Somerville High School.

"It's all the stuff with my parents' divorce. It's really messing with my head. I've been seeing a therapist and I told him about you, that I wasn't always very nice to you, and he suggested I apologize."

I am jarred by Frankie's admission. 1.) I can't believe he talks about me to his therapist. 2.) I need to remember to get his therapist's name because if he was able to do the unthinkable in getting Frankie to apologize, I bet he could work wonders with my mom.

"You're a good guy, Rod. I mean, I still think it's weird that you read books and are obsessed with Sting. But you're a good guy."

"Well, thanks...I think," I say, chuckling. "I almost met him today. Sting. Came this close," I say, holding my thumb and forefinger an inch apart. "Turns out there's a professional wrestler who also goes by Sting."

"Don't tell me you met The Stinger!" he demands.

"Wait, you know him?"

"Of course! Don't you remember how obsessed I was with wrestling as a kid? My dad would show me old matches from his era on YouTube. Sting was the man! Did he have blonde hair and colorful makeup or black hair with black and white makeup?"

"Oh crap," I interrupt, seeing that it's my dad calling. "I don't want to be rude but I've got to get this."

"See you around, Rod. And again...sorry. I'm gonna make it up to you. I don't know how, but I will."

With my heart nearly beating out of my chest, I pick up, forgoing a greeting and immediately ask my dad if he's with my mom.

"No luck, bud," he says, audibly despondent. "I was hoping she was home and you had just forgotten to call."

It's now 9:30 p.m. and dark. Not pitch-black, horror movie kind of dark, but dark enough that an older woman shouldn't be out walking the streets of town. People are bad enough drivers in the daylight; now that the sun is down, the rate of incompetent driving rises immensely. And tonight, of all nights, my mom isn't wearing white, this impromptu walk all thanks to the misguided actions of yours truly.

"What do you think we should do?" I ask my dad, hoping to hell he's got a good idea because clearly I've got nothing.

"I am not giving up. I'll stay out here all night looking for your mother if I have to. I might just have to come home for a little break. These damn meds that Dr. Payne has got me taking are making me real sleepy. I don't know if it's safe for me to be out here behind the wheel much longer."

I know that was tough for my dad to admit. He sounds like a broken man. It's clear from his tone that my dad thinks he's failing my mom in some way, that she was there with him for the entirety of his hospital stay but now he can't rescue her. Whether he'll admit it to himself or not, those circumstances were different. Yes, she was there out of the goodness of her heart. Partially. She was also there because she doesn't drive, there's no way she was going to get into a taxi to come home, and she was being waited on by my dad's nurses. My dad needs to come home and I need to figure out a way that I can take a shift on the road. I tell him that I've got a plan. Now I just need to think of one before he makes it back home.

chapter 39

*

walking on the moon

"How long has she been gone?"

"Okay, well, here's the thing. I know that a person isn't considered missing until they've been gone for forty-eight hours. But it's unlike my mom to go out on one of her walks this late at night. And I'm starting to panic because it's getting dark and—"

"What are they considered to be while it's less than forty-eight hours?" Officer Stewart asks, pulling his police cruiser out of my driveway. I'm riding shotgun.

I'm a bit surprised by the question, figuring that as a police officer, he should know. Taken aback, I give it a moment of thought before responding.

"I don't know. I guess they're just…not home."

When Officer Stewart enquires as to where I heard of this 'forty-eight-hour rule,' as he puts it, I begin to question my decision to call him. He might be the coolest guy I've ever met (remember, I haven't met Sting yet—not the real one, anyway), but his police skills seem to be slipping. This is stuff he should've learned long ago. Perhaps he's just having an off night.

"I don't know, some TV show my dad and I watched once," I tell him. "Probably *Law & Order: SVU* or something. My dad loves that one. It's a little too rapey for me, but I'll watch it with him when there's nothing else on."

"That's good of you. But Rod—"

"Yeah?"

"Don't believe everything you see on television, okay?"

Officer Stewart then asks me a series of questions that **1.)** restore my faith in his policing skills and **2.)** remind me that I am a total nimrod. He asks me what my mom was wearing when she left, if she had anything with her, what time I last saw her, where her favorite places to walk to are—things they skip over on *Law & Order: SVU*, as they tend to jump straight into the action in shows like that. Then I go and open my big dumb mouth again.

"I have a feeling she's going to be close by, probably within five or so miles of here."

"What makes you say that?" he asks, as he meanders slowly down the neighborhood streets, shining his spotlight.

I tell Officer Stewart that I read on the Internet that most car accidents happen within half a mile of a person's home. That an estimated 52% of car accidents occur within five miles of a person's home. I tell him that I'm thinking the rule might be the same for missing persons. Officer Stewart politely disputes this statistic, contending that most shark attacks happen in shallow water and, again, I'm left confused.

"It's a percentage game, isn't it? Most shark attacks aren't going to happen in deep waters because most people don't swim in deep waters, they swim in shallow waters. Same thing with car accidents. I imagine the percentage of short trips of convenience is far greater than lengthy car rides. Bringing the kids to soccer practice, going food shopping, driving to yoga class; that's stuff that's nearby the home which would support your five miles from home statistic," he says, his response filled with thought and logic, two things my theory was heavily lacking. "We don't want to get too wrapped up in Internet statistics, though. We're a couple of smart guys who both know this town pretty well. Let's go find your mom."

The first place we head for is Colin's memorial site. He drives us across the White Bridge then up River Road, the winding street on which I first made Officer Stewart's acquaintance. I tell him that my dad was out looking for about an hour and that I'm sure he probably looked at the tree already, but Officer Stewart says that doesn't mean it's not worth a second look, especially since we've got two sets of eyes and a high-powered spotlight. Walking through an unfamiliar place late at night reminds me why I don't ever watch horror movies, because being terrified is no fun at all. To ease my dread I do what I always do and fill the space with verbal diarrhea, asking how far Edison is as that's where Colin is buried or even Asbury Park, wondering if it's plausible for my mom to walk there, since it was the site of the Green Day concert from which Colin never returned.

"That's over an hour drive from here. She wouldn't be able to make it there anytime soon on foot, but we can't rule out the idea that she might try. Let's keep that in our back pocket for when we've exhausted all of our other options."

Thinking of Asbury Park makes me think of Cat. She'll be there over Labor Day weekend for Cosplay Con. I never did find out what costume she's creating. Now I never will. Here we are, standing at the tree where my brother died in search of my missing mother, and my mind keeps going back to a girl who I've known all of a week. Allowing my brain to think of nothing but Cat (and myself) for the past week is why my mom is getting dangerously close to being labeled a missing person (I never did get an exact timeframe for when she'll officially be considered that, but it's safe to say it'll be less than forty-eight hours). I need to get Cat out of my mind. For good.

Officer Stewart continues asking me questions about my mom and her walks, saying he has a few other places in mind to check out but suggests we first make a quick caffeine stop to fuel our search. He drives us through town to see if Mike has kept The Store open after hours, and as we drive past and see the lights off for the night, I use every bit of will power I can muster to avoid looking up at the roof of Follow the Sun Yoga. At Wawa, Officer Stewart treats me to a black tea (in addition to Cat, I've decided I'm giving up coffee too) and gets a coffee for himself. Our next stop is the building that sits atop the hill all the kids from town use for sledding in the winter. I've only gone maybe twice in my life with Frankie on snow days, and the unmarked building was always unoccupied. It's a small, one-story building not much bigger than the library in town and I have no idea what it's used for. Officer Stewart informs me that they make lenses for microscopes. He said it's as boring as it sounds and it's been here since he was a kid and that the most action this place sees is kids parking up here at night to get it on. He shares with me that he actually lost his virginity here. While I'm surprised at his admission, it doesn't feel crass or braggy. The way he says it is very matter-of-fact, like something a friend would share with another. This, of course, breaks my "no thinking of Cat" pact with myself, and in record time I might add. I can't help myself and ask a couple rapid-fire questions that I hope are vague enough not to let on that I'm wondering how long it'll take for my own heart to get put back together.

"Were you a mess after you two split up? How long did it take to get over her? Do you still think about her now, even when you're not up here on this hill looking for missing persons?"

"Impossible to answer those questions, Rod. I actually married her."

Well, that's disappointing.

We've been searching for hours. It's getting close to 2 a.m. I've checked in with my dad a few times, and he convinced Officer Stewart to stop by my house to pick up some food that he made for us during his shift as the lookout man at home. At this point we're both starving and could use a pick-me-up so that's what we do. My dad made spaghetti and *Beyond Meat* meatballs that he packed up in Tupperware containers. He sends us on our way after we brief him on where we've looked and what the plan is going forward. There actually isn't much of a plan other than Officer Stewart promising my dad that we will keep looking for as long as it takes. He's either a good actor or he is as confident as Sting because he sounds more sure of himself than I have ever been about anything.

As we continue combing the backroads of Neshanic Station, shoveling spaghetti down our throats, Officer Stewart suggests that some music might give us a boost. I've still got The Police box set in my cargo shorts from earlier and pull it out, offering it to him.

"CDs? Rod, you are an old soul. I like it," he says, taking out disc two and inserting it into the cruiser's stereo.

We drive up Woodfern Road, which runs parallel to the woods behind Frankie's house. Officer Stewart drives slowly, shining his spotlight into the woods. It's a good idea because if someone wanted to be alone, these woods would be a perfect place. The moon is radiant tonight, casting its shine down over my small town. I'd like to think that it's doing its part in trying to help us locate my mom. When I was young I called it the night's sun because I thought they were connected, the sun occupying the side that faced us during the day and the moon taking over at night after spinning around. Staring at the moon makes me once again think of Cat. I can't believe our time is over, that she's going back to Holmdel in two days, that we've been robbed of another month together. My short-lived time with her made me feel like we were the only two people in the world. It was truly perfect, like Sting's lyrics…

We could walk forever, walking on the moon.
We could be together, walking on, walking on the moon.

"Rod, where are ya, buddy?"

"Oh, sorry," I say, coming down from my stargazing. "I was walking on the moon."

"You're a genius."

Officer Stewart parks his police cruiser in front of The Store and I'm struck with a mixture of panic and confusion. Although unlikely, since it's nearly 3 a.m., there's the possibility that Cat still could be up on the roof and seeing her would not be a good first step in training my brain to stop thinking about her. I do a quick scan and when I don't see her my panic subsides. Still, I'm confused as to why my statement about walking on the moon brings us to The Store; we drove past hours ago and saw that it was closed, so I don't immediately follow Officer Stewart as he gets out of the car.

"Man, you guys and your Wawa loyalty," he says, sticking his head back in his open driver's side window. "Don't worry, I'm not a customer. As a police officer I've got to use all of the tools in my belt. And right now a guy with a drinking problem who wanders the train tracks late at night constitutes a tool, in more ways than one."

Because the freight train tracks run high over Neshanic Station, Officer Stewart believes they will give us a clear vantage point from which to see what's going on in town down below, almost as if we were walking on the moon. We stand outside the unlit general store as he fires off a text. Mike arrives just a few minutes later and, like the professional that he is, Officer Stewart does the talking and informs Mike of our situation.

"Oh man, I'm sorry to hear that. I'm actually about to take a walk along the tracks now. You guys are welcome to join me."

* * * * * * * *

"I'm sorry I called you."

"Don't give up on me, Rod. I know we haven't found her yet but we will. I promise."

"Oh no, no...I didn't mean it like that," I plead, mortified at how my admission came out. "It's just that I feel like lately I've been bugging you, asking for a lot of favors."

"I'm a police officer. It's literally my job to help people in need. You did the right thing by calling me."

"I just feel weird because I called your cell phone and didn't call the police station directly. I just hope this doesn't get you in trouble because you're not following protocol. Don't they need to put out an APB or something in this situation?"

"An APB? Let me guess, more lingo you picked up from watching police shows with your dad?"

Seeing Neshanic Station from this vantage point atop the train tracks is allowing me to see my hometown in a whole new light. Most days, I see Neshanic as a prison keeping me from spreading my wings and experiencing all the things the world has to offer. Not a high-security prison like the ones they depict in the movies, more the kind that rich people get sent to for cheating on their taxes. But from high above, Neshanic Station looks like one of those model towns you see at Christmastime, the kind that people set up on their fireplace mantle and decorate with fake snow. I can see the library across the street and the old man barber shop a few doors down from that, the one where Mario the barber gives only two styles of haircuts: short and buzzed. This view allows me to see nearly all the way to the post office but the Methodist Church that sits on the corner of Maple Avenue keeps me from doing so. At this moment I am immersed in the beauty of this small town—a charm that I have failed to notice until now.

It amazes me that I've spent every day of my life in this town and it only took one week to turn my world on its head. Perhaps feeding off my newfound admiration of this quaint little town, a bout of courage washes over me and I enquire as to how Mike knows my parents, the first words I've spoken to him all night. He responds, not as much *to* me as *at* me.

"THERE!"

chapter 40

*

fallout

It's been two weeks since the fateful day Cat and I ventured into New York City. Fourteen days have passed in a blur. It's almost as if I've been watching the mundane events of my life unfold as they were happening to someone else. Without Cat, life has lost its color. I feel like I'm in one of those black-and-white Laurel and Hardy movies that my dad loves, only instead of being funny, it's pure tragedy.

I'm back to Old Rod. Rod before Cat. My life these days is eerily similar to *Bee Movie*. Barry the Bee left the hive, against the advice of his family, and at first, things were great. He met a girl, fell in love, and then successfully sued the human race, getting all the nation's honey returned to the bees. But then the world turned grey. Without work the bees lost their way and without bees to pollinate them, the flowers lost their color and died. I'm no longer Rod after all; I'm much more of a Barry.

Back in the hive, I've reprised my role as my mom's emotional caretaker, staying by her side, always in range. The fallout from the night she walked off, only to return against her will inside a police car many hours later, has been severe, as I'm sure you can imagine. She's hardly spoken a word in two weeks, only communicating when absolutely necessary. She sleeps constantly and if she's not technically asleep she's in a daze, staring blankly at the TV screen, sometimes not even bothering to turn it on. Since I can remember, my mom has always been sad. Lately, though, she's been crying at the rate she usually only reaches around especially painful events like Colin's birthday or the anniversary of his death. Even then, the crying typically subsides after a day or two and then she's back to her standard level of sorrow. Now it's as if it's Colin's birthday all the time and my mom is intent on throwing him the world's most depressing party. It's his party and she'll cry if she wants to.

I'm trying everything I can think of to try to make amends, both for running off to New York City (again) and for screaming in her face. Both things have gone unspoken of but they're always there, like a bubble floating in front of our faces, waiting to be popped. I'm not a guy who curses very often so I imagine that shook her up pretty good. Perhaps this is part of what drew me to Green Day's music (for a while, anyway), that Billie Joe Armstrong curses so much. Apparently I'm drawn to things that are my exact opposite, you know, like Sting, the world's smoothest man. On multiple occasions I've asked if she'd like to take a walk together, which she's declined each time. I've gotten so desperate that I've even attempted to get her to look through her old family photo albums to remember a time when she was happy, before I arrived and rained on the parade.

There are times when I get out of the house, like when I go over to Joanne Jones's house to scoop her litter boxes or when I begrudgingly head to Frankie's to watch him play video games (what can I say? I'm a glutton for punishment), but that's about it. Taking a page out of my mom's book, I haven't listened to music since that day. Cruising around in the Catmobile, I loved listening to music. Hearing Cat passionately describe how each Green Day album was a timestamp to a different period of her life, with so many songs about escaping bad situations, each one helping her find new avenues of empowerment, was enthralling. In the moment, I felt that way too, or at least I thought I did, but now I realize I was only kidding myself. Cat and I are different people. She can wear a jacket in July and not look the least bit out of place. She goes to basement shows where one must "ask a punk" for the location. I, on the other hand, wear cargo shorts with pockets stuffed full of Larabars and mixed nuts in case I need a snack in a pinch, and spend the majority of my time alone in my room reading books about people whose lives are far more interesting than mine.

Not even Sting has been able to dig me out of this hole. The concert in Atlantic City is just around the corner and I've given up on attempting to find a way to get there, not that it was ever much of a reality anyway. I've lost faith in synchronicity. Believing Sting holds the key to my mom's happiness is absurd and borderline dangerous. Two rogue trips into New York City, one of the most densely populated cities in the United States, in blind attempts to meet him have both ended in disaster. My collateral damage knows no bounds. Sometimes we just need to accept who we are. I am a worker bee who is not meant to leave the hive.

The one positive in my return to the hive has been the bond I've formed with my dad, which, surprisingly, stemmed from him reading Sting's memoir in the hospital. He's continued losing weight and is exercising like a madman. Our favorite thing to do together is cook. I've taught him all the meals I know by heart and now we're making our way through *Forks Over Knives: The Cookbook*. He had to go in and check out a copy from the library, though, because I thought my going in there would somehow be a betrayal toward my mom.

We always invite my mom to join us when we cook together but she never takes us up on our offer. Sometimes I catch her watching us and I'm unable to discern whether she's jealous, mad, or just indifferent. Her expression never changes. Perhaps it's in my head but it seems like whenever my dad and I are having the most fun is when she most needs me to get her a glass of juice, help her work the TV, etc. I don't resent her for this, though. She's flawed, sure, but I love my mom. I actually feel like I can relate to her now more than ever. These past two weeks of trying to keep Cat out of my mind has me feeling the effects of a broken heart, which my mom has been suffering from since Colin died. Comparing my mom's broken heart, due to the death of her (favorite) son, to mine, even as a thought seems wrong so I, of course, keep it to myself.

My stomach growls, alerting me that it's time for lunch. I think I'll see if my dad wants to make stuffed tomatoes together. I'm really going to miss spending time with him when he goes back to work. The rumbling in my stomach halts; my brain needs every bit of focus it can muster to remind my lungs how to breathe as, from my bedroom window, I watch a girl walk up my driveway.

chapter 41

*

message in a bottle

The similarities between Cat and her Aunt Amy are uncanny. Being that they're related, that Amy helped raise her, and also that Cat considers Amy a role model, there are bound to be commonalities both hereditary and habitual. Physically, Amy's smile is what most reminds me of Cat. Theirs are welcoming smiles that beam not only from their mouth, but their eyes too. Whether she knows it or not, Aunt Amy has got a PMA.

Amy's unannounced visit to my house triggers a rush of emotions. It occurs to me that this is the closest I've come to contact with Cat since our day in New York. I've typed out more text messages than I'd like to admit but have ended up erasing each of them before having the courage to press send. There are so many things I want to ask Amy but I know the words will lose in a race to pass through my lips before the tears come gushing out of my eyelids like water out of a battered dam. Fortunately for me, Amy takes the lead and asks if we can chat outside for a moment.

We step out into the oppressive humidity that a New Jersey summer is happy to deliver. The weather in Jersey can be described in one word: undecided. Our summer days range from being so hot one day that sweating begins the moment a shower ends (leaving one to wonder what the heck the point was of taking one in the first place) to cool enough to require a hoodie and shorts the next. Some winters we'll be pummeled with snow to the point that school closings lose their luster before we even get to February while other winters don't require the snow shovels to leave their hooks in the garage. This particular summer has delivered more humidity than I can remember but by the time the sun goes down, things cool off enough to wear a light hoodie which is a welcome ally to help stave off the mosquitos liberating every last bit of blood they can suck from our arms. We sit in the two maroon Adirondack chairs that have resided on the side of my house for as long as I can remember, even though this is the first time I can recall sitting in them.

I've only met Amy a few times. And though I've only been in her presence a handful of times, here she is, opening up to me like I'm an old friend. Amy and her sister, Cat's mom, have never seen eye to eye on much, not since they were little girls. As children they were close, as sisters are (her words), but rather early on (too early, Amy believes) they grew apart. During middle school her sister developed a chip on her shoulder. It came about after their father took off, leaving the two girls and their mother to fend for themselves. There was no messy breakup, not even a goodbye. One day they awoke and their dad was gone. A few years later he resurfaced, but Amy tells me he never reprised his role as a father. He seemed more like a long-lost uncle who would pop into their lives as quickly as he'd leave again. After a while it became easier for Amy and her mom when he wasn't around and they began hoping he'd stay away for good. Her sister, Cat's mom, took it hard though. She needed someone to blame and Amy and her mom took turns as her target. Amy could take it. She developed a thick skin early on as a survival technique but the disdain took a toll on their mother and the more Amy stood up for their mom, the more bitter her sister grew. Their dad's disappearance into the night saddled both girls with baggage they didn't ask for but would carry into relationships with men for the rest of their lives. Amy went one way—failing to trust men, ending relationships when things were fine in an effort to beat her boyfriend to the punch, etc. Her sister went in the other direction, searching for the approval of any man that would look at her, not feeling much self-worth, if any at all. That's how she ended up pregnant at a young age by a boy (Amy's word) who refused to take responsibility for his failure to use protection during a one-night stand.

Cat's Aunt Amy stares blankly across my yard, lost in thought. We sit for a moment in comfortable silence, which is something else that reminds me of Cat. Their ability to sit in stillness without it being the least bit awkward is impressive. Perhaps it's a yoga thing? Amy apologizes for rambling on about herself and tells me that her long-winded point is that Cat means everything to her. Her own sister, she can take or leave. They will always be a part of each other's lives not because of their shared DNA but because of Cat, whom Amy adores.

"This move out here, to the middle of nowhere as far as I'm concerned, was a necessary one but it was the hardest decision I've ever made. I was running away from something, Rod. From someone, actually."

She's referring to Joe, her ex-fiancé with the drinking problem. Amy doesn't know that I'm aware of her failed engagement. She's crying now as she continues opening up her heart to me.

"I had to leave my old life behind. It's been a dream to open my own yoga studio for years and this is the only place I could find where I could make that a reality. Not only did I need to find a yoga studio, I also needed to find a place to live so I fled Keyport and came out here to Nowheresville, USA. No offense. I left behind the one person who means anything to me and no matter how much yoga I practice, I can't forgive myself for that."

I know that the person she can't forgive herself for leaving behind is Cat, not Joe. I also know that I am an emotional gimp which is preventing me from getting myself up out of this wretchedly uncomfortable chair to offer her a hug. I find myself unable to do anything other than flop my sweaty hand awkwardly onto her shoulder as Amy cradles her head in her hands in her search of solace.

"I'm getting way off track here," she says, looking up and wiping away her tears. "I'm sorry to lay this on you. I swear I brought you out here to talk about you. And Cat. You and Cat."

The way she says "you and Cat" makes it sound like there is a me and Cat. But there's not. There was, for a brief moment in time. But for some reason, in a strange plot twist in the pointless tale of my life, it turns out she is a soldier in the Green Day Army, sent to infiltrate and continue the ruination of my life. I cannot for the life of me understand why the world's most famous punk rock band is so intent on destroying my life but I'll give them this: they continue to find creative ways to carry out their mission.

Amy composes herself with a few deep breaths and, true to her word, tells me about Cat. Before signing the lease for Follow the Sun Yoga, Amy sat her sister down and persuaded her to let Cat come and spend the summer in Neshanic Station. Cat was becoming more interested in yoga and wanted to pursue her teacher training so this summer she would help Amy get the studio up and running and then next summer she would return to pursue her 200-hour teacher certification. Cat's mom acted like it was a big deal to her but Amy insists that her sister didn't care about Cat not being around.

Amy believes that Cat's mom liked the idea of holding something over her head so she made her negotiate hard for it. Amy was up to the challenge. Cat ended up being more help than Amy could've imagined, as much for her assistance in getting the studio ready as in her role as Amy's de facto therapist. This move and breakup have been harder on Amy than she had anticipated and Cat has been there for her every step of the way.

"And then my spiteful sister shows up out of the blue, breaking the deal, demanding that Cat come home immediately just because her boyfriend was going to San Francisco for three weeks on business and she couldn't bear to be alone for that long. When she threatened getting the authorities involved because Cat is not yet eighteen, I had no choice but to allow my evil sister to take her back to Holmdel. The one caveat Cat fought for tooth and nail was that she be allowed one more day so she could take you into the city to realize your dream of meeting Sting."

I sit for a while with no words making themselves available to me. Cat and Amy may have a way of making silences feel comfortable but I, on the other hand, have the opposite effect.

"I know you're hurting that Cat is gone, Rod, but know that she's hurting too. That doesn't make your pain any less but you need to know the positive effect you've had on her. I've known Cat her entire life, literally since she was a baby. She's a tough cookie. If there's one thing that runs in my family it's picking men that are no good for us and Cat seems to have inherited that trait. She knows it, and because of that, she doesn't let many people in. But she also knows you're different. You brought a brightness to her that I haven't seen in many years. She means the world to me and I am forever indebted to you for that. And I know she is too."

Hearing Amy say this is the first time I've felt good since Cat left. Sure, I've had nice moments cooking with my dad, and the new Matthew Quick novel is every bit as good as I'd hoped. But since Cat disappeared, there's been a festering feeling in my stomach. The butterflies that took refuge in my belly when Cat walked into my life were evicted to make room for a colony of termites that moved in and have been chowing down on my insides every waking moment of every day without Cat. Even in the good moments, which were few and far between, those termites were still doing their worst inside of me. Until now.

But that feeling of contentment, like most happy moments in my life, is fleeting. The black cloud (or green cloud, I should say) that looms over my head is still there. Since Cat has been gone, I've replayed every single moment that she and I spent together. I've dissected them, analyzed them, lived within them. Cat knew from the very first day, the very first conversation I ever had with her, how I felt about Green Day, of the problems they had caused my family. Why did she insist on playing them for me over and over, making them the soundtrack to our adventures? Cat, the world's biggest Green Day fan, and me, the receiver of their torment—this is more than coincidence. It's a sadistic version of synchronicity. It's sick-chronicity. This is an angle to the story, our story, that I can't figure out. It's a code that not even Officer Stewart, as good a police officer as he is, would have any chance at cracking. It's the only part of this that doesn't make any sense.

I don't share any of this with Aunt Amy. All I'm able to muster while successfully holding back tears is one sentence.

"She's still got her life, friends, cosplay events, and Green Day concerts while I'm stranded in this crappy little town, stuck here all alone."

"Seems you're not alone in being alone," she says, reaching into her bag and handing me a bottle with a handmade label that reads simply *Rodney*.

chapter 42

*

hole in my life

Dearest Rodney,

I miss you so friggin' much. You're probably extremely mad at me right now and you have every right to be. I should've reached out sooner. I should've called. I should've sent a text. I should've done a lot of things. Honestly, I don't know why I didn't do any of those things. Broken hearts do strange things to our minds. One thing I do know is that I was scared. Correction: I am scared. Scared that you'll never speak to me again. I'm hoping against hope that is not the case. You already know that my two most life-altering events were finding Green Day and cosplay. Now I've got a third event to add to that list: finding you. I know two things in which you believe strongly are synchronicity and that Green Day is out to ruin your life. Because of you, I now fully believe in the former. Hopefully because of me, you'll begin to rule out the latter.

Years ago, during a particularly contentious time in my life, my mom was dating the worst boyfriend she's ever had—quite a feat, as she's dated some real turds. She was downing wine like it was her job, which is a flawed analogy because she's been fired from every job she's ever had but if drinking wine were her job, she'd be CEO of the company. I digress. We were living with him in this disgusting little one-bedroom apartment in Keansburg. The walls were so thin that I could hear my mom and this crap bag doing disgusting things in their bedroom. My bedroom was the couch, until Crapbag wanted to watch TV, at which point I ceased to have a bedroom until he'd drunkenly stumble back into his own to pass out. All I wanted was for Aunt Amy to come and save me, for her to take me away from my mom and adopt me as her own. I know she actually tried, because she is awesome, and although she couldn't make that happen, she did come over and liberate me from that hellhole every chance she got.

One day Aunt Amy picked me up and surprised me with a trip to New York City and tickets to a Broadway show. We got all dressed up and went to this posh restaurant for lunch where we pretended we were VIPs and that we ate at places like this all the time. After lunch we walked through Times Square and she took me to the Disney Store (keep in mind, I was a little girl) where we went on a shopping spree. Then we went to the theater to see *American Idiot*. At the time, I had no idea what it was. Seeing that play was the most magical experience of my life. The charm of the old theater, the bright lights, the live acting, and best of all, the music. It was loud, powerful, and I don't know how to describe this without sounding melodramatic but when those songs were playing, it felt like a void inside me was being filled. I never wanted it to stop. It just so happens that Billie Joe Armstrong was playing the role of St. Jimmy in the show we saw. This meant nothing to me at the time but later, as I became more and more infatuated with Green Day, I realized the significance of what I had seen.

After the show I begged Aunt Amy to bring me back to the Disney Store so we could return everything she had bought me earlier. It's not that I wasn't appreciative of her buying me all of that stuff; it's just that I went into New York City that day as a girl who wanted to be Ariel from *The Little Mermaid* and I left with a singular focus: to recreate the feeling that music instilled in me, the music made by this band called Green Day. She took me to a record store so I could get *American Idiot* on CD. Then, while browsing the rack, she found and insisted on buying me another album of theirs, *21st*

Century Breakdown. It's the one that was released after *American Idiot*. That's when I had my *Bee Movie* moment. Remember how you felt when you heard that the lead character's name was Barry and it made you feel less alone? Well that's the same way I felt when Aunt Amy showed me the back of the CD and pointed to not one, but two songs that had my name, Gloria, in them! (Again, though, if you tell anyone that's my real name, I will kill you. I'm definitely more of a Cat than a Gloria).

Green Day's music saved my life. It gave me a sense of purpose. I would listen to them for hours on end. When I wasn't listening to their music I was reading about them on the Internet. There's even an amazing book about them called *Nobody Likes You* by Marc Spitz that, if you ever forgive me, I will totally lend you because I know how much you love books! Their music was, and still is, an escape for me when life got crappy. Green Day was there for me when my mom would drink too much, when she would take out her contempt for life on me, her only daughter, and when she would fight with her boyfriends, causing us to pick up and move every time the fighting got to be too much. The only constant in my life was Green Day. Any blow that life threw at me could be blocked with a pair of earbuds and a Green Day album.

Green Day opened up a new world to me. If I hadn't discovered their music I wouldn't be who I am today. I wouldn't have the friends I have, I wouldn't have found my passion for cosplay, and I wouldn't have made the connection with you. I was in a dark place when I met you, Rodney. The whole ordeal with Derek Sanders was weighing heavily on me and the last thing I wanted to do was meet a guy. But when you shared your disdain for Green Day, claiming that you were the American Idiot, I was instantly intrigued. I always believed that I shared a synchronicity with Billie Joe Armstrong, like he's writing songs directly to me, I just didn't know what to call it. When you told me about yours with Sting, even though I wasn't familiar with his music (which, by the way, I LOVE now. Well, The Police, anyway), I was instantly drawn to you. I couldn't explain it but I knew there was a connection between us and I had to see it through. And I'm glad I did. That feeling I told you about when I heard Green Day's music for the first time while seeing *American Idiot* on Broadway—the closest thing I've ever felt to that is the time I spent with you. And now without you, there's a hole in my life.

This might sound stupid, but for my entire life, every time I'd shut my eyes, I'd see my mom and she'd be looking straight past me, not seeing me standing right there in front of her. But since I met you, you're all that I see when I shut them and you're looking at me the way I've always wanted to be looked at but never thought I would be. Thank you for all that you've done for me. You make me feel like no one ever has. This isn't the end of our story, it's only a chapter. I miss you soooo much, Rodney.

Love,

Cat

chapter 43

*

brain stew

8:03 p.m.

I'm having trouble trying to sleep. I'm counting sheep but running out. Sure, it's not a huge mystery as to why I'm having so much trouble sleeping, being that it's only 8 p.m. and the sun is still clocked in, not yet ready to call it a day and let the moon take over. I'm just so confused. Of course I appreciate the effort Cat went through getting her message in a bottle to me, taping the picture that Jesse Malin took of us and Joe Strummer to the outside of the bottle, and quoting Sting's lyrics in her letter. It's exciting to think that I've influenced her in some way, that she now loves The Police (her words). At the same time, it's a little ridiculous taking credit for this. Sting's songs did the influencing. I'm just the messenger. *Need sleep.*

8:49 p.m.

My eyes feel like they're gonna bleed, dried up and bulging out of my skull. I really need to set her letter down and get some sleep. It's nice to read about how Cat discovered Green Day through their Broadway show. Her name being in two of their songs on the album *21st Century Breakdown* does very much remind me of my situation with *Bee Movie*. Still, because of Green Day, my brother is dead and my mom is an emotional mess. A well-written letter can't erase that. *Need to focus on something else. Anything else. Need to get to sleep.*

9:38 p.m.

My mind is set on overdrive. The clock is laughing in my face. The condescending red light lets me know I've been staring at it for an hour and thirty five minutes. The sun is down and I am up. I've passed the point of delirium.

In order to give my brain (and eyes) a break, I decide to head down to the den to see if my dad is still awake. My guess is he's up watching the end of the Phillies game. They're playing the hated Washington Nationals. Hated by my dad and the rest of Phillies Nation, that is. I make a deal with myself that if my dad is awake when I get down there, I'm going to put him on the spot and ask once and for all how he knows Mike. I haven't brought it up, not since witnessing the recognition between them at the hospital, which is due to a lack of courage on my part, not a lack of curiosity. I've put this off long enough. It's now or never. No one can do this for me.

On my own, here we go.

* * * * * * * * *

My dad is still awake and, while the Phillies game is on the screen, he's not paying much attention as the Fightin' Phils are getting blown out. It's just him in the den. He tells me that my mom is up in Colin's room. She's been spending a lot of time in there since the incident with Cat. Reading the look on my face, my dad insists that I have nothing to feel guilty about. Easy for him to say.

I haven't conjured the courage to come right out and ask him about Mike, I'm more of a "beat around the bush" kind of guy. My dad is in a chatty mood and tells me he's bummed to be going back to work on Monday. He confides in me that we badly need the money. It takes every bit of willpower to keep from crying as my dad tells me how much he's enjoyed the time we've spent together these past two weeks. Even though he knows it's been hard on me, having a broken heart and my mom being extra needy and leaning on me even more than usual (his words), he says that cooking together has breathed new life into him. He thanks me for leaving Sting's memoir in his hospital room, that it gave him a newfound appreciation for life which he says he owes all to me.

On the verge of crying, my brain blurts out the first thing that comes to it in a last-ditch effort to thwart off tears.

"How do you know Mike?"

The abrupt question catches my dad off guard and he pauses for what feels like an hour before answering my question with one of his own.

"Why don't you go over to The Store?"

"The Store?" I ask, making sure I heard him correctly. "You mean the competition? Didn't you tell me that all they sell is cigarettes and lottery tickets?"

"Well, Mike was the one who found your mom that night. I just thought it'd be nice to thank him, is all. And if you ask him what you just asked me, it might bring you the clarity you're searching for."

* * * * * * * * *

My mom was huddled underneath The White Bridge. Mike spotted her from high atop the train trestle, no less than fifty feet in the sky and at least the length of two football fields away. The fact that he caught a glimpse of her from that height and distance is nothing short of incredible since it was pitch black by that point. Mike says the moon reflected off the river just so, which led him to notice her and it's a good thing, too, because neither Officer Stewart nor I could see her even after Mike tried to point her out to us. With blind faith that he was right, we followed behind, descending the steep embankment from the train tracks to the river's edge.

Climbing down was insanely difficult and wildly scary, at least for me. Mike seemed to have done it a thousand times and made his way down swiftly. Officer Stewart is super athletic so it wasn't much of a problem for him. I, on the other hand, couldn't see three feet in front of my face and ended up taking a tumble into some underbrush. When they looked back, I blamed the noise on a wild animal but I'm quite certain neither Mike nor Officer Stewart bought my excuse. Finally, we made it to the bottom and, sure enough, Mike was right—it was my mom. She was lost in a zone, deeper than I've seen in a long time. Getting her into Officer Stewart's police cruiser was a challenge. Once she was in, Mike turned back and walked toward the river while Officer Stewart drove me and my mom home. I didn't even get to thank him.

Tomorrow I'm going to walk into The Store and thank Mike for finding my mom. Then I will hope that he's in an uncharacteristically conversational mood and will offer an unsolicited explanation of how the hell he knows my parents. Because I sure as shit won't have the guts to come out and ask him. Not after the confusing night I've had.

chapter 44

*

the grouch

A thick fog of smoke lingers at the front of The Store like an unwelcome mat. Peering through the mist, I see that Mike is in the back, hunched over the deli counter reading a newspaper. He doesn't look up when I come in, ignoring the bells attached to the front door hung there to alert him of a customer's arrival. Mr. B. is in his usual seat, cigarette in one hand, cup of coffee in the other. Mike sips from a Corona bottle while perusing the paper, still failing to acknowledge my presence even though I'm now just a few feet away. When he finally looks up to see me, I smile at him and he responds by chugging the remainder of his Corona in one swig—at least half a bottle.

"I need another beer."

When Mike disappears into the back room to retrieve another midday work beer, it gives me a moment to gather my wits. I need to find the perfect time to ask him how the heck he knows my parents. That's why I came here and that's what's important.

"So, Rod—"

"Cat likes Green Day!" *So much for sticking to the plan.*

"Okay."

"Can you believe that?" I ask, incredulously.

"Yes."

"What do you mean, yes?"

"Green Day is one of the biggest bands in the world. So yes,

I can absolutely believe that Cat likes Green Day. Wait, don't you like them, too? I seem to recall the two of you going on about them the day you got your ass kicked."

"Yeah, well, not anymore. Fool me once, right? Cat's gone, my head is a mess, and I haven't gotten a good night's sleep in a week, with the through line of disaster being Green Day."

"Honestly, Rod, I think you're messing up by not listening to Green Day. I can't speak to their later stuff because I gave up on listening to new music at the turn of the century, but on the records they released when I was growing up they were singing about all the things that you have going on in your life right now. No one writes better songs about trying to figure out who you are, teenage love, boredom, masturbation. They've got it all covered. All of the questions swirling around your hormonal, teenage brain—if you listen to Green Day, you might find your answers. At the very least, knowing that someone else is asking the same questions will make you feel less alone."

"They killed my brother," I say, surprising myself with the abruptness of my statement. When Mike doesn't respond I take it as a cue to continue. "Colin was my parents' pride and joy. He was a baseball star and then he got into Green Day and everything changed. If they hadn't become his favorite band, he wouldn't have gone to see them play that night and he'd probably be playing for the Phillies now and my parents would still be happy. Instead, they got stuck with me, the world's worst consolation prize."

I am full-on crying now. I try my damnedest not to but that only causes the tears to rain down with more force.

"What about that optimism you copped from Sting? If your brother hadn't passed away, you wouldn't have been born. A case could be made that if it weren't for Green Day, you wouldn't be alive."

"In which case everyone would be better off. My parents were so happy when Colin was alive. I look at their old photos and they're smiling in every one of them because the son they wanted was still alive."

At this point Mike begins to cry, which catches me completely off guard. He just keeps repeating, "I'm sorry. I'm so fucking sorry." I don't know what he means by this but we're both crying. Mr. B. is either oblivious or uncomfortable because he doesn't take his eyes off his cup of coffee.

"I knew your brother," he says, finally regaining his composure.

Mike digs out a crinkled, handwritten sign from behind the deli counter that he has clearly used before, which he affixes to the front door.

We're closed for a bit. Come back later. Or don't.
-Management

* * * * * * * * *

Mike leads me through the doorway behind the deli area of The Store. We cut through the office, which is mostly filled with empty beer boxes and Yoo-hoo bottles. I don't see a computer or paperwork anywhere so I'm not sure how exactly it qualifies as an office, but that's what he calls it so who am I to argue? Mike's interpretation of an office leads us to a narrow staircase that brings us to his second-floor apartment, directly across from the one where Cat was staying with her Aunt Amy until a week ago.

While he rummages through boxes in the other room, intent on finding something he wants to give me, Mike tells me to sit anywhere I can find a spot. I choose the arm of a chair near the window as it seems to be the least crowded place to sit (including the floor). At the risk of sounding judgmental, Mike's apartment is a wreck. Beer bottles cover the coffee table and floor, some empty and some half-full with cigarette butts drowning inside. There are ashtrays scattered all over the place, each filled to the brim. This combination permeates the apartment with a tenacious aroma of stale smoke mixed with staler beer. In addition to the cigarettes and beer bottles, there are plates holding half-eaten burritos, crumpled fast food containers, (mostly) empty pizza boxes, paper coffee cups, and wrappers upon wrappers of Tastykake brownies, which I'm certain were once a part of The Store's inventory since I've seen Mike eating them just about every time I've been in The Store.

"Sorry about the mess, the maid is on vacation," Mike says, nudging a pizza box with his foot to clear a narrow walking path.

He's clearly joking about having a maid but a small part of me holds out hope that he isn't, that her being on vacation is the explanation for the disaster area he calls his apartment. I make a promise to myself to clean my room before going to bed tonight.

"No, it's fine," I say unconvincingly. "I like it."

Mike finds what he's been searching for but doesn't give it to me. He sits on his couch, staring at the garbage-covered floor for an uncomfortable amount of time.

"They call this liquid courage but really it's quite the opposite," he says, holding up the fresh Corona he grabbed on the way up. "It should be called liquid capitulation." Mike pauses for a second, looking at me, before adding, "It means to give in."

"I know."

"Oh yeah, I forgot, you're one of those 'readers,'" he says, putting air quotes around the word readers for reasons unknown. "Your brother was a reader too, now that I think about it."

"He was?"

"Yep, he always had his nose in a book, which I thought was cool because most guys like him could hardly be bothered to read a menu, let alone a novel."

I know that Colin was a reader. Well, I know that he had a nice collection of books and assume they were more than decorative, but to hear about my brother from someone other than my parents sends a charge through my body, igniting a fire in me to immediately hear as much about him as I can— specifically, enough to find out what Mike means by "guys like him."

* * * * * * * *

Mike's first job was working here at The Store as a teenager. Back then Wawa didn't exist, at least not locally, so The Store was in its heyday. Cigarettes and lottery tickets weren't the only big sellers. Mike tells me that these were the days before people got their news from screens that fit inside their pockets, instead turning to newspapers to keep them informed. The Store carried a variety of them: *The Courier News*, *The Star Ledger*, *The New York Times*, *USA Today*, etc., and Mike would read each of them throughout the course of a day. It's a habit that continues today, he tells me, even as the newspaper business is standing on its last leg.

Beyond cigarettes, lottery tickets, and newspapers, The Store's deli counter was busy from morning until night. This is a bit hard to believe, being that I've only ever seen Mr. B. sitting there, but Mike is speaking with such passion that I'm inclined to believe him. The Dolly's Special was the bestseller. All day long they were ordered: for breakfast by people on their way into work, at midday by those on lunch breaks, and for dinner as people came back into town on their way home from a long day on the job. Sub sandwiches were another popular item in Neshanic Station, though Mike tells me that they were called hoagies and if you didn't use the correct vernacular, you'd receive your order with a sneer.

I begin to wonder why Mike is taking me on this stroll down memory lane. The last time I saw him, he had just successfully found my mom, for whom my dad, Officer Stewart, and I had been searching all night long. This visit was my opportunity to thank him for his help but when he laid eyes on me, he had turned pale as a ghost, closed The Store, and dragged me into his apartment for this beer-fueled diatribe.

That's not to say I'm not enjoying hearing about The Store's history. I'm just wondering what lit the flame. As Mike continues on with his tale, I'm the one turning a sudden shade of white.

Mike started working at The Store at age sixteen, the same age I am now (for the next few weeks, anyway). When he first applied for a job he was told they were not hiring, since they already had a kid who worked the register. A kid named Colin. Colin lived up the street from Mike and was a year older. They knew each other but were not friends, since they ran with different crowds. Even without a job opening, Mike very much enjoyed the atmosphere of The Store and began hanging around. He'd nurse a Coke for an entire afternoon, which technically made him a paying customer. He'd sit and read all the newspapers even when the owner, Sal (husband of Dolly, of Dolly's Special fame) gave him his daily reminder that "this ain't no damn library." One day Mike joked under his breath, "it's clear this place isn't a library because Sal has likely never stepped foot in one of those." The joke was uttered a tad louder than he had meant it to be. Colin heard and loved it; after that, they formed a bond built upon making fun of Sal. Colin then began giving Mike half of his daily shift meal: you guessed it, a Dolly's Special.

Eventually, as The Store got busier, Colin moved back to work behind the deli counter and he recommended that Mike take over his job at the front register. Colin and Mike became work friends. They didn't socialize much outside of The Store; Colin had his friends on the baseball team and Mike hung around with the music heads, or the River Rats, as they were called. The River Rats, he tells me, was a nickname originally put upon them as a slur, but Mike and his friends embraced it and wore it as a badge of honor. They had an "us against them" mentality. The River Rats spent their days listening to punk rock, swimming in the river, and smoking cigarettes. All who weren't River Rats were yuppies, in their eyes. Mike even lumped Colin in as one of the yuppies but thought of him as one of the good guys, an outlier from the rest of his snobbish circle of friends.

After a couple of years working together, after school and full days during the summer, Colin went off to Seton Hall University on a baseball scholarship and Mike was promoted to the deli counter. Without Colin to socialize with, Mike's only friend at The Store was Mr. B., who even back then ate the majority of his meals there. Colin would come home for breaks and pick up some shifts while home but The Store, by that point, was changing.

Hearing about Colin from someone other than my parents is intoxicating. It's like seeing two different painters' renditions of the same model. Up until now, Colin's story has been told to me, almost begrudgingly, in bits and pieces by my parents. Akin to a novel by Charles Dickens, the story itself is very rewarding but extracting it from the pages (or in my case, from the lips of my guarded parents) can be a painstaking endeavor.

"Then when he was home on summer break your brother started asking where he could get a ticket to see Green Day down in Asbury Park. It was so out of the blue," he says, taking a long pause. "I couldn't understand it," he says, finally piercing the dead air. "Because, despite what you think, Green Day wasn't Colin's favorite band. Hell, I bet he couldn't even have named one song of theirs that wasn't a single."

Mike proceeds to tell me that Green Day was *his* favorite band, not Colin's. In fact, in all the time they spent together at The Store, Colin never showed any interest in music; he was laser-focused on baseball. Mike wondered why he suddenly became interested in scoring a ticket to their sold-out show in Asbury Park. Apparently Colin's friends, the yuppies, had all recently gotten into Green Day and were going to the concert, so Colin wanted to go along.

"Green Day was huge at the time and I blamed them for yuppies like your brother's friends infiltrating my beloved punk rock scene. God, I was such a territorial asshole." He takes a long swig from his bottle and an even longer pause afterward. "It was my ticket. I gave it to him."

It takes Mike quite a while to compose himself. Long enough for it to click as to why my mom refuses to walk down Olive Street and why I've never been allowed to set foot inside The Store, the painful memory of Colin's one and only job haunting my mom for all these years. I sit across from him, my entire universe turned upside down, not knowing what to say, as usual. Mike takes a long breath before finishing, telling me that the guilt of giving Colin his ticket has never left him, not even for a day. He tells me that he drinks in an attempt to numb the pain and then he drinks more to try to drown out the guilt of knowing he drinks far too much. We are both silent again, staring in opposite directions.

"The other day when I walked into the hospital room and saw Colin's parents, realizing they were also your parents, it hit me like a ton of bricks. I came home and went on a drinking binge. That made things worse. Then I dug up my old Green Day CDs and traveled down that rabbit hole, which helped ease the pain. Other than hearing all those amazing old songs of theirs, the only thing that's come close has been talking to you."

As Mike hands me what he's been waiting to give me, what he brought me up here for in the first place, I immediately notice two nimrod symbols, both exactly the same as on the shirt of Colin's I wore—the one responsible for my nickname. It's the same lowercase black lettering with a period at the end inside of a yellow circle. There was nothing else on the shirt, but on this CD these two yellow encircled nimrod symbols sit atop faces that look like they're out of an old black and white yearbook. Green Day is typed in large print above the nimrod-covered faces. The cover art is quite sharp. He also hands me a pair of headphones that look like they're attached to an early model iHome of some sort, but Mike explains to me that it's a portable Discman, the 90s version of an iPod, which will allow me to listen to the CD in private. He *definitely* knows my mom.

As we make our way down the narrow staircase leading from his apartment back to The Store, Mike tells me that *Nimrod* is the perfect representation of Green Day. That, in fact, it's a perfect punk rock album. It's their *London Calling*, he says, which I know is an album by The Clash, the band that Joe Strummer fronted, whom I learned about when I met Jesse Malin in the city with Cat. Mike says that *Nimrod* is his favorite Green Day album but that all of their early records are excellent and instructs me to come back once I've fully digested this one and he'll tell me more Colin stories and will lend me another CD.

Before leaving, I make sure to thank Mike. It's a blanket thank-you that, from his wink and nod, I trust he understands, covers finding my mom, telling me about my brother (and his friend) Colin, and for lending me *Nimrod*.

chapter 45

*

brand new day

As I leave The Store, thoughts pinball around my brain feeling dangerously like the onset of a panic attack. Before I go home I need to find somewhere to think, to fully digest the wealth of information fed to me by Mike. As I load *Nimrod* into the Discman and try to figure out how to get this musical relic to play, I nearly barrel over Officer Stewart who's coming in the door as I'm walking out.

"Something I said?" he asks with a smile likely to charm even those he's placing under arrest.

"Oh no, not at all," I say, unnecessarily answering his rhetorical icebreaker. "Sorry, I'm just trying to figure out how to get this thing to work. Mike lent it to me but it's so old that the markings have rubbed off the buttons."

"Wow, haven't seen one of these in years," Officer Stewart says. "The play button is here and the volume is on the side. And that's pretty much the gist of it."

"Thanks a lot. All right, I've got to get going. See you around."

"You good, Rod? You look a little pale. I suppose the food here will do that to you, but I mean otherwise."

"Yep. Just a lot on my mind. Thanks for asking."

"Anytime. My phone is always on if you need me. It's a beautiful day out there, enjoy it," he says, fist bumping me goodbye.

Officer Stewart is right, it is a beautiful day. It's one of those perfect summer afternoons: hot but not sweltering, the blue sky peppered with white clouds so perfect it could be mistaken for a painting. Pressing the unmarked play button and hearing Green Day without any baggage attached I'm transported back into Cat's car, the first time she played me the song *American Idiot* which I insisted she play again and again (and again and again and again). Listening to Green Day on our way to the basement show in New Brunswick was an ear opening experience. I'd had such negative connotations attached to their music that when I finally heard it, it was not at all what I was expecting, in the best way. That entire week, each time I listened to them with Cat was euphoric and then a week later I was back to believing they were a trio of saboteurs. Hearing *Nimrod*, an album that has already had an immense impact before ever hearing a note from it (I don't recognize these songs and am positive Cat didn't play this one for me), is another earth-shattering experience.

Rather than stand in front of The Store, staring aimlessly ahead of me like a lunatic, I head east on Olive Street while brainstorming a place to go to get some thinking done. The library immediately comes to mind but Mary will be there and, as much as I enjoy chatting with her, that won't help me clear my head. There's got to be a place more secluded. The roof of Follow the Sun Yoga is where Cat went to be alone but since I just left it'd be weird to walk back that way and risk being spotted by Mike and/or Officer Stewart. Plus, I don't trust myself getting up on the roof. Even if I did manage to defy the odds and make it up safely, there'd still be the tall task of climbing down. Agility is not a quality I'll be including in my Instagram bio when I get around to creating an account. Underneath the White Bridge is a possibility but with it being the place where my mom ended up the night she walked off, there's no telling if that was a one-time thing or if she makes a habit of going there and it'd be awkward, to say the least, to run into her there so let's scratch that from the list. The woods behind Frankie's house seem like a place where someone could get some thinking done. I don't want to risk Frankie spotting me though, especially if he's run out of spoofs and is blowing his pot smoke out his bedroom window, as he's been known to do.

The combination of Green Day's music blasting through the borrowed headphones and the realization that this band is not responsible for Colin's death, nor are they my own personal black cloud, feels like shackles have been released. It's a feeling of freedom that I've never experienced, a sensation I want to hold onto forever. Green Day is a punk band, plain and simple. A phenomenal one, for sure, though I can't help but feel foolish and maybe even a bit egotistical believing for so long that I was the target of their ire. A vast majority of kids I've gone to school with my entire life don't even know my real name but the world's most famous punk band has it out for me? The absurdity of that idea exudes a chuckle out of me. This, of course, also means that Cat wasn't wrapped up in any of my delusions either.

Suddenly I realize that I'm on Fairview Road, on the outskirts of town, right near Greg DeSanto's house. He was one of the first friends I made in elementary school. I went to his house a few times in second grade but our friendship came to its conclusion the day he ate Play-Doh, threw it up all over his bedroom floor, and blamed it on me when his mom asked. I can't believe I walked this far without realizing it. I'm sweating but I've never felt better. Perhaps my mom is onto something with this walking business, that there's a method to her madness. At this moment, I feel closer to her than ever before and, for the first time that I can remember, I actually wish my phone would ring so I can share with her how much I'm enjoying her favorite (and, come to think of it, only) hobby. As I retrieve my phone from my pocket, I wonder if she'd be open to hearing all the things that Mike told me about Colin.

chapter 46

*

2000 light years away

"I'm so glad you called me!"

"Did you know that Green Day has a song about a teenager who is in love with someone who lives super far away and the distance between them is killing him?" I ask, eschewing a standard greeting, my excitement far too great for that.

"I swear I've listened to that song two thousand times since I last saw you."

Cat tells me she's been waiting for me to call every day for weeks, but right now she's at work and can't talk. She got a job at a vegan restaurant in Keyport called Nature's Plate where she works the register and makes juices and smoothies. I want to tell her how incredible it is to hear her voice, that the feeling she got from first hearing Green Day's music on Broadway, when the notes filled the void inside of her—that's what her voice on the other end of the phone does to me. And also that Green Day isn't the catalyst for sending Colin's life into a downward spiral—that his accident was just that, an accident. It could've happened on his way home from a baseball game and it had nothing to do with Green Day. But because I'm me, I'm unable to muster anything but an "awesome!" in response to her working at a vegan restaurant. Cat asks me to come visit her, but I remind her that while my seventeenth birthday is getting close, I have neither a license nor much hope of getting one any time soon.

"You need to change that. You've got to get your license when you turn seventeen so you can come visit me. And when you're not visiting me, I'll come visit you."

"Deal." My brain is only capable of one-word responses at the moment. I hear her boss call for her in the background.

"Crap, I've got to make a Live Lemonade. Will you be around in a couple hours? I'll call you the minute I get out of work!"

"Definitely." You've heard of a two-pump chump? Well I'm the one-word nerd.

"Rodney, one more thing. The Police—they're incredible!"

"Aren't they?" Two words this time. I'm moving up in the world.

"Cat!" her boss calls out in the background.

"Okay, I gotta go. I'm soooooo glad you called!"

chapter 47

*

i can't stop thinking about you

When I first started masturbating, I would do so sitting upright on my bed with the bedspread draped over me. I must've looked like Casper the Wanking Ghost. This was back in the seventh grade, when I was still Catholic. I don't know what I am now. Undecided, I suppose. In Catholicism, at least as far as I understood it, masturbation is considered a sin, so I used the bedspread as a shield in order to prevent God (and Colin) up in heaven from seeing me do the deed. I already had parents who were disappointed in me; I didn't need the big guy upstairs or my deceased brother thinking I was some kind of perv. I'm not saying it was rational, I'm just saying that's what I did. Years removed from my introductory wank sessions, I'm up to my old tricks again, only this time the bedspread is being used to hide the headphones that are blasting Green Day into my skull at a thunderous volume. If either of my parents should walk in, my plan is to lie and tell them I was masturbating.

Typically, the last few days of summer are complete torture for me. The looming school year brings with it reminders of early wake-ups, homework, and probing questions in the cafeteria ("so what do you do for protein?"). Usually I go into mental hibernation around this time each summer, but this year is different. I haven't had time to stress about the start of my senior year. I've only been able to think of two things of late: Cat and Green Day.

Since I don't drive and she's been working every day since we reconnected, we haven't seen each other, so I've been spending all of my time in my bedroom talking to, texting, or G-chatting with Cat. Every other waking second of my day, mostly while Cat is at work, has been spent listening to Green Day. Obviously I don't want my parents (especially my mom) to hear me listening to Green Day because they are still under the impression that it was Colin's favorite band and are to blame for his death. I have not yet figured out a way to tell them otherwise. My mom isn't exactly the easiest person to talk to about all things Colin. This is why I listen to Green Day behind closed doors (and under a blanket) on the Discman that Mike lent me. It was his suggestion that I stay off YouTube and instead listen to *Nimrod* in full, from front to back. He says that YouTube causes musical ADD, that an album is meant to be listened to just like a book is meant to be read—from cover to cover. At first, I heeded his suggestion and only listened to *Nimrod*. But then, with Cat's guidance, I began branching out and listening to their other albums, some I'd heard in her car on our adventures and others that were brand new to me. I shared Mike's recommendation to listen to each album as it was intended rather than skipping around from song to song, and while she was adamant about not wanting to give the Grouch one iota of credit, she conceded that this was an idea she could get behind.

Labor Day is just around the corner, the last hurrah of summer. Cosplay Con in Asbury Park is rapidly approaching and Cat wants me to come along more than anything. But not only is this in the same city Colin traveled to for that fateful Green Day concert, never to return, but the cosplay event of the year (her words) is taking place inside the same exact venue where the concert took place: Asbury Park Convention Hall. There isn't even a remote chance that my mom would allow me to go and I've given up on stealth adventures to cities, New York or otherwise. Still, the prospect of seeing Cat is enough for me to run through ideas of how I *could* get down there, as far-fetched as they may be.

The other day on my way to the library, I popped into The

Store to see Mike. My dad and I had made black bean and rice wraps, purposely making enough so that I could deliver some to Mike and Mr. B. They both went wild for them ("I cannot fucking believe these are vegan," were Mike's exact words. "What in the Sam Hill is a vegan?" were Mr. B.'s). After hearing some stories about Colin, my favorite being about how he could fit an entire egg inside his mouth without cracking it, a party trick he and Mike would perform in The Store, betting customers whether he could do it, I broached the idea of heading down to Asbury Park on Sunday. Mike told me that there's no way in hell he'd ever go to the Jersey Shore on Labor Day Weekend, the most crowded weekend of the summer, to spend it next to oiled up 'roid heads from Staten Island listening to their club music while drinking piss-warm fancy beer (his words). On top of that, he's the only one currently employed at The Store since Cat left him high and dry (also his words), so he'll be working from open to close all weekend.

Cat thought it'd be a good idea to ask her Aunt Amy if she'd be interested in going to Cosplay Con and if so I could travel down to Asbury Park with her. While I wasn't against the idea of spending time in the car with Amy, as she does have a comforting quality that not many possess, never in a million years would I have the guts to ask her. Before I was able to finish typing out my concerns through G-chat, Cat informed me that she had called Amy and, while she said she'd otherwise love to, she's going to be away at a yoga retreat in Vermont all weekend.

Officer Stewart's name came up in passing but that idea was dead on arrival. While I've gotten to the point where he's one of the first people I will call in an emergency (and I'm talking his cell phone, not at the police station), asking him to hang out as a friend is out of the question. Cat must've been on the same page because she didn't even make a case for it. Cutting through the sound barrier that is my bedspread and over top of the blazing barre chords of Green Day, I hear a faint tap at my door.

"Hey bud, got a minute?"

"Sure, Dad. Uhh...just give me a second," I say, exiting my G-chat and shoving Mike's Discman under a pillow.

"Definitely. No problemo. Take all the time you need. Get cleaned up...if that's what you need to do. I'll wait here until you're decent. Take your time."

When I open the door my dad stands outside my room, nervously peering inside, looking around before deeming it fit to enter. He's holding a brown lunch bag which he's trying, and failing, to keep out of my sight.

"So, umm...listen, bud. I think it's time we had a little talk. I just want you to know I don't come here in judgement. I know I'm a little older than the other kids' dads, but we still had the same...uhh...hobbies when we were kids."

"What's in the bag, Dad?"

"Oh...uhh...this? Yeah, this is kind of what I wanted to talk to you about. So I know it's totally normal for boys, uh, *guys* your age to spend a lot of time in your room...alone...exploring..."

"Oh god—"

"And that's totally cool," he persists, the speed of his verbal output accelerating. "I just don't want to see you hurt yourself so..." He then pulls a bottle of lotion out of the bag. Most kids my age would be confronted by their concerned parent for sneaking booze or vape pens. Mine thinks I'm a chronic masturbater. An enthusiast, perhaps, but chronic I am not.

"Dad, that's not it."

"Oh, if there's another brand you'd prefer, just say the word. I felt a little funny buying straight lube but if that's what the kids are using these days..."

In an effort to never again hear my dad use the word lube, I start talking. Quickly. I tell him that I reconnected with Cat and that I've also been listening to Green Day. I explain to him that, despite what Mom thinks, Cat isn't a bad influence. She's the only person that's made me feel...well, anything and I want to feel like that again and before he has the chance to drop the tired cliché that there are more fish in the sea, I tell him that I don't want any other fish; I only want Cat. Because he's my dad, he sneaks in a catfish joke which I barrel over and keep talking. I then give him an abbreviated version of the story Mike shared with me about Colin not even being a Green Day fan, that he only went to the concert because his buddies were going. After sixteen years of believing that Green Day has been the black cloud hovering over my existence, I now think misery can be altered to fit our motives. I tell him that I haven't felt like myself since the blow up with Mom, or rather that I *have* felt like my old self and that's part of the problem. As unlikely as it seems, Green Day's music is the only thing that makes me feel like the person I was when I was with Cat. The person I liked being.

My dad sits for a moment in silence, absorbing the blast from the bomb I just dropped. He chuckles as he looks at the bottle of lotion in his hand, giving it to me and telling me to keep it just in case. Then he gets really sweet and tells me how happy he is that I seem to be on the up-and-up, that he was worried about me for the couple of weeks when my heart was in pieces and that, even though it was a long time ago, he's been through his share of relationships so if I ever need anyone to talk to, he's my guy. Then he tells me something that bounces around my head like a pinball wondering where he's getting his intel.

"I know about the trip. And I think you should go."

chapter 48

*

oh love

My dad doesn't have ESP, nor does he possess the know-how (or desire) to monitor my G-chat conversations. Heck, I would bet my book collection that he doesn't even know what Gmail is. The trip he suggested would do me some good was not the one to Asbury Park to visit Cat. The reason my dad came into my room that day, the day he delivered me a bottle of hand lotion, was because Frankie had shown up at our front door. He'd been texting me for a few days leading up to that, but I was too far down the Green Day rabbit hole to be willing to endure watching him play video games while smoking copious amounts of marijuana so I didn't bother responding. Geez, how ungrateful do I sound toward the guy who came to my house to offer me tickets to see Sting in Atlantic City?

Remember when I told you that Frankie's dad, the Blowhard, owns a car dealership and is kind of a big shot (at least in his own mind)? Well, owning a car dealership has its perks. Besides all of the money he rakes in, one of those perks is getting free tickets to all kinds of events. This time, third row seats to Sting's concert in Atlantic City (or AC, as people around here refer to it) fell right into his lap and although he couldn't give two craps about Sting (Frankie's dad's words), he never passed up an opportunity to hit the tables for a night of debauchery (again, his words...though Frankie thankfully left these words out of his pitch when telling my dad about the tickets, while I was still in my room listening to Green Day undercover). I don't know how my dad convinced my mom that letting me go was a good idea, especially since he has to work and can't come along, but here I am, getting ready to visit Atlantic City for the first time to see my hero in concert. We don't have backstage passes but Frankie said that his dad is "working on it" (which to me sounds like big shot talk, though stranger things have happened).

At the risk of sounding like a Debbie Downer, there is a downside to Frankie getting me a free ticket and perhaps my best chance to meet Sting. Actually, there are two. The first one is that he made good on his promise to make it up to me (it being the years of making fun of me for no good reason) and now he gets to hold that over my head. This is not me being salty; he's already brought it up multiple times ("Can you *believe* I made this happen?!" *Yes, I can, because you've mentioned it forty-five times already*). The other negative is that today just so happens to be the day that Cosplay Con is taking place. While neither of us truly believed I'd be able to make my way down there to go with her, I do think Cat was a bit disappointed hearing that rather than seeing her for the first time in weeks, I'd be with Frankie headed to realize my dream, the one that she and I were so close to attaining together. Cat swears she's okay with me going to the concert instead of the cosplay convention, but I know it stings that Asbury Park is on the way to Atlantic City and I won't even be able to stop by quickly to see her. Even though we're leaving Neshanic Station early in the day, Frankie tells me that we won't have time for any pit stops because his dad wants to get in as much gambling as possible. It irks me that he refers to Cat as a "pit stop" despite the fact that he has no idea he did, since I didn't mention Cat's name when asking about the possibility of stopping off somewhere on the way. Logic and love don't always see eye to eye.

Since the day Mike sent me home with his *Nimrod* CD, I haven't listened to Sting. As a matter of fact, I haven't listened to anything other than Green Day (in private, of course). Mary the librarian let me borrow her copy of *My Songs* so that I could listen to it on the way down to AC to get myself into the right mindset. Before hopping into Frankie's dad's car, I decide it's best to leave the Discman in one of the oversized pockets of my cargo shorts; I don't want to appear rude or ungrateful, opting to zone into my Sting CD rather than engaging with my hosts.

"No way, Nimrod," Frankie says when I open the back door of his dad's car. "You're up front. I need space to stretch my legs."

Before we reach the end of our street, Frankie is sprawled out horizontally across the backseat, with noise-cancelling headphones plugged into the Nintendo Switch that he's playing while his dad, in the driver's seat, is listening to a podcast about how to win big at blackjack through a pair of earbuds of his own. Now seems as good a time as any to bust out the Discman and reacquaint myself with some of the greatest songs ever written.

The drive from Neshanic Station to Atlantic City should take two hours, almost on the nose. As we inch down the Garden State Parkway, I realize that Mike wasn't exaggerating about Labor Day Weekend being the Jersey Shore's busiest of the season, making the commute an absolute nightmare. We are an hour and a half into our journey, sitting in dead-stopped traffic. I'm staring at a sign for Exit 105 to Long Branch, which Frankie's dad's GPS tells me is just about the halfway point from Neshanic Station to Atlantic City. Even more disconcerting than the sluggish traffic is the fact that *My Songs* isn't doing a damn thing for me, leaving me wishing I had gone with my gut and brought along *Nimrod* as a backup in case this happened. Don't get me wrong; I love the album and Sting doesn't have to worry about being dethroned as the Coolest Man in the World in my mind, but music is all about time and place (Cat's words) and at this time I want nothing more than to hear Green Day.

Moments after I begin thinking about Green Day I receive a text from Cat wishing me good luck, encouraging me to tell Sting about our run-in with the other Sting, that it's a hell of an icebreaker. Notice that she didn't preface her statement with "*If* you meet him," instead treating it as a foregone conclusion. Cat has got a PMA. After finally giving up on *My Songs*, I ask Frankie's dad if it's all right to put on the radio, and he shoots me a look that leads me to believe he forgot I was even there. He can't be bothered to remove his earbuds so I motion toward the radio, pretending to turn it on, which makes him shrug and look away, the universal sign for "I don't give a shit."

Frankie's dad's pre-programmed channels don't come in, as we're far out of range of our local signal, so I scan through the channels, quickly moving through the majority that are pumping out music with eerily similar dance beats to those blaring out of the cars on either side of us. My station-surfing is halted the moment I hear an actual guitar and, while I don't recognize the song, there is no question that the voice belongs to Billie Joe Armstrong. I am transfixed by the words coming out of his mouth.

Oh love, oh love
Won't you rain on me tonight?
Oh life, oh life
Please don't pass me by
Don't stop, don't stop
Don't stop when the red lights flash
Oh ride, free ride
Won't you take me close to you

We only caught the end of the song so even if I did have a smartphone with an app to tell me what song it was, which I don't, there likely wouldn't have been time to make it happen. Fortunately, the station's DJ does me a solid.

"You're listening to 90.5 The Night, Brookdale Public Radio, and that was *Oh Love* by Green Day. Oh love, indeed. The Beatles suggested that it's all you need and Billie Joe and the boys seem to agree. I'm your DJ, Jeff Raspe, join me tonight at the world famous

Stone Pony in beautiful Asbury Park as 90.5 The Night Presents: Jesse Malin live in concert."

With this crystal clear sign of synchronicity I do what any love-struck teenager in search of a sign would do: I fake an emergency call from home. Both Frankie and his dad are lost in their own worlds to the point where I have to turn the acting (and the volume) up a notch as I pretend to receive an urgent call from my dad telling me that I need to get to Asbury Park immediately. My debut acting role may have been as Skunk #2 in *Noah's Ark*, but nothing about this phone performance stunk (at least not to an apathetic audience of one).

"That was your dad on the phone?"

"Yessir."

"And he wants me to drop you off in Asbury Park?" Frankie's dad asks, remarkably indifferent.

"Yes."

"Good enough for me."

Half an hour later, I'm standing in the parking lot of the Asbury Park Train Station. As his dad's car pulls away, Frankie, from the backseat, offers me a dubious look, clearly not buying my family emergency story. He mouths a one-word question "Cat?" to which I'm unable to contain my grin, producing a smirk and a thumbs-up from my oldest frenemy.

chapter 49

*

last of the american girls

An affable cab driver informs me that it'll take a good twenty-five minutes to walk from the train station to Convention Hall but he can get me there in five. His friendliness evaporates and he seems personally offended by my decision to walk but I couldn't have asked for a more beautiful day for a stroll through a bona fide New Jersey beach town. My family are not beach people. I don't think I'd ever seen my dad in a pair of shorts until recently, let alone a bathing suit. Since his operation, he wears shorts all the time. He's been eating right and working out like a madman and has lost 35 pounds! He truly looks like a new man. I still can't see him sitting on a beach, though, and my mom—forget it. It's laughable to try to picture my mom anywhere near a beach (though it would seemingly be the perfect place for a long walk). I walk along Cookman Avenue and so far I don't see anything that looks like the beach or even beach-like. That said, Cookman Avenue is incredible. It reminds me a bit of New York City, only cleaner and without all the skyscrapers. What it does share in common with New York is the amount of shops that I have never seen before. While driving along the highway where I live, you'll see the same stores you see everywhere else you go: Target, Starbucks, McDonald's. Here in Asbury Park, there are restaurants all over the place and not one is named TGI Fridays. On my stroll I also pass a record store, a paranormal gift shop, an independent bookstore, and not one but two coffee shops, one of which I stop into for some caffeine courage, as the closer I get to reuniting with Cat, the more nervous I become. It's the first cup of coffee I've had since that day we spent in NYC. I'd gone back to being a tea guy since then but for some reason it feels blasphemous to order tea at a Jersey Shore coffee shop.

The further I travel up Cookman Ave., the fewer shops and restaurants there are. I've now entered a section where the buildings are occupied with swanky-looking apartments, the kind I will never be able to afford. I can tell I'm getting closer to the boardwalk as the unmistakable aroma of the beach begins to seep into my senses. It's nothing short of amazing the way the ocean's distinct smell can identify itself to a person who has been there fewer times than can be counted on one hand.

While I don't have anything to compare it to, the boardwalk seems quite busy today. With it being the last weekend of summer I expected a large crowd but the sheer number of people out here, basking in the sun's seemingly infinite warmth, walking the wooden boards that run parallel to the beach, and patronizing the countless pizza counters and beach bars that line the boardwalk is borderline overwhelming. As I make my way down the boardwalk, dodging people as if it's my job, I know I'm getting closer to Convention Hall as I begin passing cosplayers adorned in their costumes. So far I've seen Harley Quinn, a sexy version of Velma from Scooby Doo, The Mandalorian carrying Baby Yoda, and a plethora of anime and superhero characters, none of which I can name.

Convention Hall is a massive structure at the end of Asbury Park's boardwalk. The majority of the building is composed of brick, carrying the character and charm of something built long ago. There are multiple entrance points that can be accessed from the street, the boardwalk, or the beach. Directly in front of me is an entrance that spans the width of the boardwalk, easily one hundred feet across. Ten or so sets of double glass doors stand ready, willing, and able to accommodate the multitude of costumed cosplayers arriving en masse, searching for solace from the sun. Above the doors there look to be five hundred window panes, each outlined with the same seafoam green wood trim that surrounds the doors below them. It's truly a sight to behold. As I stare at this beautiful architecture from the past, it hits me that this is the last place Colin ever came in his short life. Just as my emotions begin to get the better of me, I'm approached by Harry Potter and Hermione Granger.

"Rod, is that you?"

It hits me that this Harry is a much taller version than the one I pictured while reading the books (yes, all seven of them). Then comes the confusion that this towering Harry seems to somehow know me.

"It's me, Will. Cat's friend. We met in New Brunswick," he says, as Hermione, clearly bored with our encounter, excuses herself, telling Harry to find her inside.

It's so good to see and catch up with Will. He tells me that he didn't want to dress up but he's glad the others convinced him to because as soon as he walked inside the convention, Hermione came up to him, proclaiming that they're meant to be together.

"I don't even know her real name. This place is magical! Wait, what are you doing here?"

"I came to surprise Cat," I inform him.

"That's awesome! Do you have a ticket?"

Apparently Cosplay Con is long sold out. At this point I realize I haven't thought this through. In my defense, a spur-of-the-moment decision, by definition, doesn't involve forethought. Undeterred, Will walks me a few blocks away to where his car is parked, right next to the Catmobile. He sets me up inside, turning on the air conditioning and radio for me, and tells me he'll be back with Cat and the others as soon as he can. Will says to keep an eye out and when I see them approaching to lean the seat back so I can give Cat a good surprise. It really is good to see him again.

* * * * * * * *

I believe I already told you that I'm not much of an air conditioning guy. There's nothing redeemable to me about fabricated cold air being forced into my face so I opt to use the windows instead. I figure it'll give me better odds of noticing Cat before she notices me since I'll be able to hear them coming. I'm glad I did, because as I see Sonic the Hedgehog and Tails approaching, I don't recognize that it's Wheels and Ellie in costume until I hear Cat's unmistakable voice coming from behind them.

"Are you gonna tell me what's so important that I *had* to come out to the car right now?"

"Aren't you due for a costume change soon? I want to be a good friend and stand in front of the windows so no one sees you changing but Hermione is all over me so if she grabs me and starts making out with me in the corner, I can't promise I'd have the willpower to break away."

My entire body experiences pins and needles at the sound of her voice, rendering me unable to follow the plan of leaning back in the seat, getting myself out of sight. In fact, I've forgotten all about the plan until the moment Cat screams as our eyes lock, reminding me that she wasn't expecting me to be sitting in Will's car like a dog with the window cracked for him. After I fumble to disengage the seat belt (why I had the seat belt on in the first place is a question I wish I had an answer for), Cat takes my face in her hands.

"What are you doing here?!"

"Leaving the hive."

"What about Atlantic City? What about Sting?"

"He's not you."

With that, she pulls me close to her. Our embrace lasts a good long while. Usually I'd be mortified to be standing in front of other people putting our affection on display. Today, though, I feel no such shame. I've been waiting to hold Cat for 2,000 light years, leaving me perfectly content to cherish our embrace and I'll be damned if I'm the one to break it off.

"Is it me, or did we just reenact the cover art of *21st Century Breakdown*?" I ask, referring to Green Day's 2009 album—the one containing two Gloria-based song titles. The most beautiful smile imaginable appears on her face.

"Very close. It's just missing one thing," she says, pulling me in for a kiss that makes my knees feel as if they're made of tofu (and not the extra firm variety).

Once I'm able to remember my name (and my manners), I greet Wheels and Ellie, telling them how much I love their costumes. Ellie thanks me, adding that she should've been Sonic, since Wheels sounds more like Tails.

"That may be, but I look more like Sonic."

"What a thing to brag about," Ellie rebuts.

Just like at the basement show, the conversation with Cat's friends is refreshingly natural. They feel like *my* friends too and if I weren't already over the moon about seeing Cat, whose hand I just now notice is enwrapped in mine, this exchange with them would have made my day. Will is itching to get inside to reunite with Hermione, so along with Wheels and Ellie, he heads back into Convention Hall while Cat tells them she'll catch up soon.

"So, what do you think of my costume?" Cat asks when we're alone together for the first time in what feels like forever.

"I love it! What are you?"

She laughs, saying she'll give me a hint, that she's a character from an album I've already mentioned.

"Okay, so *21st Century Breakdown*. Oh wow, you're Gloria!"

"Good guess, but no. Try again."

I step back, taking inventory of what she's wearing. A blue dress with white stars underneath a black jacket, but not the one she usually wears. This one is longer, like an overcoat, and she spins around so that I can see a large American Flag sewn on the back with an anarchy symbol in place of the stars. She's wearing Doc Martens, which I've learned are the name of the yellow-stitched boots that I love. I'm a bit stumped, attempting to run through the song titles on the album while putting clues together based on what she's wearing. Slung over her right shoulder, she's holding one of those old timey sticks with a sack at the end like you'd see a runaway in Huck Finn's time carrying their belongings inside. The sack on hers has dollar signs on it and in her other hand she's holding a book. She turns it toward me and I can see the title: *Little Book of Conspiracies*, which is the clue that makes it click.

"You're the Last of the American Girls!"

"Ding ding! We have a winner. Now step forward and accept your prize," she says, kissing me again as the bassline from *Walking on the Moon* plays on a loop in my mind while our lips lock.

"This costume is amazing!" I say once I'm able to regain my wits. "But what happened to the wings I saw you wearing on the roof that day? And the question mark tie you bought at the thrift store?"

"A boy who actually pays attention. Where did you come from?" she asks before explaining that she couldn't decide so she actually has two costumes, which I realize is what she and Will were discussing while approaching the car.

She'll be changing into her next one shortly and because she'll be sending me off for a bit before she changes in the backseat, Cat tells me about this one instead of giving me another quiz. For the second half of Cosplay Con, Cat will be going as Whatsername from *American Idiot*. She'll wear a vigilante mask over her eyes a la The Lone Ranger. Handcrafted bus transfers from Chicago to Toronto will poke out of her red jacket with its collar flipped because, unlike James Dean, she's a rebel *with* a cause. Underneath she'll have on a black, short-sleeved collared shirt with a red question mark necktie, the question mark signifying Whatsername while also being a nod to Billie Joe Armstrong at Woodstock '94. On top of the jacket will be the wings and on her hand Ellie will be painting a red hand grenade heart.

"Speaking of which, I should really get back inside. I wish you could come in but it's sold out and security is tight."

The convention will be over and Cat will be "all mine" at 5 p.m., two hours from now. I assure Cat with a thumbs-up that I'll be fine, adding that I'm a master at killing time and that I'll take the opportunity to explore Asbury Park and read *Nobody Likes You*, pulling it out of my cargo shorts pocket.

"You're reading it! Let me see that real quick."

Mary was able to get a copy of *Nobody Likes You: Inside the Turbulent Life, Times, and Music of Green Day* sent over from the county library (this time I insisted on teaching her how to initiate the transfer on the computer so she couldn't pull another fast one and spend her hard-earned money on me). Cat flips through the pages in a frantic but controlled manner until the knowing smile on her face lets me know that she's found exactly what she's searching for. She hands the book back to me, open to page 152, and says rather cryptically, "Our next adventure."

"Oh my gosh, I almost forgot!" she says, opening the backdoor of the Catmobile. She hands me a jacket that feels so familiar, like a word on the tip of the tongue, but I cannot figure out what's familiar about it. It's a black jacket with a short, unfolded, stand-up collar, the kind often seen on motorcycle jackets. Across the chest are two yellow stripes, the top one thicker than the bottom. It hits me.

"Wait, is this a Pollen Jock jacket?" I ask, referring to the jackets worn in *Bee Movie* by the bees who left the hive.

"Wow, you really *have* seen that movie a lot! And yep, sure is. But it's modified to suit you. I haven't thought of a clever name for it, so if you come up with anything I'm all ears."

I'm stunned at how much it looks like the jacket from the movie. Pinned to the left breast, above the stripes, is a yellow circle with white wings and has PMA sewn in cursive inside the circle. Cat explains that the Nimrod patch fastened to the jacket's back is from the very shirt that got me my nickname, admitting that's why she went into Colin's room that day after meeting the other Sting. She didn't know at the time exactly what she was going to do with it, but she thought it was a shame that a perfectly good Green Day shirt, and a rare one at that, had been sitting at the bottom of a drawer for five years.

"It's not exactly cosplay, but it's gonna look great on you. But I'll keep it in the Catmobile for you until later. It's too damn hot to be wearing a jacket out here."

Immediately, she catches my sideways glance, peering at her overcoat.

"Hey, fashion over function. Besides, it's air conditioned in there," she says, nodding toward Convention Hall.

"I love this. But what made you bring it here? You couldn't have known I was going to be here. Hell, *I* didn't know until an hour ago."

"I kept a PMA."

chapter 50

*

welcome to paradise

If you're going to be stuck somewhere with two hours to kill, may I suggest that somewhere be Asbury Park? This place is paradise. From the shops and restaurants on Cookman Ave. to the beach and boardwalk also brimming with shops and restaurants of its own, Asbury Park has got it all. I make a mental note to check if there's a college nearby, thinking I could enroll and live down here once I graduate high school. That, though, is a task for another day; my goal at this juncture is to locate The Stone Pony so that I can surprise Cat with tickets to see Jesse Malin.

No smartphone means no app to guide me to where our old photographer friend from NYC is playing tonight. That leaves me with only one option: to ask someone for directions. People-watching is an activity I thoroughly enjoy but don't get to do nearly as often as I'd like. Neshanic Station is a mundane little town in which, even on the rare occasion that I venture off my normal route (from my house to the library, to Joanne Jones's, to Frankie's, and back), I see the same small-town faces all the time. Here in Asbury Park, the people look different—exotic. There are surfers with sun-bleached hair carrying surfboards underarm, their wetsuits hanging halfway off at the waist, looking perfectly cool in a way that cannot be learned. I pass countless scantily-clad girls causing a certain (very persuasive) part of my body to frantically alert my brain, pleading for me to glance over at them, but my embarrassment prevails, forcing me to look in the other direction (a battle I'll never forgive my conscience for winning). Little kids walk by with one hand resting inside a parent's while the other clutches a cartoon-sized balloon or an ice cream cone. Then there are the khaki wearers—more than I would've thought. These are people who perhaps have made a promise to themselves never to don a pair of short pants or else they didn't get the memo that Asbury Park is a beach and is hotter than all get-out. Whatever their reasoning, they're here and they're trapping a lot of heat inside those chinos. My cargo shorts may be painfully out of fashion but at least they breathe.

I home in on a well-dressed man with a kind face looking out over the boardwalk railing at the ocean. He's wearing a floral print, short-sleeved, button-down shirt underneath a black vest that looks a lot cooler than my description portrays. Another person who is not a fan of shorts, he's wearing black dress pants and a black hat that I can only describe as a mix between a fedora and a cowboy hat. My guess is that he's either **A)** a musician, **B)** a fan of rock 'n roll, or **C)** European. The first two options point to him knowing how to get to The Stone Pony but even option C gives me a chance as it's a famous landmark and would likely be included on a sightseeing itinerary thanks to Bruce Springsteen cutting his teeth there. Even though I don't know much about music, if you're born in New Jersey, you know about the Boss.

New Rod seems to be having a resurgence—my instinct was right. In addition to being dressed to kill, this guy also had a kind demeanor and a keen sense of direction, and gladly provided me with directions to The Stone Pony: walk straight down the boardwalk for five minutes and look on the right for the sign that reads The Stone Pony. *Simple enough.*

With a good hour and a half to kill and a short five-minute walk ahead of me, I take heed of the signals being offered to me—a rumbling stomach and a vegan food cart fifty feet to my left—and grab some lunch. Finding an open seat where I can devour my chickpea-tuna sub, I plant myself upon the vacant bench and take in the volleyball match being played on the beach in front of me. We play volleyball in school but this match is a far cry from what we do in the gymnasium of Somerville High School, where three to four people know what they're doing while the rest of us do our best to avoid getting spiked with the ball. The game on the beach is made up of beautiful people playing in their bathing suits, the men all shirtless and the women not far off. Most of their torsos (both the men's and the women's) sport abs that look like they were painted on. Both teams are fiercely competitive, high-fiving when their team scores a point or turning on one another, arguing and passive-aggressively placing blame when the opposing side gains the upper hand.

While both teams take a water break, I remember Cat's claim that our next adventure can be found on page 152 of *Nobody Likes You*. Opening to the page, I see that chapter ten is entitled *Captain Underpants* and am riddled with intrigue. My wonder has to wait as my phone rings; just by the sound, I know it's my mom. I don't want to lie to her anymore. My deceit has caused enough trouble already. That said, I don't want to send her into cardiac arrest, which I'm sure is what will happen if I tell her that instead of being in Atlantic City with Frankie and his dad, as was the plan, I'm actually in Asbury Park, mere feet from the last building Colin ever stepped foot inside. Rather than lie, I decide to play the semantics game. I tell my mom that I'm on the boardwalk eating a sandwich, getting some fresh air, and enjoying some time to myself away from Frankie. Technically none of what I said is a lie. I spend the rest of the call deflecting questions, telling her how much I miss her too and that I promise to check in later.

* * * * * * * *

The Stone Pony resides across the street from the boardwalk. The brick building is painted white with black Stone Pony signs on both sides and another above the white awning that hangs over the front entrance. And if that weren't evidence enough, the marquee to the right of the front door confirms that I'm in the right place:

90.5 The Night Presents: Jesse Malin

For a second I'm thrown for a bit of a loop when I don't see a line of people waiting to get in, since that's what I always pictured a rock 'n roll club to look like, but then it occurs to me that it's just past 3 p.m. so the show likely won't be starting for hours. The only person causing any fanfare is a little girl around four years old who is mystified by the large black pony painted on the left side of the building. She's jumping up and down, giggling and swatting at the painted pony, while her parents laugh and encourage her, each taking a video of her with their phones. It strikes me as odd that both parents are shooting videos of the event. Wouldn't one parent capturing the moment be sufficient? The videographer could surely share the captured images of their little girl's joyful moment with the other in an instant. But who am I to judge?

Caught (once again) peering into a window, this time into the tinted front door of The Stone Pony, a high-pitched squeal is (once again) startled out of me. When I turn around, I see that it's the stylish guy from the boardwalk.

"Hey man, I don't think the box office is open yet. I know there's a bartender in the back stocking the bar but she's not gonna hear you at the front door. Do you want me to go get her for you?"

"Oh, okay. Cool."

"Cool as in you want me to go get her?"

"No, it's cool."

"Oh. So, cool, you don't want me to go get her?"

"Yeah, no," I utter. *Jesus, this is not going well.* Fortunately the guitar he's holding catches my eye, leading me to successfully form a coherent sentence. "So you *are* a musician."

"What gave it away? The hat? Man, rock 'n roll clothes and the beach don't mix. I was trying to talk myself into putting my feet in the ocean but I'm afraid I'll burst into flames if I walk out onto the beach in these clothes and I didn't think to bring a bathing suit. I'm Derek, by the way."

"Nice to meet you, Derek. I'm Rod."

"Are you going to the show tonight?"

"I didn't know it was happening until an hour ago so I'm trying to find out how much tickets are. If I can afford them I'd love to get them for me and my girl—well, technically she's not my girlfriend. She almost was and then I nearly screwed it up because of Green Day. For years I was convinced they were attempting to ruin my life. Now they're my favorite band and I'm hanging out with her later today for the first time in weeks. Cat is her name." *And I'm Rod, the American (babbling) Idiot.*

"That's a cool story. I know the guys from Green Day. You won't meet nicer, more down-to-earth guys than them. Except maybe for Jesse Malin, that is."

"Crazily enough, we did meet Jesse, only we didn't know who he was at the time," I tell him. "It was the last time I hung out with Cat actually. We were in New York City and Jesse offered to take a picture of us in front of a Joe Strummer mural. He's the singer for The Clash, not The Ramones."

"Well, the bad news, Rod, is that the show is sold out. But the good news is that I play guitar in Jesse's band and I'd be happy to put you and Cat on our guestlist."

My mind has forgotten all words.

"Doors don't open until 7 p.m. but come back any time after that and tell them you're on our list. You won't need an actual ticket."

"Very cool. Better for the environment, which I'm a big fan of. So is Sting." *Why do I even speak?*

"Sting? Yeah, I've heard that about him," he says, chuckling.

"So 7 p.m., no ticket, just tell them I'm on your guestlist. Will you do me a favor and tell Jesse that the Sunset Kids say hi?"

"Sure thing, Rod. Nice to meet you and enjoy the show."

"Oh, and Derek...break a leg!" I exclaim, instantly regretting my parting words.

As Derek picks up his guitar and heads toward the back of the building, my brain is unable to fully process the enormity of what just happened but it's easy to understand that it was AWESOME. I look to my left, making eye contact with the little girl who moments ago was so enamored of the painted pony and realize that at this moment, we are the two happiest people on the planet.

chapter 51

*

castaway

Cat's unflappable nature is one of her many traits that I admire. That said, her exclamation of being a cradle robber in response to me reminding her that I'm not of legal driving age and do not have a car of my own, here or anywhere, is the last thing my panicked brain needs to hear at this moment. I'd much rather focus on the fact that the Catmobile is here in Asbury Park, still in its spot over by Convention Hall, but whose ever-important keys are in Ellie's possession. Normally this wouldn't be a big deal except that she, Will, and Wheels are en route to Philadelphia, where they'll be spending the night at a friend's place. They left directly from Cosplay Con over an hour ago, which means they'll probably be pulling into the City of Brotherly Love any minute now.

I'm entering a state of shock while Cat sips her coffee with a nonchalance that only adds to my anxiety. We sit at a high-top table at Café Volan, the same coffee shop I visited upon my arrival in Asbury Park. Part of me feels like the barista shot me a sideways glance for being back here so soon, though the massive surge of caffeine rushing through my bloodstream coupled with the dread of being stranded in an unfamiliar city could certainly be the cause of my pseudo-paranoia.

My mind jumps to a year from now, Cat and I castaways in Asbury Park. We walk the beach in the same clothes we're wearing today though they're tattered beyond recognition. Cat's hair is long and dreadlocked while mine has been naturally bleached by the sun, unlike the lifeguards who clearly spend a hefty portion of their paychecks having their tips frosted ever so slightly in an effort to appear touched by the sun. We sleep underneath the boardwalk, surviving on discarded containers of tater tots and the kindness of strangers who aid and abet us in acquiring the remaining nutrients our bodies require, occasionally purchasing for us vegan burritos and bottles of water.

"Rod...where are you?" Cat asks, pulling my mind out from under the boardwalk.

"I can't believe I did this. I am such an idiot. See...I told you...I'm the American Idiot," I say, dejected.

"Stop blaming yourself. You're not the one who asked Ellie to hold your keys so you could get a picture with Groot. If anyone is to blame, it's me."

"Yeah, but if I hadn't come you wouldn't have been distracted, walking down the boardwalk to find me. You'd have gone straight to your car with your friends, realized Ellie still had your keys, and you'd be back home in Holmdel by now instead of being left in the lurch with me, worrying about where your next meal is coming from or if the stranger poisoned the burrito before giving it to you."

"Okay, first off, you're switching to decaf," she says, sliding my cup away from me. "Now, stop worrying. I will totally get us home after the concert."

"The concert? How can you even think about going? We need to spend our time figuring out how to get home, not rocking out with Jesse Malin, as awesome as that sounds."

"We'll take a train back to Holmdel after the show. I'll use my mom's boyfriend's car to drive you home and then Ellie will return my keys tomorrow and give me a ride back down here to pick up the Catmobile. Voilà."

My brain wants to reject this idea. It searches for miscalculations, overlooked details, holes to poke to expose the weakness of the scheme that Cat has so cavalierly cooked up. But it comes up empty handed. It's a fool-proof idea. So solid, in fact, that when Cat arrives at an obstacle, I'm the one who shoos it away like a fly, exerting such little thought and effort it would impress even the blasé barista behind the counter whose vernacular for coffee is "a cup of hot."

"The only problem is that your parents think you're in Atlantic City with Weasel-Face Frankie. What'll you tell them when you walk in the door a day early?"

"My mom will be so ecstatic that I'm home it won't matter what I say. In fact, next time she calls, which I assume will be happening any minute, I'll tell her that Frankie is driving me up a wall as a way of greasing the wheels, if you will."

Cat's composure begins to level off my nerves from the wave of caffeine they've been riding for the past couple hours. Her plan is picture perfect and I'm kicking myself for not thinking of it first, especially considering that I've already been to the train station when Frankie's dad dropped me off earlier. It was my first Asbury Park experience. The station seemed to be a bit of a seedy place at two in the afternoon so I imagine we'll be seeing some interesting characters there tonight after the show, but Cat doesn't seem concerned. I've decided I'm going to fake my way to serenity starting with appreciating my good fortune that now I won't have to learn how to make fire using a couple of sticks and forage for my own food (a true challenge for a vegan) after all. From trouble-bound to lost and found in the time it takes to drink a cup of joe. Three cheers for public transportation!

chapter 52

*

strangers & thieves

Making Cat happy makes me happy. I used to think all those people who at Christmastime claim to enjoy the act of giving a gift more than receiving one were a bunch of phonies. But seeing how excited she is about being on Jesse Malin's guestlist for his sold-out show tonight, I'm thinking that maybe they're onto something.

"I know this is going to sound uber-pretentious so forgive me, but Jesse Malin's music is the perfect soundtrack for reflection. His slice-of-life lyrics, the way he intersperses rockin' songs with slow songs throughout his albums...I don't know many artists that are able to set a mood like he does. Mostly for me, the louder and faster music is, the better. The power of punk rock helps to drown out the rest of the world. But when I discovered *Sunset Kids* after we met him, I realized that a song doesn't have to be fast or loud to be heavy."

As is so easy to do, I get lost in Cat's words. I love hearing the passion in her voice, seeing the excitement in her eyes, and watching her mouth fight to keep up with her brain that is firing off neurons expeditiously. We talk like this for hours, first over coffee and then as we slowly make our way up Cookman Avenue, occasionally popping into one of its many (non-chain) stores for some good old-fashioned browsing. Inside Holdfast Records, Cat purchases a used copy of *Zenyatta Mondatta* by The Police on CD, saying that she's been listening to the shit out of them (her words) on Spotify and now it's time to hear them in the Catmobile.

"With the windows down and the volume up," I add, landing me on the receiving end of another magical kiss. I am momentarily enamored of the idea that I am now a bona fide Green Day fan and Cat is a fan of The Police. My elation halts as panic sets in that we're going to miss the show, as it has every ten minutes for the past hour. Each time, Cat calmly insists that we're fine, assuring me that Jesse is the headliner and won't take the stage until at least 10 p.m.

* * * * * * * *

As we enter The Stone Pony, the opening band is wrapping up their set, which Cat says is the best time to get a spot on the floor in front of the stage, since many attendees will be rushing off to get drinks from the bar or to the bathroom. Likely both, in fact. There's a bar to our left as we make our way inside, which causes me to naively ask Cat whether we are allowed to buy a bottle of water from there or if one must be twenty-one to make a purchase. Do you ever ask a question that seems logical enough as it's forming in your brain but as soon as the first word leaves your mouth, you cringe at the rest that follow? Questions like these are my most frequently asked. Cat assures me that if we can pay for it, we can order anything non-alcoholic that we want, that they only check wrist bands to make sure you're twenty-one if you're attempting to buy booze. Cat says her mom makes a game out of trying to look (and sound) as young as possible when ordering from a bar or liquor store and makes a big spectacle on the rare occasion she does get asked for ID. The bar is so crowded that I rethink my idea of having a bottle of water to nurse while we watch Jesse play. When the lines are as long as they are, thirst can wait.

Cat and I find a spot on the standing-room-only floor, virtually dead center, about six rows of people back from the stage. In front of us are mostly women, intensely enthusiastic and, for the most part, suggestively dressed. A few of them brought dates along who are visibly less enthusiastic and certainly more modestly dressed. I've never thought much about what the inside of a rock 'n roll club would look like, but if I had, I would have pictured the exact interior of The Stone Pony. I scan the dark room, seeing that there's another bar in the far corner of the club in a section set back from the dance floor we are standing on (*do they call them dance floors? Will there be dancing?*). There are bathrooms to the left of the second bar, a line outside the ladies room and a revolving door of men going in and out of their own undoubtedly less hygienic restroom. I begin to wonder what the outside patio area looks like as I gaze through the open doors about fifty feet behind where we are standing when I feel Cat's elbow nudge my ribs and I turn to see that Jesse and Co. are taking the stage.

"My name is Jesse Malin and this song is called *Turn Up the Mains*," he announces before he and his band punch me and the entirety of the sold-out Stone Pony crowd in the face with a wall of sound. For the next hour and a half I feel privileged to be a part of this crowd as we are treated to perfectly crafted songs of punk rock 'n roll (Cat's words), Jesse's engaging and hilarious storytelling (did you know the word gig stands for "get it going?"), and even a PMA chant led by Jesse. I am sweating and smiling more, at least simultaneously, than I ever have before and I can tell Cat is having the time of her life as well, which makes this night that much more special.

Between songs, Jesse thanks the crowd for coming out to the show and for showing him and the band the love and support that they always do. He says that getting out of the house, stepping away from screens, seeing live music, and being together with real people is more important than ever. He's as kind and genuine as he was the day in NYC, a day I'll never forget. Apparently Jesse hasn't forgotten either.

"I hear there are a couple of Sunset Kids out in the audience. Where are you guys?"

The only reason I know I'm not in one of my daydreams is that Cat shakes me furiously in excitement, which surely would've snapped me back into reality. We scream and raise our hands and in our close proximity to the stage, Jesse spots us right away.

"From what my main man Derek tells me, you guys are big fans of Green Day. This next song is one I wrote with a good friend of mine, one of the most genuine people I know, who has never changed even after all the fame, glory, and adulation he's received, and that's Billie Joe Armstrong. This one is called *Strangers and Thieves* and it goes out to Rod and Cat."

"ARE YOU FUCKING KIDDING ME?!" Cat joyfully screams into my face. Then the two of us scream unison and dance with each other and everyone around us.

* * * * * * * *

"Okay...don't freak out," Cat says, putting my brain on high alert for a freak-out. "But we missed the last train out of here."

Commence freak-out.

After Jesse Malin and his band wrapped up their preposterously amazing set, Cat and I knew we had to hustle over to the train station. They played until a little after 11:30 p.m. Cat figured we needed to get to the train station by midnight but that there was a chance we might get lucky with the trains running later than usual for the holiday weekend. Our plan was to catch a cab which would get us to the station in plenty of time, since it's only just shy of a mile from The Stone Pony. Unlike in New York City, where taxi cabs can be seen whipping around nearly every corner, outside The Stone Pony there were none to be found. Neither of us has a credit card so Uber and Lyft weren't an option. Thus, we started jogging. Our output was not going to get either one of us recruited onto our respective school's track team, but we kept a pretty impressive pace, if I do say so myself. Impressive, maybe, but not fast enough.

We find ourselves standing on the platform, Cat doing her best to keep cool and collected as I do my best to avoid a full-fledged panic attack. The platform is not empty, though. In fact, it's filled with far more people than I would expect if it's indeed true that the last train has already come and gone. I optimistically share my observation with Cat, hoping that she misread the schedule, which conjures a half smile as she quietly points out that the people we find ourselves amongst are not waiting for trains—they've already arrived at their destination, either for the next couple hours or for the night. I scan the platform, subjectively this time, and find synchronicity in the fact that Jesse Malin sent out to us a song titled *Strangers and Thieves*, though I find it best to keep this observation to myself.

We decide that the best thing to do is walk back toward the boardwalk where it's well lit and the people are...how do I say this without sounding too judgmental? Well, they're not the people who hang around a train station past midnight. Our walk takes us, once again, up Cookman Avenue. We were here not too long ago but we were jogging our hearts out trying to catch the last train so I didn't take notice of how beautiful this street is at night. There are far fewer people than when we had gotten coffee before the show but it's by no means abandoned or as intimidating as the train station. There are people outside bars smoking and chatting and people leaving bars headed toward whatever the rest of the night has in store for them. The thought crosses my mind that perhaps we should ask one of these people for a ride back to Holmdel, but logic quickly takes over, reminding me that they are 1) strangers and 2) in the process of leaving a bar so there's good reason to believe that they're not the best fit for a ride home. But then I have a better idea.

"What about a cab?" I ask, hopefully. "I know we didn't see one outside The Stone Pony but we could look up the name of a taxi service on your phone and call them for a ride!"

"How much money do you have on you? It'll take about half an hour to get back to Holmdel so I'm guessing it'll cost somewhere around thirty bucks. Maybe less if they take pity on us."

Grabbing my wallet from my shorts, which at first doesn't want to come out because of the stubborn button attached to my back pocket, I open it up to find that I have exactly four dollars. Pooled together with Cat's money, we have $13, which isn't anywhere close to what we would need even if we were lucky enough to get a taxi to pick us up in the first place.

"What about your mom?" I ask, an idea so obvious I'm appalled it didn't come to me earlier. "Can't she come and pick us up? I know it's late but if it's only half an hour away, it shouldn't be too big a deal, right?"

"Normally it wouldn't. I mean, she'd make it into a big deal that she would hold over my head for the next couple of years, which would give her great satisfaction, but she flew out to California to visit the other Sting's biggest fan for the weekend."

Mike already started drinking hours ago. Earlier he sent me a text asking how things were going (which I thought was quite thoughtful of him) and then he told me The Store was super busy and that he was closing up shop at 9 p.m. because that's Miller Time. There's only one person left to call. I know it and Cat knows it. She also knows how reluctant I am to make the call, so she takes my phone and says she will.

While she steps away to use my phone, I try to remember if Cat has ever met Officer Stewart but I can't recall. She's heard about him ad nauseam so she must feel like she knows him. It was kind of gutless of me to have her do my dirty work, especially if she's never met him. It's just that I've leaned on him so much lately and now to call him after midnight to come all the way to Asbury Park? That's just more than I can face, even over the phone. I overhear Cat give her assurance that we will be waiting on the bench on the boardwalk directly across from The Stone Pony, promising that we will not move from that spot.

chapter 53

*

driven to tears

As you well know by now, twenty years ago my brother, Colin, died on his way home from Asbury Park after leaving a Green Day concert. After he passed away, my mom never drove again. So perhaps you can imagine the sheer magnitude of the earthquake erupting inside my skull, shattering everything I thought I knew, as I sit on the boardwalk bench across the street from The Stone Pony and watch my mom pull my dad's car into the parking spot directly in front of us. My mom drove herself here to pick up Cat and me with the intention of driving us home. This is not a drill, this is real life. At some point my brain is going to have to believe what my eyes are seeing.

Minutes are passing but not in real-time. A moment ago I was on a bench staring at my mom through the windshield of my dad's car, reasoning with myself that I was hallucinating, that it could not be my mother sitting there behind the wheel. Now I find myself in the backseat of said vehicle, yet I do not remember climbing in. I do know that Cat is in the front seat speaking calmly to my mom but from my vantage point in the backseat, I see that my mom is shaking like a leaf. Her knuckles, snaked around the steering wheel, are as white as ghosts and her elbows are shaking so dramatically they look like they are about to take flight.

"I can't do this," my mom says barely above a whisper.

"Yes, you can," Cat says, laying her hand on top of one of my mom's.

"I made it here on pure adrenaline," she says through labored breathing, nearing the point of hysterics. "But this is all I had in me. You have to drive us home. I can't do it."

"You can do this," Cat says. I notice her retrieving *Zenyatta Mondatta* from her bag with her right hand, the one not being held captive by my mom's death grip, and sliding it into the car's CD player.

The three of us sit in my dad's car, idling in the parking spot in front of the boardwalk bench on which Cat and I spent so much time waiting tonight. My mom's gaze does not leave the steering wheel while Cat gently strokes her hand and mouths "Shhh" to me in the backseat, extinguishing my gut instinct to fill the dead air. Mercifully, the silence is broken about midway through the opening track, *Don't Stand So Close to Me*.

"This is the song that played in *Friends*, isn't it, sweetheart?" my mom asks, still not looking away from the steering wheel.

"Yep. Sure is, Mom."

Don't Stand So Close to Me fades out. The silence between songs is deafening, lasting a thousand years. The next song, *Driven to Tears*, begins with Stewart Copeland clubbing the drums as if he were mad at them, snapping the stillness like a twig, and the moment Sting's bassline kicks in, my mom and I declare in unison, "I love this song." Our eyes lock in the rearview mirror and she sees me again, for the very first time. Without another word spoken, my mom shifts the car into reverse and, with an abundance of caution, backs out of the parking spot.

Before Sting can finish telling us what has driven him to tears, Cat asks my mom to pull over, though she was driving slowly enough that Cat seemingly could have rolled right out of the passenger seat onto the pavement without suffering much damage. I'm confused by her request, especially after seeing that Cat has directed my mom to drive us to where the Catmobile is parked.

"Cat, what the hell is going on?" I ask, following her lead and getting out of my dad's car. "Are those your keys?" I ask, dumbfounded, as she unlocks her door. "And what's my mom doing here? I thought the plan was to call Officer Stewart."

"How many times do I have to tell you that plans are boring?" Noticing the tortured despair on my face, she continues. "While I was performing my costume change in the backseat earlier this afternoon, I was thinking about how sweet it was for you to surprise me. And also about how much trouble you were probably facing, being that this is the one place most forbidden by your mom. Then it occurred to me that if the Catmobile weren't available, you'd need a ride home. You'd need someone to save you. And saving you might save her."

Hearing this leads me to wonder if we actually did miss the last train, or if Cat made that up to carry out this plan of hers. I wonder how she knew I wouldn't have the courage to call Officer Stewart myself, allowing her to pretend to call him when, in fact, she was calling my mom. Speaking of which, I wonder how that conversation went and how my mom convinced my dad that she was fit to drive herself to Asbury Park. But most of all, I wonder how I got so lucky to have someone like Cat in my life.

"I don't know how you do it," I say.

"Do what?"

"Continuously top yourself with amazing adventures."

"The adventures are amazing because they're *ours*. Without you, today would've been good. With you, it was the best day of summer, hands down. Thank you for surprising me at Cosplay Con and for taking me to see Jesse Malin. And thank you for being interesting. Every time I'm around you, good things happen. You are such a positive influence on my life."

I use every bit of resolve in my body to fight back the tears on the verge of a mutiny, threatening to blitz the gates in an attempt to make their way out of my face. I feel a single tear escape and travel down my cheek, the first detractor, which I swiftly wipe, hopefully before Cat can notice.

"Speaking of adventures," she adds, "don't forget to read chapter ten."

"*Captain Underpants*," I say. "Got it."

"Goodbye, Mrs. Williams," Cat says, leaning into the open passenger-side door of my dad's car.

"Don't forget your album," my mom says, ejecting *Zenyatta Mondatta* from the CD player.

"No, you keep this. You guys can listen to it on your way home. Rod can give it to me next time I see him."

"No, honey, this is yours," my mom insists, noticeably more composed than when she first arrived. "He and I have some catching up to do. It's been a while since we've talked." A rare smile fights to form on her lips as she hands the CD to Cat. "And Cat...thank you. Thank you from the bottom of my heart. You gave me a gift that I prayed for every day for twenty years. A gift I didn't think was possible to receive. Because of you, I'm able to get my son home safely from Asbury Park. I am forever indebted to you."

At this point I am powerless against the tears that make a jailbreak from the overflowing ducts in my eyes. I find myself full-on crying after hearing my mom refer to me as her son for the first time ever.

* * * * * * * * *

You've surely heard the phrase "it's like riding a bike," suggesting that once a skill is learned, it's never forgotten. What the phrase fails to mention is the rust that needs to be scraped off, especially after twenty years of not practicing a particular skill. My mom pushes on and lets off the gas pedal as if she's attempting to emulate the rhythm of Stewart Copeland's feet thumping the bass drum that we heard a short while ago. Each set of headlights traveling down the opposite side of the road cause my mom to slow down and begin to veer into the shoulder. Once we merge onto the Garden State Parkway, my mom flinches as if she's dodging a bullet every time a car passes us.

None of that matters, though—the choppy driving, the nervousness around other vehicles, the time added to our journey. All that matters is that we are on the parkway and that my mom is in the process of getting us home. She informs me that it's my job to distract her from the dread harboring in her chest and requests that I talk to her without stopping until we get back to Neshanic Station. Never has a person been so fit for a job as I am for this one.

Deciding to start from the beginning, I share with her the origins of my fascination with Sting, reminding her of the time she and I danced together to the music of The Police and when she hummed along after hearing their song on *Friends*. That because of those instances I believed that Sting held the key that would unlock the inner happiness that was buried deep inside her, and thus my ambition to meet him was born. Next I tell her about how I met Cat, being caught peering into the window of the new yoga studio in town. I tell my mom about our adventures together: seeing a basement show and singing with the band in New Brunswick, my dustup with Derek Sanders, and about meeting the other Sting in NYC. About how she insisted upon driving me to the hospital either before or after each adventure, where she sat patiently in the waiting room while I visited Dad, and that it's Cat I have to thank for introducing me to Green Day, whose music has unearthed emotions buried deep inside me, feelings incapable of being expressed in words. Between Cat introducing me to their music and Mike informing me that Colin was only a casual Green Day fan, mainly at their concert that night only for "something to do," I began to question my assertion that they were the black cloud hanging over my life. Then I spoke about how, once I'd finally listened to them, it didn't take long for me to realize that they are the greatest band rock 'n roll has ever seen, even better than The Police. My mom chuckles at this notion, saying that she has some Beatles records that may make me change my tune on that proclamation, and we agree that one day I'll play her my favorite Green Day songs and she'll play me her favorites by The Beatles.

Despite our excursion taking us nearly an hour longer than it should have, once home in our driveway, we stay put in the car and continue our conversation. After a while my dad joins us, hopping into the backseat, even attempting to throw The Eagles into the mix for the greatest rock 'n roll group of all time, which my mom and I both quickly veto. As my family sits inside my dad's car, parked in our driveway, talking like excited teenagers while the early morning sun gets a start on its day, I realize that Cat is right—plans are boring. Excitement lies in the unknown and it's the small things that happen in the in-between that make for life's biggest moments.

chapter 54

*

i was a teenage teenager

Today is the first day of winter break, the final one of my public-school career. I've spent the better part of the morning in my room playing my bass in an attempt to keep my mind busy and block out what's happening later this afternoon. For my birthday in September, my dad took me to Guitar Center to check out their bass selection. He liked that I was interested in learning how to play an instrument and made a deal with me that he'd match whatever money I was able to pony up (his words). I had a hundred bucks saved from scooping litter boxes and Guitar Center had the sweetest-looking P-bass, which is the nickname for a Fender Precision Bass, though if you're an idiot like me, you might get nervous and ask the largely disinterested associate if you can "test out the F-bass," gifting him something to chuckle about with the rest of the snooty guitar salesmen in the back room.

Knowing less than nothing about instruments, the decision to get a P-bass was an easy one once I learned that both Sting and Mike Dirnt from Green Day play P-basses. Mine is a Squier Affinity Precision Bass that was $230, the least expensive one they had (my dad bent his own rule and threw in the extra $30; he's a good guy like that). I don't care if it's a knock-off because it's still a P-bass (*not* an F-bass) and it's black with a white pickguard, just like the one Mike Dirnt plays. And it rules.

The transformation that my dad has made since the beginning

of summer is nothing short of incredible. He's down seventy-five pounds, he exercises almost every day (sometimes accompanying my mom on her walks), and (even though I'm not supposed to say anything because he doesn't want me to jinx it) he's in talks with Mike about buying into partnership in The Store and taking over the deli/grill area, where he plans to redo the menu to healthy plant-based foods and serve as head chef. Fingers crossed that he can make it happen so he can finally quit his two jobs to do something he enjoys. I know he's going to make it happen and so does he. My dad, the new-and-improved version, has got a PMA.

You're probably wondering about my mom, huh? Well, they say Rome wasn't built in a day. In the same regard, a twenty-year Xanax dependency isn't cured in three months. My dad's nurse, Roxanne, suggested that he adopt the mindset of "Day one, not one day." My mom has applied this to her situation as well. The way she describes it, a light went on inside her after coming to save me from Asbury Park (my words...which my mom *loves* to hear) and Day One of changing her life came the next day (well, the next night, really, because she slept a good twelve hours after we finally went inside that morning). It hasn't been easy. Some days are better than others. My mom understands that she has a long road ahead of her and she is putting in the work. She's seeing a new therapist, who has her on a program with the goal of weaning her off her medications, or at least reducing them to a manageable dosage. She's even begun practicing yoga, using the Sting yoga mat that had been gathering dust in the corner since the day the other Sting gave it to me. While in our driveway that morning, I told her about Cat's Aunt Amy and her yoga studio being named after the song *I'll Follow the Sun* by The Beatles, and although she hasn't yet built up the courage to take a class at the studio, Amy teaches her private lessons online. My mom has her mat set up in Colin's room, which she suggested we partially rearrange (a major breakthrough for her). That was a rough day but we made it through. She had me and my dad put Colin's bed in the attic, which was the biggest pain ever. We almost killed ourselves on those damn stairs but we eventually managed to get it up there. The walls are still decorated the way Colin had them, his Phillies poster and trophies hanging, only now there's an open space in the center of the room where my mom practices yoga and there's an elliptical in the corner that my dad found on Facebook Marketplace for next to nothing. He and I just had to go and pick it up, which was another massive undertaking but well worth it in the end. My parents offered to let me keep my bass in Colin's (old) room but I play in mine instead, with the door closed, and will until I get good enough to be comfortable letting other people hear me play. My mom and I never did have that Green Day listening party that we spoke of in the car; she says she's not quite ready. She did play me *Help!* by The Beatles and, while they're not as good as Green Day (or The Police, for that matter), they've got some pretty catchy tunes. I'm learning to play *I've Just Seen a Face*, which is her favorite song by The Beatles. It's an amazing song that I'm learning to play the way The Beatles play it as a surprise for her birthday. After that I'm going to try to play it Green Day-style for me (as in how the song would sound if they were to play it, which would sound incredible!).

As for Sting-chronicity, that remains a bit of a mystery. Much like Carl Jung's ideas, I understand bits and pieces but accept the fact that I will never be intelligent enough to fully grasp them. And that's part of the fun, isn't it? No, I didn't end up meeting Sting and while my stance on him being the be-all end-all resolution to all of my (and my mom's) problems may have loosened, his influence is the catalyst to everything in my life. While I was scouring his lyrics for clues, his songs ended up making me fall in love with music (without me even realizing it in the moment). His passion for yoga is what led me to meet Cat and now my mom even does yoga—on a Sting yoga mat. And his memoir stirred up some old memories in my dad, which commenced his evolution. I'm taking Environmental Science this year in an effort to learn more about the rainforest and see what I can do to help be part of the solution. Perhaps one day I'll find myself working for the Rainforest Fund, the organization founded by Sting and his wife, Trudie. Who can say what the future holds? Sting has been the greatest teacher of my life and although I'm no longer obsessively pursuing meeting him, I still hope to one day tell him as much.

For the first time in my life, I feel like I'm getting to be a teenager. Nothing more, nothing less. In school I formed a club called the Teenage Teenager Club, which doesn't have a specific agenda or requirements to join. Our vision for the club is for kids who feel as if they belong nowhere to feel welcome with us. It's actually beginning to build some steam. We get together and talk about all kinds of interests, whatever anyone in the club wants to discuss: books, music, food, yoga, the rainforest, anything really. That's where I met Dave, a kid from my grade that plays guitar in the jazz band. He has a band that needs a bass player and, while I'm not confident enough yet, hopefully soon I'll be ready to jam with them.

After school three days a week and on weekends, I work at The Store, which I thoroughly enjoy. I work the register, I cook on the grill (Officer Stewart is my best customer), Mike tells me stories about Colin, and we listen to Green Day. Lots of Green Day. The only bad part is that I haven't seen Cat nearly as much as I'd like now that we're both back in school and working but today I'm taking my first step in changing that. Speaking of Cat…

"Hey!"

"Hey, you! I'm just calling to wish you luck. How are you feeling?"

"Well, my hands are sweating so much that I'm barely able to hold onto my bass."

"Being nervous is *totally* natural. You're going to rock this. And after you do, we're still on for later, right?"

"Yep. I start work at two so come in any time after that."

"What about the Grouch?"

"He goes to a daily meeting at three so he'll be gone by then and won't be back for at least an hour and a half."

"Perfect. These plans are top secret so no one can know."

"Until we're ready," I say, clarifying that our secrecy is

temporary; I made a promise to my parents not to keep any more secrets or sneak out on any adventures without telling them. They're allowing me a lot more leeway in leaving the house and being able to be a teenager, so long as I'm honest with them. We've even retired the walkie-talkies.

"Yes, until we're ready, for sure," she agrees. "Once we've crossed the t's and dotted the i's we'll work on a pitch to sell this plan to our parents."

"Most definitely," I agree. "It'll probably just be Mr. B. in The Store with me, maybe Officer Stewart too if he pops in for coffee. It's highly unlikely that he'll be paying attention but just a head's up that both Mr. B. and Mike are doing the vape thing in an effort to quit smoking cigarettes and they've been a little more on edge than usual, so I suggest refraining from bringing up cigarettes. Or valentines, for that matter. Instead, maybe we should come up with a name for our adventure. Something like...I don't know...Operation RodCat?"

"Well, Skunk #2, you're still a terrible actor. Tell me the truth, Rodney, how long have you been cooking that one up?" she asks, seeing right through me (even over the phone).

"Dammit, I can't lie to you. I thought of it last week and have been dying to use it," I admit.

"I do appreciate your honesty but the name could use some work. How about Operation CatRod instead?"

"That sounds like a part of a feline's anatomy," I counter.

"You're not wrong."

"What about Operation Underpants?"

"Now there's a name I can get behind! Okay, go do your thing. You got this! See you in a few hours."

Cat and I hang up at the perfect time, just as the driving instructor pulls into my driveway. I'm seventeen now and, while I wasn't able to get my license on my birthday because I didn't sign up in time, today is my first day of driving lessons. Once I complete my lessons, I'll be eligible to take my driver's test and hopefully get my license. Then I'll really feel like a teenager. Having my license is going to provide me with so much freedom. I can drive to Holmdel to visit Cat whenever I'm not working, I'll be able to help my dad by doing some of the grocery shopping, and I'll be able to split driving duties with Cat when we take our road trip to California over spring break, the aforementioned adventure tentatively referred to as Operation Underpants. Remember the Green Day book, *Nobody Loves You*, that Cat kept urging me to read? Chapter 10: *Captain Underpants* tells the story of a lost Green Day album from 2003 entitled *Cigarettes and Valentines*. Very few people have ever heard this album other than the band and some people within their inner circle. There's a mystery surrounding the album's whereabouts. Some believe that the master tapes were stolen while others surmise that the band is holding onto them with no plans to ever release the album. Cat and I have made a vow to venture out to California and not return until we've solved the mystery…or until school starts back up, whichever happens first.

ACKNOWLEDGMENTS

Many thanks to the following people, without whom this book would not exist:

Gia and Will for being the source of my PMA. So many ideas in this story belong to Gia that she probably deserves a co-writing credit.

Sarah Waverka for painstakingly correcting my grammar, curbing my comma-dependency, and for making me look like a far better writer than I am.

Craig Cirinelli at HouseWithoutWalls Design whose talent and patience never cease to amaze me.

Phoebe Torsilieri, Rob McAllister, Matt Witte, Chris Calabrese, and Joe Cullinan for reading early versions of *Nimrod* and for their honest feedback.

Mom, Dad, Jac, Tindy, Colleen, Frank, and Diane for being such a fun and supportive family.

David Gamage at Earth Island Publishing for believing in my work and for answering every one of my many (many) questions.

All the bands and writers that continue to inspire me, keeping me young inside, and all those fighting the good fight for animals and the environment.

"Well, I think when all is said and done, just cuz we were young doesn't mean we were wrong."

-Propagandhi, *Rock for Sustainable Capitalism*

CPSIA information can be obtained
at www.ICGtesting.com
Printed in the USA
BVHW050229080223
658128BV00012B/524

9 781739 795597